Blessed
by Time

May God bless you!
Anne

Endorsements

Just when you thought there couldn't be another original time-travel book, along comes *Blessed by Time* by Anne Baxter Campbell and proves you wrong. A gripping yet delightful tale of a couple torn between two lifetimes while mourning the loss of their daughter, *Blessed by Time* will challenge you with the timelessness of the gospel and the healing love of the Savior, which spans centuries and continents. A great read for yourself—and a wonderful gift for others!

—**Kathi Macias** (www.kathimacias.com), award-winning author of more than fifty books, including the 2011 Golden Scrolls Novel of the Year, *Red Ink.*

Anne delivers a spell-binding tale of time travel back to Jesus's day where the faith of a child brings hope and belief to a community. Loved it!

—**Terri Wangard**, author of *Wheresoever They May Be.*

I just finished reading *Blessed by Time*. And ... WOW! This is like nothing I've ever read before, and I've been an avid reader since I was three! I'm amazed at how Anne Baxter Campbell put this all together. Awesome job, Anne!

—**Peggy Blann Phifer**, author of *To See the Sun*.

Blessed
by Time

Anne Baxter Campbell

Elk Lake
PUBLISHING, INC.
35 Dogwood Drive
Plymouth, MA 02360

Cover Design: Jeff Gifford
Interior Design: Cheryl L. Childers
Editors: René Holt, Deb Haggerty

PUBLISHED BY: Elk Lake Publishing, Inc., 35 Dogwood Dr., Plymouth, MA 02360

Library Cataloging Data
Names: Campbell, Anne Baxter (Anne Baxter Campbell)
Blessed by Time / Anne Baxter Campbell
332 p. 23cm × 15cm (9in × 6 in.)
Description: *A child's faith, a woman's grief, and a man's search*
Sarah Johnson is a woman deep in grief over the loss of her only child, three-year-old Tamara. Six months' time hasn't lessened the pain. She left for work early one morning and hasn't been seen since. Her husband Paul, professor of languages and counselor at Arizona State University, also grieves but is moving on. How far on? When Sarah disappears, he's suspected of getting rid of her in favor of a luscious redhead. How can he convince the police he's innocent? And where—or when—on God's green earth did Sarah go?
Identifiers: ISBN-13: 978-1-946638-77-9 (trade) | 978-1-946638-78-6 (POD) | 978-1-946638-79-3 (e-book.)
Key Words: time slip, first century, death of a child, Jesus, redemption, second chances, love story
LCCN: 2018932440 Fiction

Dedication

I dedicate this book to my husband, Jack. He prepared meals, did fix-its, made suggestions, and constantly believed in my ability to write even when I lost that hope and shelved the manuscript in a dusty file.

Not until he'd graduated to heaven ahead of me did I dig out, dust off, redraft, and deliver *Blessed by Time* to Elk Lake Publishing, Inc. I hope Jesus will let him read the book, and I hope the story still has his approval.

Acknowledgments

First and foremost, I am grateful to the Lord. He's the author and finisher of my faith, and He's the constant companion who gives me the ideas that fly through my fingertips on the keyboard.

I deeply love and appreciate the people who provided edits. They turned what would have been a sloppy manuscript into this finished product:

The Scribes, a wonderful group of fellow writers (critters) from American Christian Fiction Writers.

Laurie Penner, a wonderful writer herself, a dear friend, and an able editor!

René Holt, another terrific and talented editor who found the invisible typos still in the manuscript.

Numerous beta readers, who found even more of the invisible typos!

And, of course, my wonderful publisher, Deb Ogle Haggerty of Elk Lake Publishing Inc, who gave me hope this book I gave up on had a chance.

Thanks to each of you from the bottom of my heart. May God hold each of you close and grant you His very best blessing!

Prologue

Sarah Johnson stood alone at one side of three-year-old Tamara's hospital bed, gently wiping her little one's face with a cool, damp cloth. Her husband, Paul, and his mother, Halena, hovered on the other side. Tammy's body shook with increasing violence and frequency, and the chills racking her small frame rattled the bed between seizures. Sweat soaked the child's hospital gown and the sheets.

The hospice staff tried; they'd done all they could to make her more comfortable. The tumor crowding her brain wasn't operable, and she couldn't tolerate any more chemo or radiation. As the cancer spread, her body had begun to shut down. The morphine, dripping through the intravenous tube, kept the pain at bay, but nothing could halt the monster in her head. That morning, the doctors had warned the family they shouldn't expect Tamara to live through another night.

Sarah's mind kept rerunning events from the past weeks in the hospital. Tamara had asked for her favorite toys, and then, one by one, handed them to other children. She was doing what she loved to do—give. Now their sweet child lay dying, her skin so hot it felt like a July sidewalk in downtown Phoenix. Life just wasn't fair. Sarah stroked the regrowing downy blonde fuzz on her baby's head, terrified of that moment when Tamara would be gone forever.

Tammy opened her eyes a smidgen. She looked at her family through lackluster eyes, and her lips tilted up in a weak greeting before moving her gaze toward something or someone at the foot of her bed. Sarah glanced in that direction but saw nothing. A soft voice murmured something unintelligible nearby, and a faint floral scent drifted through the room, briefly masking the antiseptic smells. A visitor with fresh perfume walking past, maybe.

A look of delight widened Tammy's eyes and smile, and she lifted one hand maybe a half inch before it dropped back. Her eyes closed, her last breath soft on the sheet under her chin, the smile still on her lips.

"Oh, no," moaned Sarah. "Please, Tammy, stay. Don't go."

Paul and his mother cried out in unison, and they turned to each other's shoulders to weep in ragged sobs. Tears blinded Sarah as she bent down to gather Tamara's limp form into her arms and rock her one last time.

Chapter 1

April AD 2008

Sarah woke to the sweet scent of blooming jasmine and a breeze blowing through the room. How could that happen? No windows were open. She was instantly wide awake, despite the sleeping pill she took before retiring. She sat up, her heart jack-hammering. Paul muttered in his sleep and turned over. She glanced at the clock on the nightstand—12:05 a.m.

She'd had some vivid nightmares over the past months. In her dreams, Tamara would be alive but sick, and then her child would die again, over and over. According to the grief therapist, these should be ending or at least diminishing by now. Sarah lay back on the pillow, knowing she'd wake to the same dreary world in the morning. *Sleep only helps when I don't have these stupid nightmares.*

Sleep didn't return. She tossed until two a.m., then gave up.

Paul was never at his cheeriest when awakened, so she eased herself out of bed with as little disturbance as possible. She could take a shower when she got back home. *Or not. Who cares, anyway?*

She pulled clothes from the closet and walked barefooted into the living room to dress.

Going into work early couldn't hurt. The pile of papers on her desk assured enough to keep her busy until next winter. Busyness had been a good thing. Busyness kept her from thinking about her baby girl lying under six feet of hard ground—and about her disintegrating marriage. She brushed a straggly tangle of hair back from her face. If only she could hit an "undo" key and erase the past six months. No, make that a year, to back before Tammy had been diagnosed with cancer.

The drive from their Wickenburg home to her office in north Phoenix provided way too much time to reflect. Turning the radio to KNIX, she sang along with the music. She couldn't think about problems while singing.

She yawned. *Sing louder.* Reaching for the knob, she turned up the volume.

Sarah heard a low rumbling sound, more like a distant, deep voice than thunder. The smell of jasmine returned with a ripping sensation, and she closed her eyes for a split second. When she opened her eyes again, her hands froze on the steering wheel. She couldn't see the road! The moonlit highway and even the car surrounding her had blown away.

A hand reached out to her, and she grasped it with a desperation that belied the suicidal thoughts that had plagued her since that day in the hospital. As though from a distance, Sarah heard the smack and screech of metal against rocks and trees, a heavy splash, and then nothing. Black silence. *Got to get out of this car.* She couldn't feel anything but the comforting hand. *Am I dead?*

Chapter 2

April AD 30

This is crazy!

No flowery smell, no wind, no flimsy net, no steadying hand. She sat at the edge of a hard, wooden pallet, maybe four or five inches off the floor, her head swirling with confused, contradictory thoughts. She was in a house, but a dwelling different from any she'd ever been in before. Or maybe she had? Rough rock walls were held together by sloppy mortar, and the single-room dwelling had a dirt floor. Furnishings were almost nonexistent—a wooden table with the top only about eighteen inches from the floor, a couple of pallets, a fireplace of sorts, and a shelf nailed to the wall. She rose and walked toward the larger and lower of two windows. Light filtered in, but she didn't know whether daybreak or twilight.

Daybreak.

The room didn't feel too chilly, considering that sagging shutters, fastened to a wooden window frame with leather hinges, hung open. A bird sang an unfamiliar song from a nearby tree. Or maybe she had heard the tune before? A dog barked in the distance.

A little girl slept on a straw-covered wooden pallet under the window. Sarah stepped closer to the child and stared. She looked like Tamara: long, honey-blonde hair in a bright tangle on the pillow.

Of course.

Hands trembling, Sarah knelt next to the child, taking in every detail, inhaling the sleeping child's scent. She gently lifted the hair away from the little one's face. *Tammy? Tammy!* She stroked the toddler's cheek with the back of a finger.

The child's eyes opened, and she lifted both hands and smoothed Sarah's cheeks. "Mama, why are you crying?"

Sarah hungrily gathered her daughter into her arms. Suddenly the little girl's back arched and she began to jerk. *Oh, no. Please, not a convulsion. Get me out of this dream!*

In a few brief seconds, the muscle spasms quit, and the child lay quiet. Her breathing evened, and she appeared to have gone back to sleep. Gently, Sarah hugged Tammy and then laid her back down.

Only then did Sarah notice the man lying on the other pallet—the one she had just risen from. He had his back to her. She stood and walked closer to him. Longish dark beard, shoulder-length black hair. Still, something about the shape of his shoulders or the way his hair curled around his neck reminded her of Paul.

Okay, time to wake up. She pinched herself hard and yelped. The dream didn't go away, and the man awoke.

He muttered something under his breath, scratched his beard. "Woman, why did you wake me? The sun is barely out of its bed. I could have rested until you returned from the villa."

His language was strange, so how did she understand what he said? But his voice—he sounded just like Paul, complete with the gravelly, early morning grouchiness. Sarah gawked at him. He looked like Paul. He sounded like Paul. She shrugged. *Really, why wouldn't he be in the dream?*

Paulos, not Paul.

"Tammy—Tamara's sick." She kept her voice soft. "We need to find a physician."

Now what? She had responded in the same language. This nightmare got more bizarre by the second. First, she didn't know what was happening, and then she did. Was arguing with yourself crazy?

A pounding of fear brushed her heart. *Demons!*

Demons? Now, that is crazy!

The man glanced toward Tammy and lowered his voice. "You Canaanites. Do you think we should run for a healer every time a child is ill? I don't understand the way you think."

A Canaanite? Whatever. "Don't you care that Tammy is sick? She just had a seizure. A fit. And her skin is hot. Don't you understand? She needs a physician."

"Of course I understand, but we're not wealthy, wife." He acted as though he were explaining something to a particularly dull child. "People like us get over illnesses, or they don't. We don't have enough coins for a healer, and they don't get rid of demons anyway. Speaking of coins, the mistress will be angry if you're not there to prepare her family's morning meal. You know we need their favor. If you lose this position, we won't eat, and we won't have a place to live. The money I get from begging won't support us." A brittle hardness tainted his voice.

You think she has a demon? You've got to be kidding.

Everyone knows demons cause fits.

The man pushed back the ragged blanket and dragged himself across the floor to Tamara, grinding his teeth. He touched her cheek with his lips and leaned back on his elbow, his brow crinkling.

Sarah stared in astonishment at his right leg. The foot turned outward at an awkward angle. The limb was swollen and tied to a rough board with strips of dirty cloth. The same leg Paul had broken in a fall while replacing some tile on their roof four months ago, but in the "real" world, the leg had been set and healed properly.

The drunken healer didn't do it right.

"Sarah, did you hear me? Go to the master's house and prepare their meal. I'll stay with Tamara until you get back. Do we have any cheese left? I can give her some bread and cheese if she wakes before you return."

"I don't know. You'll have to look." She picked up a dirty brown headscarf, tied it over her hair, and marched out the door. *Now, what did I do that for?* She started to pull the scarf back off, then shook her head. *Follow the dream—I think I'm supposed to wear this ugly thing.*

She assumed her hair was still the same dishwater blonde, but this guy's hair looked black instead of brown, like Paul had. Maybe the dim light in the hovel made the color look darker.

Taking a deep breath as she stepped outside, Sarah almost gagged at the odor wafting from the stables. She hurried to the rear gate behind the spacious brick home and through a courtyard, releasing her held breath. The large yard was filled with fragrant flowers, bushes, grape vines, a vegetable garden, a fountain, a sundial, and carved stone benches. A rooster chased a hen past the sundial, and three tethered goats grazed on the bushes.

One path led from the gate into a partially open, rock-walled cooking area outside the house, enclosed on three sides. A wooden roof, extending about a foot above the top of the walls and supported at the four corners by poles, sheltered the fireplace and workbenches. The stone walls had several gaps as well, and she wondered why.

For use in the summer. To allow smoke out and air in.

"Huh. So now I'm answering my own questions?" she muttered.

Next to this structure was the entrance to the villa. She walked inside. Another fireplace, this one in the center of the room, and an oven in one outside wall with a flue venting the smoke outside. Open windows high on the walls let smoke out from the fire in the center.

With a sense of familiarity, she placed small chunks of wood on the coals banked below the oven, blew on the coals to start the fire flaming. When the oven was hot enough, she plastered the rounds of raised bread dough to the sides of the oven to bake, began cooking some oatmeal-like cereal in an iron pot over the other fireplace, and set out cheese, apricots, and goat's milk. How did she know to do all this? She had never done anything like this before. Or had she? Memories surfaced of doing exactly this daily routine for years.

When the loaves were done, she placed the food on a serving platter alongside olive oil in a dish and carried the platter to a room where a family would break their night's fast.

The interior of the house was elegant. Colorful strings of beads, so thick she couldn't see through to the other side, hung across doorways leading to other rooms. Multicolored marble tiles were laid in swirling patterns on the floor. Family members were dressed in tunics ranging from royal blue to deep purple, while Sarah's garb was a plain and serviceable brown. The matriarch of the family wore a long, loose tunic, expensive and elegant. The garment was embroidered with gold leaves around the neck and on the matching sash, which circled a trim waist.

Sarah's emotions varied from awe-struck to exasperation over being awe-struck. Every thought that ran through her head contradicted itself in the next instant.

At least none of these faces are familiar. Well, not from the modern world, anyway. Just from this dream.

Why do I insist it's a dream?

The slender woman stood an inch taller than Sarah's five foot two, her thick, dark hair elaborately coiled with vibrant jewels on the crown of her head. Her expressive, large, brown eyes were framed by eyelashes so long and thick they looked like they were layered in mascara.

Mascara? Oh—kohl.

The man was maybe five feet six or seven and a little overweight. His brown hair and beard were neatly trimmed. Sarah had served these people before, at least in the dream.

Three children trotted into the room, followed by a puppy, and all four hurried to the table. The pup was black with a tan stripe across his shoulders, and he wagged his tail at a constant and furious rate, obviously anticipating the spare crumbs that fell accidentally or on purpose from the table.

"Apricots!" The older of the two boys landed in his chair.

"Darius?" his mother said, her left eyebrow lifting.

"Oh, yes. Thank you, Sarah!"

The other two children echoed his thanks.

Sarah smiled at the children: seven-year-old Darius, six-year-old Gideon, and four-year-old Orphah. *Now, how did I know that?* She shook her head. With wavy dark hair and large dark brown eyes, all three resembled their mother. Sarah waited in silence for the family to finish eating, refilling their glasses of watered wine or goat's milk when needed.

"Well done, Sarah, as usual." The father patted his stomach. Again, Sarah "remembered," the names of the children's mother and father—Dorcas and Hamath. The look in the master's eyes expressed more than just appreciation for the food as they drifted down her tunic. Sarah saw her mistress's eyes narrow, and Sarah hoped the suspicion didn't extend to her.

"Take the remaining food for your family, Sarah," the woman said.

Sarah bowed in thanks, gathered the leftovers, and left the room. A creepy feeling crawled up the back of her neck. She suspected the master's gaze followed her.

She prepared plainer fare—cheese, bread, and raisins—for the several servants and slaves of the household. Another servant took the meal to their dining area. After cleaning the kitchen, Sarah wrapped the extra food from the family's meal in a clean linen cloth and retraced her steps to their so-called house.

Chapter 3

April AD 30

Paulos glanced up as she entered but uttered no word of greeting. Sarah wondered if their relationship in this dream world was as distant as in the real world. There, Paul had adopted formal speech with her, no friendly camaraderie anymore. Even before Tamara died, they'd become cool with each other. That chilly distance had only increased with their child's death. They didn't have much in common other than Tamara, and then she was gone.

Odd to be lonely in the middle of a marriage. A couple of years ago, she had adored him, and he her. She supposed she still loved him, but she was reluctant to expose herself to outright rejection by telling him so.

Loved? He never loved. I was chosen for him.

"I'm going now. I'll be by the gate." Paul—*no, Paulos*—ignored the plate of food she put in front of him. "Maybe people there will be more generous. No one at the marketplace cared enough to add a single coin to my basket yesterday."

"Have you eaten?"

"No. Maybe later." Paulos stood, using two stout forked tree limbs to brace himself. He looked so thin. He'd never been heavy, but now, prominent bones pressed his worn tunic into ridges and hollows. Grunting and stumbling, he made his way through the doorway, ducking his head to miss the top of the frame.

Tamara stood by her pallet, her face flushed.

"Mama, I don't feel good," she whimpered. She fell to the floor, convulsing again. Sarah ran to her and tried to hold her, but the stiff, jerking muscles made Sarah fear she would do more harm than good. Sarah placed her body between her daughter and the wall, absorbing the energy of jerking arms and legs. When the seizure ended, she lifted the child's limp form to her chest, rocking her child as she brushed tears from her own cheeks.

Tamara opened her eyes. Sarah held the youngster close and waited for her own heart to steady to a normal beat.

"Can you eat a little bit of fruit?" Sarah asked, offering the child some raisins.

Tammy shook her head weakly.

"Juice?"

Tamara nodded. After moving her to the pallet, Sarah squeezed some withered grapes and brought the clay cup to Tamara. The toddler drank the proffered juice, then crawled into her mother's lap and closed her eyes. While Sarah nibbled on the fruit and cheese, she wondered what to do with these family members—one ill of body, the other ill in both mind and body. She wished she had someone wise to talk to. She'd given up on the Sunday school notions of a benevolent God years ago *(or was it a few thousand years in the future?)*, so that option was out. She knew no one here in this distant past dream world other than her husband, her daughter, and her employers. *And other servants.* Who knew where this dream would take her next?

The day passed in a surreal haze. Sarah found herself doing work by rote—cooking, cleaning the kitchen, going back and forth between her house and her employers' villa, all the while keeping a close watch on Tamara. The child had recovered, and now she played with Orphah and the puppy, Kedar, in the warm sunshine. Sarah recalled that Tammy had started calling him Keddy, and the other children followed suit.

As Sarah prepared the final meal of the day, Tamara played with a wooden doll in the courtyard. Sarah pictured Paulos carving the doll for Tamara's name day last September. Name day? Oh, right. Almost the same thing as birthday, only a few days later—the date she was named.

The master came from the dining room and stood behind Sarah. She moved to the flour bin to start preparing tomorrow's bread, frowning as she considered his increasing interest in her. *Not like he's movie star material. And not as though I'm some kind of hot mama, either.* She pictured herself—short, ten pounds overweight, muddy brown eyes, dishwater blonde hair, two slightly crooked teeth—and wished he'd leave her alone. *His own wife's a lot prettier!*

"You don't have to be so afraid of me." His voice dripped honey. "You know I wouldn't hurt you. I enjoy watching you at work. Is that frightening? And I *am* your employer, remember? As my servant, you're subject to my wishes."

Sarah wasn't too sure about the legality of his ideas, but how would she find out in this ancient dream world? No internet, no computers, no library. *Maybe I should just dream up a computer and internet.* She began kneading the bread dough, using a starter from the morning's dough for leavening.

"I'm sure you wouldn't want to dishonor me, sir. I'm a married woman, and you're an honorable master." She mentally crossed her fingers and hoped he agreed.

13

"True, Sarah, but Paulos grows weaker, and he might not live much longer. If you please me, I might take you into my household as a concubine." He stepped closer, lifting one hand toward her face.

Sarah dodged again. "Paulos just feels depr-, uh, sad because he's crippled." *Depressed probably wouldn't be understood by this oaf.* "I expect him to begin eating more soon. And perhaps a physician might be able to fix his leg."

"How would you pay for a physician?" The master folded his arms across his chest and leaned against the wall. "Is my servant Sarah a secretly rich woman?"

Humph. He sounds just like Paulos did this morning. She had an idea. *Maybe* ... "Wasn't Paulos injured while he did work you ordered him to do? Maybe it's your responsibility to provide a physician."

The master's jaw dropped. "Is it possible you've forgotten I did find a healer for him?"

Another memory. "You sent for the cheapest charlatan you could find. Is that who you'd call for your family? He was drunk when he arrived. Some physician."

"Woman, I remind you that you're not a member of my family and not entitled to the same quality of physician such as would be warranted by my own kin. Your uncivil tongue could earn you a beating." His eyes had turned cold and sharp.

Oops. That didn't exactly work. "Forgive me, sir. It's only that I'm so concerned about my husband that I forget my position." She bowed her head in what she hoped was a submissive attitude. "He can do very little work for you in his present condition. If his leg were straightened and healed properly, he could be of use to you again."

The master's eyes narrowed. "Maybe you're right. I'll think about this and give you my answer tomorrow." With this, he left the kitchen. Sarah breathed a sigh of relief, as much for the man leaving the area as for the hope he might consider hiring a decent physician.

After finishing her evening chores, she knelt and held Tamara close to her heart. "I love you," she murmured, her throat tight.

"Me too, Mama," Tamara whispered. She squeezed her mother's neck.

Sarah packed up the remains of the evening meal, then, holding Tamara's hand, she walked back to the miserable hovel they called home. She noticed with gratitude the lamp lit in the window. Even with a full moon in a clear sky, the lamp would be needed inside the dark house.

Oh, well. I'll probably wake up in the morning to find this dream over, anyway. This has to be the most vivid one yet. But then again, this nightmare is better than the others. At least Tamara is alive here—wherever "here" is.

Tyre. In Phoenicia.

She watched Tammy, memorizing details so she could savor this moment when she woke tomorrow morning in her own bed.

Paulos lay on his pallet. Sarah said nothing about the master's promise to think over resetting his leg. No point in getting his hopes up, in case their employer decided against the idea. Besides, tomorrow was probably not going to happen here, anyway.

Tamara ran to her father and hugged him. "Papa, do you feel better yet?"

"No, my little one. Do you feel better?" Paulos reached up and stroked her hair with a gentle hand.

"I'm all better." She yawned. "'Cept I'm sleepy."

"Then it might be a good time to go to bed." Paulos nodded toward her pallet by the window.

"Okay, soon as I squeeze you and Mama." She hugged him again and trotted to her mother.

Sarah lifted her and held her close. She placed Tamara on the pallet, then sat beside her, combing the little one's soft hair with her fingers and humming softly until the child fell asleep. She wished this part of her dream would last forever.

Sarah sighed as she left Tammy's side. She placed meat, bread, and cheese on a small platter and set the food on the low table next to Paul, then brought another helping for herself. Paul—*Paulos*—ate only a few bites. "Food doesn't taste as good as it used to."

"I worry that you're getting thinner and weaker, husband. Couldn't you eat a little more? You need the protein and vitamins to get stronger."

"The what?" He turned over the meat and cheese as though something might be hidden beneath.

"Oh, uh, things in food that are good for you." *Oops again. Oh, dear, how do I get out of this gaffe?*

"Is this another Canaanite notion?" He set the cheese down.

"Yes, uh, Canaanite. My parents told me this." She kept her gaze on the piece of mutton on her plate, using fingers and a knife to trim off the fat and cut the meat into bite-sized pieces.

"I don't care about my strength. I don't care about much of anything. Of what use am I? If I died, you'd be free to seek a husband who could properly provide for his family."

"Please, Paulos, don't say that. What other man would love Tamara as you do? She'd miss you so much. Please try, for her sake." Sarah touched his hand across the table.

"And you? Would you miss me?" He asked softly, not meeting her eyes.

"Of course!" She pulled her hand back. "Now eat!" She pushed the platter closer to him.

"I'm not hungry." He lay down, turning his back to her.

Wrong response again. She must sound more like his nursemaid than his wife. Would they ever learn how to talk to each other again? *We didn't have any problem talking when we first got married. When did we stop? We act like strangers.*

Crossing the room, she knelt by Tamara's pallet. She brushed wisps of hair away from her daughter's eyes. Careful not to awaken her, she kissed Tammy's forehead. Tears slid down Sarah's cheeks as she watched the child sleep. When weariness overtook her, she almost fell across Tamara. She wished for something to lie on other than a dirt floor to be next to her baby girl.

Standing, she crossed the room and trimmed the lamp before lying down on the pallet next to Paulos, not touching, separated by an icy gulf too wide to cross.

Chapter 4

April AD 2008

Paul woke at his usual six a.m., though it seemed like midnight. Despite a full night's sleep, he felt groggy and grouchy. On the dresser, the old-fashioned alarm clock clanged. Scowling, he threw the blanket back and put his feet on the floor. *There.*

Standing, he turned off the alarm and scratched his whiskers. He stretched to his full six feet, feeling every muscle in his body, and turned to see if Sarah was awake. Her side of the bed looked smooth and flat. No sounds in the house. *Must have gone in early again. Just as well. I don't feel much like carrying on a conversation.*

Sometimes he wondered why they bothered to stay together. That new professor of zoology, Maureen, acted more interested in him than his wife had in a long time. Sarah seldom spoke to him if she didn't have to. If it hadn't been for Tamara, they probably would have separated a year ago. After she died, neither of them had enough gumption to move out. If they did separate, he could move in with his mother until he found somewhere else to live. *Sarah probably wouldn't even notice I was gone.*

He started a pot of coffee brewing, then headed for the shower. *She didn't even fix the coffee before she left. Probably stopped at Starbucks. She keeps telling me not to get so impatient with her, that she's still grieving. Big deal. So am I, but at least I make enough coffee for both of us.*

"I'll just work a little later this afternoon," he muttered. "Maybe past dinnertime, grab a bite at the Burger Shack. Suits me just fine. Let her wonder where I am and be a little inconvenienced, for a switch." *Maybe even a drink after work with Maureen?* Maybe not. Office romances could get sticky. He didn't want to get into that scene, even if Sarah and he were distant. *Well, not unless we separate.*

Maybe I should talk about that with Dr. Howard, he mused, thinking of their grief therapist. Why hang onto a marriage that is sinking into the pits? Obviously, their marriage didn't mean anything to her either. She sure wasn't making any effort to improve things. *Not that you have, either, Johnson. Let's be honest.*

Paul left for work, bemoaning the long commute from Wickenburg. Even using the freeways, getting to work took two hours—and two hours back—or more when traffic was bad. The drive wasn't so long for Sarah, only an hour. If he moved in with his mom in Tempe, his commute would only be a half hour.

Paul walked into his building on the Arizona State University campus at 8:55. As he turned the corner from the elevator, he saw Maureen standing outside his office door.

"Good morning, Paul." She greeted him with that throaty voice she used on him. "I thought maybe you'd like to know the latest news. Have you heard Trish Pettigrew is retiring?"

"Good morning, Maureen. Nice suit. Electric blue is definitely your color. And yes, I did hear about Trish."

"Thanks. You look pretty hot yourself." Maureen looked up at him flirtatiously. "Did you also know several of us are taking Trish to TGI Friday's after work today?"

"No, I hadn't heard that." Paul unlocked the door and walked into his office. Maureen shadowed him, and he turned to face her.

"Your tie is a bit crooked. Shall I fix it for you?" She stepped closer and reached for the offending object. Too close. He could smell the sensuous perfume on her long, wavy, red hair. His cheeks burned and sweat dampened his armpits.

After she straightened his supposedly crooked tie, Paul backed up a step. She lifted her eyes to his.

"Uh, thanks," he said. "Excuse me, I've got a class."

"Wait—would you like to help Trish celebrate? I could give you a ride over there and bring you back here to your car later." She moistened her upper lip with a pointed pink tongue. "Maybe much later."

He hesitated, more tempted than he cared to admit. "I don't think I should, as much as I'd like to."

"Why not? Afraid of little ol' me?" She stepped closer again and grinned. "I've yet to bite anyone. Nibble, maybe."

"Maureen, I'm scared to death of *little ol' you*, and that's precisely why I can't go with you," Paul answered with a grin. "Now I have to go, so out the door with you."

"Well, then, take your own car, but come to the party."

"Again, no thanks. See you later, Maureen." Paul squeezed her shoulders, then turned her and pushed her out the door, locking it and heading down the hall before she could talk him into changing his mind. He congratulated himself on declining Maureen's invitation. And kicked himself at the same time. *Hmm, great minds running in the same channels? Well, if Sarah and I split ...* He grinned as he speculated on what could happen.

When Paul arrived home, Sarah wasn't there. Neither had she written him a note to say where she was. Distant though they were, she usually had enough courtesy to leave word if she'd be late. No message on the answering machine either, just a couple of sales calls and one from their investment counselor. And one from his mother. He called her back, and she chatted at length: "Wasn't that a lovely thunderstorm last evening?" and "How about coming to dinner next Sunday?" Halena had moved to Arizona from Greece in the sixties, and her barely discernable accent colored her words.

"Okay, Mom, dinner Sunday sounds good to me. By the way, you didn't hear from Sarah today, did you?"

"No, dear. Why?"

"She's not home. She left before I got up this morning. I don't know where she is."

"That's odd. No note, no message on the voice mail?"

"No."

"Did you try her cell?"

"Not yet. That's next."

"If you don't reach her that way, you might try that girlfriend at her office—what's her name … Betty? You know, the gray-haired lady who came to Tammy's funeral and stood talking to Sarah for such a long time after."

"Yeah, Betty. If I can find her number, I'll call her. It's after nine, and I don't think anyone would still be at their office. Guess I should call there first, though. They could be working on a bid."

"Let me know what you find out. Sarah's been so down since Tammy died … I worry about her. I keep wondering if she's thinking about doing something to herself."

"I don't think she'd ever do that, Mom. She probably just got busy and forgot. I'll call you later and let you know."

Paul hung up and pushed the speed dial for Sarah's cell, but the call immediately switched to voice mail. He left a short message, asking her to call back, then called her office. As he was pretty sure would happen, the answering machine picked up. He didn't leave a message. *Now, where would Sarah keep Betty's home number? The address list on the computer, maybe.*

He logged on, checking his emails just in case Sarah had sent him a message that way. *Nope.* He searched through the document files and found one called *Addresses*. Finding Betty's name, he punched in the number.

"Hello?" Lawrence, Betty's brother, answered the phone. Since the deaths of his wife and her husband, the two of them shared a three-bedroom house in Glendale. Betty was near retirement age, quite a bit older than Sarah's thirty, but she and Sarah were close. Maybe Betty sort of replaced Sarah's mother, who passed away during Sarah's teen years.

"Hi, Lawrence. Paul Johnson. Betty there?"

"Yeah, sure, Paul. Hang on a sec."

"Hello, Paul. How are you?" Betty sounded as if she might be finishing a bite of food.

"Fine. I was just wondering—have you seen Sarah today?" Paul ran his hands through his hair.

"No, she wasn't at the office, and she didn't call in. Is something wrong?"

"She left early this morning, and she isn't home yet. I'm getting a little concerned."

"A *little* concerned, Paul? Maybe it's time you got a *lot* concerned. Have you called the police?"

"Not yet. That's the next call. I just wanted to find out if maybe the office worked late on a bid or something."

"Uh-oh. Now I feel awful," Betty said. "I should have called you at work when she didn't show up this morning. I did try to call her at home, but no one answered, and I didn't leave a message. I thought she might have wanted a day off. She's still so disheartened. Maybe she went to the zoo or something."

"Yeah, maybe. I hope so. See you, Betty."

"Bye, Paul. Let me know what you find out."

The Phoenix Zoo. Sarah's favorite place. They'd spent a lot of happy hours there with Tamara. While that could be a possibility, she would be back by now. The zoo closed at five.

He dialed the Maricopa County Sheriff's Office and asked to talk to someone about a missing person.

"Lieutenant Jones speaking. How may I help you?"

"Hello, this is Paul Johnson in Wickenburg. I'm calling to report my wife, Sarah, missing. She left the house early this morning and hasn't come home or left a message. How early I don't really know because she was gone before I woke up."

"Has your wife ever been late getting home before?"

"Yeah. She works at a construction office, and sometimes they work late on bids, but she always lets me know. This time there was no one at her office. I called there, and then I tried one of her co-workers, but she said Sarah hadn't come in."

"If you will give us a description of Mrs. Johnson, including what she wore today and her car and license number, we'll put it into our system. A police officer will be out to interview you as soon as one is available. Right now, they're tied up with other investigations. It might be late before we can get one out your way. Meantime, call us back if she shows up. If it's any comfort, most missing spouses show up or notify family within twenty-four hours. Now, how tall is she?"

"She's five-two, about a hundred and twenty pounds; dark blonde hair, straight and shoulder length; brown eyes; thirty years old. I don't know what she's wearing. She has a personalized plate on her car: '1 Sarah.' The car is a 2006 gold Ford Taurus."

"Thank you, sir. We'll start the ball rolling on this end. As soon as one can be freed up from more urgent duties, we'll send an officer to your house to interview you."

"Okay, thanks." Paul hung up and stared at the photograph of Sarah and himself on their wedding day. Next to it was one of Tammy and Sarah when Tammy was about a year old. He sighed. *If only ...*

Paul pulled off and threw his tie across the room. He rubbed his forehead and tried to think of anyone else Sarah might have gone to see. Two cousins—Mildred in Carefree and Wilma in Kingman. *Late now, but maybe they would still be up.* He called Mildred first. She answered on the first ring, and he repeated his questions. Wilma had been asleep, but was instantly awake once he asked her. Neither of the cousins had seen or heard from Sarah.

He stared at the floor. Who else could he call? Sarah had been sort of a loner, not many close friends. They had a lot of casual acquaintances, but there were none he could think of she'd spend the entire day with.

Unless ... could she be seeing another man? Didn't sound like her. Besides, if a person had a new love interest, wouldn't they be getting spiffed up? If anything, she did the opposite. She didn't take any care with her appearance anymore, even going casual to work. Most of her co-workers went casual, but Sarah never did until after

Tammy died. So, an affair wasn't likely. *This leaves only two options: She was injured so badly she couldn't use her cell phone or she is, she is ...*

Paul sat on the edge of the bed with his head in his hands. *Was it only this morning I thought about asking for a divorce? What kind of idiot am I?*

The phone rang, and he grabbed it without checking the Caller ID. "Hello?"

"Hi, it's me," his mother said. "Have you heard anything?"

"Oh. Hi, Mom." Disappointment flooded him. "No, nothing."

"I had another thought. Doesn't Sarah have a college roommate named Dorothy? I think she was Sarah's maid of honor when you got married, and she came to the funeral too."

"Oh, yeah, good, I forgot about her. I'll call her. In fact, I think maybe Sarah heard from her a couple of days ago. The number should still be in the received calls."

"Bye, sweetheart. Call me when you find out anything."

Paul paged through incoming calls on the land line, and sure enough, there was Dorothy's number. He pushed send, and it rang several times. When the answering machine picked up, he had opened his mouth to leave a message when Dorothy's sleepy voice answered.

"Hi, Sarah. What's up?"

"Hi, Dorothy. No, not Sarah, It's me, Paul. Sarah's missing, and I'm contacting anyone who might have heard from her. Have you?"

"What? Missing? No, I haven't talked to her since Monday. How long has she been gone?"

"Since early this morning."

"You know, Paul, I've been really worried about her since Tamara died. She can't get past Tammy's death. This is not something I even want to think about, but you don't think she might have ... that is, she wouldn't try to ..."

"No. I mean, I don't think so, but I'm worried. She's never done anything like this before. I think if they'd found an accident, the police would've notified me by now, but I haven't heard anything. I called them a couple of hours ago, and they said they would send someone out to interview me when an officer was free. They haven't called back or showed up yet."

"They probably think she'll show up on her own. If she went off the road, though, there are a hundred places where her car wouldn't be visible, and it's dark now."

"Yeah, and if she went off the road somewhere between here and town, she could be hurt bad or ... or worse. Probably they just haven't found the car or whatever. I wish I knew. I wish I knew where to even start."

"I'm here if you want to talk, and I mean that. At any time, day or night."

"Thanks, Dorothy. I think I'll call Dr. Howard tomorrow. He's the therapist we've been going to since Tamara died. He has a pretty good feel for what goes on inside my head. Maybe better than I do. I haven't talked to him in a while, but maybe I should. So, now I need to get off the phone in case anyone calls me back."

"Sure, Paul, I understand. Hang in there. Bye."

He tried Sarah's cell again. No luck.

Chapter 5

April AD 30

Sarah woke the next day disoriented. The early morning sun shone through the single window in the house. She pushed her hair out of her eyes and sat up, remembering her dream of the night before. When she shifted her weight, the hard wood of the pallet registered. Another one of her nightmares? Or a continuation of the one before?

Rising from her bed, she found a carved comb. She'd kept her hair at shoulder-length, but now it hung nearly to her waist in a long braid. Loosening her hair, she combed and rebraided it, noting it was still the same dark blonde shade, but greasy. *I could sure use a shower. Hah! Fat chance of finding a shower, but maybe a river or something.* Again, as she wondered, another thought slipped into her head, this time of a path to a pond ... *no, a shallow well* ... where the local women and children went who didn't have servants to carry water for a bath. *I guess that's me.*

She touched Paulos's shoulder to wake him. "Mmpphh?" He winced and groaned as he rolled over.

"I have to go prepare the morning meal. Would you stay till I return? Tamara's still asleep."

"Of course." Squinting in the early morning sunshine, he yawned and scratched his beard.

As Sarah came through the door into the villa, a woman trotted into the kitchen. Sarah remembered her name was Martha, the head housekeeper. Short, stout, and fiftyish, Martha was a chatty, goodhearted woman who didn't have a mean molecule in her whole body, but telling Martha anything was a good way to let the whole city know by the next morning.

"Good morning, Martha. You're up early."

"Good morning, Sarah. The mistress asked that I go with you to the market this morning. They—the mistress and master, I mean—expect her mother and father to arrive today, and she wants extra provisions. She—the mistress—thought you might need help bringing them back from the marketplace. The provisions, that is. They—her parents—sent word by her brother Marcus. The mistress's brother, you know. He arrived last night after dinner. I offered to bring him something to eat, but he said no."

Martha rose on her toes to peek through one of the high windows. "The mistress's brother, I mean. Now, I need to clean up the guest quarters and tend to the garden in the courtyard. Since Paulos can't work, Hamath expects me to buy glass and have someone replace the broken window, as well." She glanced over her shoulder. "I guess I should ask the mistress to hire another worker or ask the master to free up one of the stable slaves to help, since I know nothing about how to replace windows. Do you? No, I don't suppose so." She nodded her head so vigorously her chins bounced. "You're a woman too, and besides that, you're a cook, not a handy man. Do you—"

"Paulos might know of someone," Sarah interrupted, thinking if she didn't, she might not get a chance to speak for a week. "Or he might be able to instruct you. If you can't do the repair yourself, I could help you. I'll ask him after the morning meal is finished. By the way, I'm going to the well to bathe. Do you want to go too, or would you rather I came back, and then you and I go to the marketplace?"

"Today will be much too busy, so if you'd come back, that would be best." Martha brushed a crumb off the work table. "There are so many things to do to get ready for everyone, you know. Air out the rooms, get out clean bed clothes, basins of water in the rooms, flowers in vases, that sort of thing. Oh, yes, and dusting and sweeping and mopping. And I should clean the upper guest quarters too. They might rather sleep up there on the roof. Oh, dear, oh, dear, so much to do."

With that, Martha bustled back into the house. She reminded Sarah of a squirrel hurrying here and there in short, energetic bursts, stopping to chatter between each burst.

Sarah hurried to prepare and serve the morning meal and then cleaned the kitchen. When she stepped into their house, Paulos sat slicing some cheese for Tamara. Tammy bounced around like the energetic three-year-old she'd been before the headaches began.

"Have you eaten yet?" she asked Paulos. "I brought melon from the house."

"I ate some cheese. I might eat a little melon, though."

"I thought you might. You liked them before, uh, before your accident. By the way, I'm going to the well to bathe this morning, and I'll take Tamara with me."

"Bathe?" he asked, nonplussed. "Why?"

"I ... um ... the mistress asked me to because she has visitors coming." Frequent bathing must be a thing of the distant future. Except for when women bathed after their monthly cycles, cleansing the body might be considered taboo. *I guess I could have said something*

*about it being two days since I last had a shower, but I don't suppose that
would fly any farther than our wooden pallet.*

Sarah wondered if Tamara knew anything about another life.
This little trek might be a good time to find out.

"Oh, the mistress wants the window in the guest room repaired.
I know you can't do the work yourself, but if you'd direct us, Martha
and I can do the repair while you give instructions. Would you do
that for us?"

Paulos's eyes brightened a little. "Of course."

Sarah suspected he'd be happy to do anything other than begging.
He'd been a strong, able man, and now he was reduced to a crippled
beggar, unable to provide for his family, and worse, dependent upon
his wife—no doubt emasculating in this time. No wonder he acted
so depressed.

"I'm going to take Tamara to the well now." She held out her
hand to Tamara, who skipped happily beside her. *Hmm. Skipping?*
She wondered if skipping was part of the distant past too. Or did
Tammy remember how to skip from when Sarah taught her last fall?

The path was a long one. They crossed the lengthy, narrow
land bridge to the mainland and weaved through trees and rocks
to a secluded cove. They walked behind two women and four other
children to the cove and met others along the pathway. Several
women were there before her with their children. Tamara splashed
happily with them. None seemed even a little concerned about
modesty.

Sarah wasn't quite so uninhibited in her thin inner tunic, so she
quickly finished and redressed, struggling with pulling her cloak on
over the still-wet tunic. More women and children arrived and left
constantly, so this was no time to talk to Tamara about memories.
She allowed a few minutes more for Tamera to play, then called her
to get dressed.

The toddler crossed her arms and pouted. "No, Mama. We're still having fun. I don't want to go yet." Sarah laughed and waded out to capture the child. When Tammy tried to avoid her, Sarah caught her and tickled her feet.

By the time they reached the shore, Tammy was squirming and giggling. Sarah helped her dress, then they hurried back up the path. Back home, she left Tamara with Paulos and went to find Martha. The master stopped her as she entered the courtyard.

"I've thought over bringing a physician for Paulos, Sarah." His teeth bared, but she wouldn't call it a smile. "As you said, he is of no use to me the way he is. I'll send for a physician to be here tomorrow morning."

Sarah lowered her head and smiled. "Thank you, sir."

"The physician will examine him in the courtyard, rather than in your house. I don't think he'd be willing to go into your dwelling."

Sarah didn't really care how the man felt about their little shack. She was so happy she almost skipped like Tamara. When she entered the villa, she saw Martha in the hallway.

"Martha, you will never guess! The master promised to bring a real physician for Paulos to make his leg straight!" She grabbed Martha's hands and danced her around.

Martha laughed but quickly sobered. "Child, you shouldn't get your hopes up. Even a good physician might not be able to make Paulos's leg straight, and he will go through terrible pain while the physician breaks and resets it. One of my brothers has a friend who died from such an operation a few years ago. Think before you do something that might do more hurt than good."

Sarah drew in a quick breath. "Oh, Martha, I didn't think of that. Paul—um, Paulos—is so weak now. What if he dies?" She frowned, then straightened her shoulders. "No, I won't think that way. He hates his existence now. I'm afraid if something doesn't change, he might decide to take his own life. I'll take good care of him. I won't let him die. Now, let's go get the provisions for the visitors."

Leading the donkey, they made their way to the marketplace, stacking the little wagon high with food. Then they talked to the craftsman who assured them he'd deliver the glass cut to size.

Martha chattered all the way to and from the marketplace, allowing Sarah's thoughts to dwell on Paulos and the coming physician. She could scarcely wait to tell him that they could reset his leg. As soon as they put away the food, she hurried to their home.

"Paulos, I have good news!" she called out before stepping across the threshold. He was still lying on the pallet with Tamara by his side.

"Papa doesn't feel good, so I'm taking care of him. See? I've got some water and aspirins." She showed her mother two tiny pieces of cheese and a cup of water. "Soon he'll feel all better."

Sarah's shock must have registered on her face. Paulos managed a wan smile. "I don't know what *as-prins* are, but Tamara assures me I'll feel much better if I take them. So, I must eat this remedy she gives me. What is your good news, wife?"

"The master agreed to bring in a physician to reset your leg, Paulos. You might yet be able to walk again."

His smile disappeared, and he blanched. "Have you lost your mind? Haven't I endured enough pain without submitting myself to another healer? Does the man hate me so that he'd make me go through this again? Or maybe even kill me?"

He paused, eyes narrowed. "Was this your idea, woman? Did you convince him to do this?"

Sarah felt as if he'd slapped her. "I was only thinking of you. I know how you hate begging. I want you to be whole again."

Paulos blew out his breath and turned away. "Or perhaps you'd like to be rid of me. I'm sure you have no use for me in this condition, since I'm *less than whole*. Maybe you would be better off if I were gone."

"No, no! I didn't mean that. Paulos, please listen to me. The master said he will get a real physician, not another charlatan. He promised."

"And what did you have to promise him in return? Don't you think I've seen the way he looks at you?"

She responded to him through clenched teeth. "I promised him nothing more than a whole servant back who could work for him. Believe that or don't, but quit shouting." She tilted her head toward Tamara. "Look at your daughter," she whispered.

Paulos glanced at Tammy, cringing in the corner, her eyes wide and frightened. He dropped his head.

"Forgive me." He held out his hand toward Tamara, but she shook her head, shrinking back to the wall.

When the silence stretched uncomfortably, he mumbled, "Let's go fix the window." He gathered up his crutches and made his way through the doorway, groaning through gritted teeth.

Sarah knelt beside Tamara. "We didn't mean to scare you, Tammy."

"You yelled at Papa, and he yelled at you. Don't you love Papa? Does he hate you?"

"We were angry, but we're not angry any more. Sometimes even grownups get mad at each other. It's not a good thing to do, but we won't hurt each other." Sarah held out her hand to the child. "Let's go help Papa, okay?"

Tamara hesitated. "Okay," she murmured." She stood and followed Sarah out the door. Before they caught up with Paulos, Keddy bounded out to greet her, licking her hands and face and wriggling in his happy puppy way. Tammy's sunny disposition resurfaced, and she giggled as she hugged the dog around his shaggy neck.

Chapter 6

April AD 2008

Paul didn't sleep much that night. Cars passing the house, dogs barking, the house creaking—the least noise snapped him awake. At five, he gave up and crawled out of bed. After trying Sarah's cell again, he started the coffee, took a shower, poured some juice—each step in his routine carrying him heavily from one action to the next.

He tried her cell one more time and then called the police. This time a different officer took his call, a Sergeant Willis. In contrast to the gravelly voice of Lieutenant Jones, this female officer's voice was pleasant and friendly. Paul repeated the story and added, "Sergeant, I'm anxious about my wife. If she *is* lying hurt somewhere, the time is passing when she could be rescued."

"I understand. I'll take most of the information over the phone. It's quicker. The report says an officer became available about four a.m., but we waited in case you might be asleep."

"I couldn't sleep. My wife has been missing since early yesterday morning, and I've called every relative and acquaintance I can think of, with no luck. A telephone call or visit from the police would have been welcome, even in the middle of the night."

"Okay, and I agree it's time to pursue every angle. Does she have a cell phone?"

"Yes, but I don't think it's turned on. I've tried calling her several times, but it keeps going to voice mail. She left yesterday before I woke up at six. Usually she doesn't turn her phone on until she gets to work. She doesn't like to answer it while she's driving, but she would have it with her. Can you locate her that way?"

"Sometimes, if everything comes together right. What's the number?"

Paul gave it to her.

"And what was she wearing?"

Paul walked to the closet, phone in hand. "I don't know. I was asleep when she left. I looked through her clothes last night but can't tell what isn't there. Her closet looks full to me, hardly anything in the hamper. I'm looking again now. Wait ... I don't see a certain shirt I know she likes. It's kind of a light sea green with a darker green watery-looking pattern, buttons up the front. Probably blue jeans with it. Or tan jeans, maybe."

"Do you know where she was going?"

He sat on the bed and rubbed his temples. "My guess is to work. She works at Greymeyers Construction Company, Black Canyon Highway and Union Hills. She usually drives south from our home in Wickenburg on 60, turns onto Carefree Highway, then onto 17, then south to Union Hills. She might not have been heading for work, but she didn't wake me up to tell me any different. She normally would have done that or at least left a note."

"I think we have enough information now, Mr. Johnson. How can we get in touch with you? Will you be at home?"

"Yes. I'll wait here for your call."

"Do you have a cell?"

Paul gave Sergeant Willis every telephone number where he might be reached: his cell, his home, his work, and his mother's house.

When he got off the phone with the police, Paul called his office secretary, Evelyn McPhersen.

"Hi, Evie. This is Paul. I won't be in today." He fought back a quaver in his voice. "Sarah is missing."

"Sarah's missing? Oh, no, Paul; that's awful! Is there anything I can do?"

"No, just let the rest of the crew know I won't be in. Please don't tell anyone but the boss why, okay? If the others get nosy, just say I'm not feeling so hot."

"Yeah, got that. Gossip mills fly hard and fast here. I'll put you on my prayer list, Paul."

"Yeah, thanks. Bye."

Prayer list. Sure. Like that would help. Pray to the ceiling all you like, Evie. It's a nice thought, and I wish it would work.

Paul walked to the computer. He'd forgotten to turn it off the night before. He checked his emails, deleted most of them. Nothing.

Realizing he hadn't eaten since that burger the day before, he opened the refrigerator door and stared at the contents. Nothing looked even vaguely interesting, but he had to eat something. He pulled out the bread, stuck a couple of slices in the toaster, and ate them plain, washed down with another cup of coffee.

He strode outside and back in with the newspaper in record time, not wanting to miss any calls. He read the entire paper. Or at least he guessed he had. He hoped no one would give him a test on the contents.

The day dragged on, but the only calls came from Sarah's friends and relatives he had contacted the night before. The policeman he talked to first finally called back at seven p.m.

"Hello, Mr. Johnson, this is Lieutenant Jones. I'd like to come out to your house and talk to you. We haven't found anything, and the car hasn't been sighted."

"I don't know what more you can do here than you can do from there, but I'd appreciate if you'd come. Maybe you can find something I haven't."

When he arrived, the officer introduced himself as Bart Jones and asked Paul to call him by his first name. The lieutenant, about an inch or two shorter than Paul and a few pounds heavier, spotted the computer and walked to it, limping slightly. "This hers or yours?"

"Both."

"You got her password?"

"Well, no, but I think she has the password remembered on the computer. Her username is sarahjohnson and a bunch of numbers @ aol.com. I went through my email, but I didn't think about checking hers."

Bart sat down at the computer, ran one hand through greying dark hair, and logged on. She had fifty-six emails.

"Wow, that's more than I get in a month," Paul commented, looking over the lieutenant's shoulder.

"Do you know who any of these are from?"

Paul leaned in and scanned the email names. "Not many of them. Some look like ads or spam to me. Maybe some office stuff, but I don't know who the people are ... except this one, Dot Pierce. That has to be her college roomie, Dorothy. The rest of the user names look unfamiliar. I'd never get on her account because it would feel like I'm snooping through her personal stuff."

"Sergeant Willis said you contacted everyone you could think of. Would you please go over that list for me? I want their telephone numbers too."

Paul gave him the list and numbers, then offered Bart a cup of coffee.

"Sure. Sounds good. Got milk and sugar?"

Paul rubbed his chin. "I should've thought about this when I asked. My brain isn't functioning too well. We do have some flavored creamer and some sugar, but the regular milk may be out of date."

"The creamer's fine, but skip the sugar."

"I hope you can find something on that computer that helps." He went to brew the coffee and brought back two mugs.

Bart walked to the bedroom, carrying the cup. Paul followed.

He opened a closet door. "Have you noticed whether any of her clothes or suitcases are gone? I'm assuming her purse isn't here."

"I thought of that and did check. The suitcases are here, and the dresser and closet are full of her clothes. I don't think she planned a trip. And yeah, her purse isn't here."

"Do you have a list of her credit cards? We can check to see if they've been used anywhere."

"Yes, I think so. There should be a list on the computer of both our credit cards."

Paul frowned. "There is one thing I didn't mention before. Six months ago, our three-year-old daughter, Tamara, died. Sarah's had a tough time. I mean, we both did and both of us went to therapy, but Sarah doesn't seem to be getting any better. For instance, she always used to be a sharp dresser. Even though nearly everyone else at her office dresses casual, she always used to wear pressed slacks or a skirt and a dressy blouse, sometimes a suit if she had to meet with anyone outside the office. Now she just throws on whatever's easiest, usually jeans and a tee shirt. She never wore much makeup, but now she wears none. In other words, she acts depressed."

"You say she was … is … in therapy. Who's her therapist?"

"Dr. Art Howard, same one I'm seeing." Paul got him the office name and phone number. The lieutenant opened drawers, checked the nightstands, even looked under the bed. Paul stood out of the way, beginning to feel uncomfortable.

"What's this stain here on the carpet?" Bart knelt next to a brownish stain.

"Coffee. I spilled some this morning and didn't clean it up. Guess I should do that." Paul turned toward the hall closet where they kept the carpet cleaner spray.

"Never mind. We'll need to test that stain before you do anything with it." Bart brushed his fingers across the stain and held them to his nose.

Paul stopped in his tracks. "Test it?"

"With any disappearance, we always check out the victim's house and people close to him or her. That includes testing stains on the rugs, furniture, etcetera, that might turn out to be blood."

"Blood? You think I'd hurt Sarah?"

The lieutenant let out an exasperated sigh. "Mr. Johnson … Paul … I never met you before today, but even if I'd known you all your life and could swear you were a terrific guy, I'd still have to test this stain. We'll need to look over your car too. It's just procedure, sir."

"I didn't think of that. But I guess I've heard the spouse often winds up being a suspect."

"Do you have other children?"

"No." Paul cleared his throat. "We only had the one."

"Does Mrs. Johnson have siblings, parents still alive?"

"No, neither. Sarah was a late-life surprise to her parents. They never intended to have children, and her mother was in her mid-forties when Sarah was born. Her father was about ten years older. Her mother died of brain cancer when Sarah was a teenager, and her father died a little over three years ago, a week after Tamara was born. Sarah doesn't have any brothers or sisters, but she has a couple of cousins she's close to. Their names and numbers are on the list I gave you."

"All right. I'll look over the car, and then I'll get out of your hair for tonight. Is your car in the garage?"

"Yes. Follow me." Paul led him through the kitchen, opened the door into the garage, and turned on the light.

Bart walked around the blue Lexus. Pointing to the dent on the left front bumper, he asked, "What's this? It looks recent." He pulled a flashlight from a holster on his belt. "Collide with a tan car?"

"Yeah, last week. I came home late one night and bumped Sarah's car when I pulled into the garage. I think her car was a little too close to the middle, but I've got to tell you, she really gave me the dickens about that." Paul shook his head, smiling.

"Had you been drinking?"

"No, just bone tired."

Bart's eyes narrowed, but he made no comment. He opened the car doors one at a time and shined the light around and under the seats, repeating the search in the trunk.

"Well, that's all I have for tonight. I suggest you try to get some sleep and that you go to work tomorrow. We'll keep looking for Mrs. Johnson, of course, and keep you informed."

Paul shoved his hands into his pockets and frowned at the floor. "Yeah, okay. It's been an eternity since I got home yesterday. Maybe time will go faster if I go back to work."

Chapter 7

April AD 30

With Paulos's directions, Sarah and Martha were able to put the new glass in the guest room window. *He really knows his craft. Just like Paul knows his in the modern world.*

When they finished, Paulos struggled to his feet. "I'm going to the city gate," he muttered as he made his painful way out the door.

After helping Martha clean up, Sarah began preparing a beef stew for the evening meal. The huge blackened kettle hanging over the fireplace, filled with a haunch of beef and a variety of vegetables, should provide enough for everyone. As she added more leeks and seasoning, the aroma from the savory stew made her mouth water.

The mistress's mother and father, Proteus and Thecla, arrived in a curtained litter, carried by six slaves and followed by their personal servants. The couple settled in the guest room with the servants' assistance. Martha showed the men to their sleeping quarters close to the stable. Thecla's personal servant, Mary, the only woman, would sleep in the villa in Martha's room.

Sarah was glad she'd made such a big kettle of stew and more bread than she had expected to need. She'd have to bake even more than this tomorrow. Not counting the guests and their other slaves, she was sure those six strong men who carried the litter could have eaten them out of groceries in one sitting.

One of the poles had slipped from a ring on the litter, leaving a ragged cut on the arm of a young Hebrew slave named Benoni. Sarah cleaned and applied salve and a bandage to the muscular seventeen-year-old's wound. With the extra cooking, cleaning, and tending to the young man's injury, there'd been no time to talk to Tamara about giving her papa aspirin.

By the time the work day was complete, Sarah was exhausted. She picked up Tamara, asleep on a fur mat near the fireplace, and carried her back to their house, thankful for the moonlight coming in the window. She wondered why Paulos hadn't left a lamp lit for them. Tenderly, she laid the sleeping child on her pallet and pulled a soft lamb's wool blanket to her shoulders.

As Sarah felt her way through the shadows to their pallet, she called softly, "Paulos?" No answer. She lit the lamp on the table, and saw the bed was empty. It didn't look like he'd been home since the window repair that morning. A sense of panic rose in her throat. *Where could he be? Had he been beaten and robbed of his pittance? Had he fallen and been unable to get back up? Was he still angry and maybe stopped at a tavern?* That didn't sound like the man she knew, but this was a different world and Paulos a different man.

Different?

Sarah sat down. Which way did he say he'd go—to the city gate? She knew Tyre was an island connected to the mainland by a long and narrow earth causeway. Therefore, Tyre's only gate would have to be on the east side of town. She decided to ask Martha to stay with Tamara while she went to look for him. She found her friend in the courtyard, chatting with the young slave, Benoni.

"Please forgive me for interrupting, but Martha, would you please stay with Tamara for a while? I have to look for Paulos. He's not home yet."

"Not home? But why? He should be home by now." Martha scowled, hands propped on her hips. As she opened her mouth to continue, Benoni stood up.

"Who is Paulos?" he asked, turning toward Sarah.

"My husband. He's crippled."

"My master is through with my services for the day. Maybe I could help. It would be well if you have someone along to help you bring your husband home."

"Won't you be in trouble with your master if you leave?" Sarah asked.

"So long as I'm here when they want me in the morning, he's lenient with my time."

Martha hurried back to Sarah's house, assuring her she'd stay with Tamara until they got back.

As Sarah and Benoni hurried toward the city gate, the young man glanced at Sarah. "I'm praying for your husband. You mustn't worry. God is telling me you just need faith."

"Faith? Your God is telling you I need faith. I heard no voice," she answered sarcastically.

He smiled. "God speaks to my heart. I don't hear a voice, either."

"They only thing my heart feels is fear. My husband hasn't ever done anything like this before." She shook her head. "I don't believe in your God, or any god. I haven't believed in God since I lost my mother to cancer when I was thirteen."

"Did you find her?"

"What?"

"Your mother. Did you find her?"

"No, I meant she died from cancer."

"I'm sorry. You must have been sad. Tell me, what is 'cancer'?"

"It's a disease that makes people die a very slow and painful death. But that was long ago." Sarah changed the subject, not wanting to discuss something that could still bring her to tears. "Paulos could have fallen and be lying horribly injured somewhere, or maybe somebody mugged ... I mean attacked him, stealing what few coins he'd been given. He's probably lying on the ground somewhere, knocked out."

"In Israel, there is a famous healer who is able to cure anyone." Benoni pointed toward the southeast, as though she could see if she looked. "I heard him speak one night when my owners were in Samaria. He stopped there with his disciples and asked a woman for a drink of water. Then he told the woman her life history, so she ran into the village, insisting that the whole town come and listen to this prophet. He spoke to all of them several times, and he healed a man who couldn't hear or speak and other people too. I was there."

Sarah felt a chill go down her spine. "What was his name?" She shouldn't have asked. She knew the answer before Benoni spoke.

"Jesus," he said.

They had arrived at the gate, sparing Sarah the need to reply. They saw only one other person, walking toward an inn not far from the gate. He looked like a merchant, but he must have arrived after sundown. He didn't have any camels or entourage with him.

Sarah stayed behind while Benoni approached him. "Have you seen a man with a lame leg?"

"No. I just got here. I haven't seen anyone but you, except for a few men going into the tavern there, which is where I'm going." He pointed his chin toward a building where a dim light, sour odor, and raucous noise spilled from an open door.

Benoni and Sarah followed him toward the building.

"You should stay outside, Sarah." Benoni grasped her elbow and stopped her from entering. "No good woman should ever go into a tavern. Wait for me here."

Sarah stepped aside into the dark shadow of the building, holding her chilled arms and worrying silently.

As soon as Benoni reappeared, Sarah stepped back into the moonlight.

"No one has seen him." He shook his head. "Let's go check the ports."

On the way, Benoni chattered on. "Jesus is the Christ, you know. The Messiah. The Son of God. The Expected One. He's probably known by even more titles than that. I'm hoping to earn my freedom so I can follow him and be one of his disciples. I've heard so many stories about him. He's wonderful, and everybody's so amazed by him, except the temple rulers and Pharisees and Sadducees. They don't like him because he criticizes their pompous attitudes. He could be the expected leader of the Jews and lead us to freedom from Rome, but the religious leaders keep harassing him."

Sarah paid little attention to his ramblings. With anxious eyes, she searched every ditch, doorway, and shadow. Her imagination invented terrible scenes.

In the end, they searched in vain. They found no sign of Paulos, and the few people they found at the ports knew nothing. Hoping maybe Paulos had returned home while they sought him, Sarah hurried her steps. *Benoni is still babbling about his precious friend. I've had my fill of the boy's constant blathering about Jesus, Jesus, Jesus.* A tinge of guilt needled her. *Although I do appreciate this boy's help, so there. A woman walking alone at night could be in danger, even in this place and in these times, I suppose.*

49

When they arrived back at her house, Paulos still hadn't returned. Sarah thanked Benoni and Martha and sent them back to their own beds. She lay down on her pallet in despair. What could she do now? She lay sleepless on her bed. This was so unlike him. Or, at least, so unlike the Paul—*Paulos*—she knew. Even though they were distant with each other, he would never leave without saying anything to anyone. Such an action just didn't fit his character. Which meant he was hurt, kidnapped, or ... but who would kidnap such a badly crippled man? She couldn't pay any kind of ransom for him, and their master wouldn't.

She decided to ask people in the marketplace the next morning if anyone had seen Paulos. Surely plenty of people knew him by sight. Traveling merchants arrived and left all the time. Maybe Martha could help. Someone must have seen him. *There's still hope, isn't there? I can't give up hope.*

Chapter 8

April AD 30

The night seemed to last forever, but at last morning came. Sarah woke Tamara, who rubbed her eyes and yawned. Peering over at their pallet, she scowled. "Where's Papa?"

"I'm not sure where he is, honey. Come with me. We need to go to the big house, so I can fix the morning meal."

"But I want Papa. He didn't hug me yet, and he always makes my breakfast."

"I know, but he didn't come home last night. I'm sorry."

Tammy pouted as she pulled her tunic over her head. While Sarah tried to comb her little one's hair, the girl picked up her doll and stuffed her thumb into her mouth. "Ow, Mama. Stop hurting my hair," she whined.

"I'm sorry, baby. Your hair is all tangled after you wake up. So is mine, see?" Sarah ran the comb over her own head until she encountered a rat's nest, untangling the hair with pulls that made her want to whine too. What she wouldn't give for some hair conditioner.

Oil.

Oil?

Olive oil. Perfumed oil is for the rich.

No wonder her hair looked greasy.

Sarah sighed. They walked out of the house and shut the door behind them. Tamara ran ahead of her mother but stopped in the courtyard to play with Keddy.

As soon as Sarah completed her morning duties, she went looking for Martha. The master stopped her.

"Where is your husband?" he asked. "Why isn't he out here? The physician will arrive within the hour."

"Paulos didn't return last night, sir," Sarah said, her voice catching. "I'm afraid he might be lying hurt somewhere. I searched for him last night but couldn't find him."

Hamath responded with anger. "After I went to the trouble to locate a knowledgeable physician? Is he a coward or just an ungrateful lout? Well, don't ask for any more favors for Paulos. If he ever returns, he can beg for his bread forever. Maybe you should begin eating with the other servants and leave him to fend for himself." The master turned and stomped into the great room.

Sarah stared after him. Somehow his fury felt a little overdone. *Probably just my suspicious nature.* She shrugged, then went to find Martha.

Martha was on her knees in one of the bedrooms, scrubbing the rock floor with old rags. "Martha, I'm going to go ask the shopkeepers if they've seen Paulos. Would you come with me? You know more of them than I do."

Martha shook her head. "I'm sorry, Sarah. Dorcas wants me to make four new drapes for the windows when I'm done here."

"So be it." Sarah sighed. "Would it be all right to leave Tamara in your keeping?"

"Of course. I enjoy her company. Such a dear child, no trouble at all. She plays so well with the other children and with the puppy too. Everybody loves her. Why, just yesterday—"

Sarah took a step backwards. "I'll return in time to prepare the next meal."

"I certainly hope you find Paulos, Sarah. I know you're anxious about him. He's such a good man, and Tamara will be so unhappy if you don't find him. Widows sometimes starve to death, you know, without a husband or a son to provide for them. What will you do if he's gone forever?" Martha wrung her hands.

Nodding, then waving, Sarah backed away and made her escape. She hurried to the marketplace and asked every merchant and shopper she saw if they'd noticed Paulos anywhere the day before.

Esther, a vendor of chickens and other types of fowl, remembered seeing him. She glanced up as she pulled feathers from a scalded fowl. "I saw him over by the city gate yesterday afternoon. He was talking to a cloth merchant, probably asking for coins. I don't know anything more. I couldn't hear what they were saying, and then I had to chase one of the geese that got away from me."

"Is the cloth merchant still here?" Sarah asked.

"I don't know. I didn't see him this morning. If you ask Jonas over there, he might know." Esther tilted her head and pointed with her elbow toward a vendor's shop that displayed brightly colored materials.

Sarah hurried across the street to where a man leaned over a crate, sorting through bolts of fabrics. "Hello. Are you Jonas?"

A deeply tanned man with a short, neat beard looked up from his work. "Yes. May I be of help to you?" His voice was so deep it seemed to rise up from his sandals.

"I'm looking for my husband. Do you know Paulos, one of Hamath's servants?"

Jonas squinted as he looked at her, and Sarah wondered if he were a little nearsighted. "Is he the one who has the broken leg?" He straightened, and Sarah could see the fortyish man was thin, three or four inches taller than she.

"Yes. Did you see him yesterday or today?" Catching herself wringing her hands, she dropped them to her side.

"I saw him yesterday, talking to one of the merchants I sell materials to, but I haven't seen him today."

"Do you know if the merchant is still in Tyre?" Her fingers twisted the edge of her cloak.

"No. He left yesterday just before the gates closed." Warm brown eyes looked intently into hers. His voice softened. "Is your husband gone?"

"Yes." Sarah's eyes filled with tears. She'd never been a weepy female, and here she was tearing up in front of a stranger. Impatiently, she dashed the tears away.

"I'm so sorry." He rubbed his chin whiskers as he turned his gaze to a bolt of cloth. "I don't believe I saw your husband again after the merchant left. Might he have gone with them?"

"No. Or at least I don't think so. I'm sure he wouldn't have left with anyone. We have a daughter, and he adores her. He wouldn't leave her fatherless on purpose. I don't think, anyway."

Jonas tilted his head to one side, one eyebrow raised in question. "You don't say anything about him adoring you. Tell me, did you argue?"

His soft question was too much for Sarah. If the man had been scornful, critical, or just curious, Sarah could have handled it, but his obvious concern undid her resolve. She burst into sobs she couldn't control. She turned to run, but Jonas caught her arm.

"Here, act as though you're looking over the fabric," he whispered. "This isn't easy to hear, I know, but the cloth merchant won't return for several months. However, some other vendor here might have seen more. Try all the sellers, at least those within sight of the gate. Or would you like for me to do that?"

Sarah nodded, not trusting her voice.

"Stay here at my shop, and I'll ask the others. If a customer comes in, tell them I'll be back in a short time."

Sarah's tears continued falling, but she nodded and struggled to get herself under control. "Thank you," she croaked.

When Jonas returned a half-hour later, two customers waited. Sarah had dried her tears, but her eyes still stung. She waited while Jonas bargained with the two women and again when another arrived. When he finished taking care of them and they were out of earshot, he turned to Sarah.

"I don't have good news. No one saw Paulos after the merchant left with his caravan. Ismael the silversmith said several men—he thought they were from the caravan—gathered around Paulos. Then he had a customer and lost track of what happened. He said the same as the others—he didn't see Paulos after the merchant left."

"Where did the caravan go, do you know?" Sarah thought her heart would tear in two, but she would *not* lose control again.

"I don't know. They packed all their camels with materials to sell. They could have gone north or south. Once they sell most or all the merchandise, they will return to Tyre to restock. Does your husband have any family in another village?"

Sarah almost shook her head but hesitated. "Yes. He has two brothers, one in Paphos on Cyprus and the other in Berytus. He has a sister in Ptolemais. I'll send word to them somehow. Perhaps he went to one of them, although I still can't believe he'd leave without a word. Thank you for your help, Jonas. You've been more than kind."

Jonas shrugged. "No more than anyone would do. If I hear anything further, I'll send word to you or come myself to tell you. Where do you live? Are you also one of Hamath's servants?"

"Yes. I'm often here buying food for the household."

He nodded. "I thought I'd seen you with Martha."

"Yes, Martha and I sometimes walk together. I'll check with you whenever I come here." She paused and took a deep breath. "I can't thank you enough. Thank you for listening, thank you for checking with the other vendors, and thank you most of all for caring."

"I might understand what you're going through. My wife is missing too. She was abducted and placed into slavery by thieves ten years ago." His eyes moistened. "I couldn't find out any more about her than that, even though my brothers and I spent four years searching this coast and several of the inland villages. And I'm not the only one. Several others here in Tyre have had older children, spouses, and parents disappear. There seems to be a monger who finds his slaves in this area."

"That's horrifying! I'm so sorry, Jonas." Sarah yearned for a computer, police, modern search-and-rescue officials, and a cell phone. Not that those always found the victims either.

"Even though it's been ten years, I still have a raw place in my heart. I will never give up hope of finding her. Her name is Mariah." Jonas rubbed his chest. "You shouldn't give up either."

"I hope she'll be found and returned to you, Jonas. I hope we both find our lost loved ones, and soon. I don't know how, but we have to find them."

Chapter 9

April AD 30

Mehida could feel every bone in her old, bent body. Her aching joints protested as she trudged along the road from the village of Nain to her home. She switched the loaded market basket from one arm to the other every few steps. If only her old donkey hadn't died. If only she had many children and grandchildren around to carry for her.

"I'm an old woman," she muttered to herself. "I shouldn't have to do this myself. I should have a strong son to take care of me, but here I am, the mother of one ungrateful daughter who ran off with that fisherman. My husband died, and now there's no one to take care of me but me."

She was so intent on not falling as she walked, she didn't see the man's still form beside the road. Didn't see him, that is, until she almost fell over his extended leg. She thought he must have moved his leg out in front of her; but then, her eyes weren't as sharp as they used to be.

A soft moan escaped the man's lips. Moving closer, Mehida knelt on creaky knees next to his thin form. "Who are you? And why are you lying here in the middle of the road? Are you trying to trip an old woman?"

He groaned again.

"If you don't get up, someone will run over you with a wagon," the toothless woman scolded. She poked him with a boney finger. "Are you listening to me?"

No response.

"Well then, I'm going to pull you off the road." Mehida tugged on one arm, but she couldn't budge him. She set her basket down, grasped both his arms and pulled again.

"Come on, you have to help me." She heaved until her aching body was soaked with sweat.

Opening his eyes in a pained squint, the man scowled at her.

Mehida placed her hand on his forehead. "You're burning with fever. Did you know that?"

He nodded almost imperceptibly, then his eyes drifted shut.

She shook her head. "I can't help you if you won't walk. Wait here. I'll find someone who can carry you."

The man regarded her though one bleary eye, then closed it again.

Paulos woke to searing pain jolting him from toenails to hair tips. Two men lifted him, one by the arms and the other his legs. He screamed. "Don't! My leg, my leg!"

"Wait," said the taller man. He lifted Paulos's tunic. The board bracing his leg had slipped to a point where it did no good at all, and the now open fracture just above his knee was swollen and red.

"My name is Joel. I'm a physician. This man is Abidon, my apprentice." The tall man spoke in a low, comforting tone. "Your leg doesn't look good, my friend. We'll carry you off this road, and then we'll set this and see what we can do about getting rid of the infection."

Paulos opened his mouth to speak, but all he could do was groan. How could one leg hurt so much?

Joel placed the board where the leg would be held stable and bound the board in place. He turned to the woman. "Where do you live?"

"My house is under that smoke." She pointed to a gray plume rising above the trees. The two men formed a cradle with their arms and carried Paulos, who couldn't keep from moaning through gritted teeth. When they arrived at the house, they laid him on the Roman-style bed, nearly three cubits high. Joel pulled up the tunic again. Paulos grabbed at his leg and raised his head. A line of white showed where the broken bone cut the skin. The leg felt hot and oozed pus and blood.

The physician shot a glance at Abidon, shaking his head. Joel motioned his assistant over to the far side of the bed. "You have to be as still as possible," he told Paulos. "Abidon will also hold you, but please try not to struggle. We have to reset this bone. It will hurt."

Glancing at the old woman, he asked, "Do you have any wine?"

She cackled. "Of course." She scurried to where a skin of wine hung on a peg next to the door. After pouring a healthy amount into a metal cup, she handed the cup to Joel.

"Good, that will do." He held the wine to Paul's lips. "Take a great drink, my friend. It will lessen the pain. Old woman, don't put the wine away. We'll need it again later."

She eyed him. "Are you sure you're a physician?"

"Yes." Joel nodded. "From Nazareth."

"Well, all right then. Just so you don't drink all my wine yourself after this young man finishes his portion. I'll have need of it myself later, and it's too heavy to carry every day from the village. I'm an old woman, you know."

Joel and Abidon both grinned at her. "We hadn't noticed." Abidon said, patting her arm.

Shaking her head, she chortled merrily and squatted on the floor by her table.

From the first incision, Paulos screamed through the entire operation, stopping only long enough to gasp for air. He tried to still his muscles, but they seemed to have a will of their own.

Apparently, Joel and his apprentice were accustomed to working with each other, because Abidon knew exactly what to do and when. They pulled on the leg until the bone snapped into place. Just when Paulos thought the pain could get no worse, the physician sewed the open wound and dumped wine over the stitches. He screamed one last time and passed out.

When they finished, Joel took a step back and looked over his patient from his head to his feet. Mehida guessed they were searching for evidence of another wound, but she hadn't seen any other blood staining the clothing, just a minor bruise on his head. Joel stepped forward again and felt the man's arms, trunk, and other leg. He turned to Mehida, who had watched with avid interest.

"Well, old woman, do you think you can take care of this man now?"

"Yes, I can. I know a little from my father. He was a healer too. I'm glad you lifted this man to the bed and set his leg, because I'm not as strong as when I was young." For once, Mehida didn't laugh.

"We'll be back through here next week, and we'll stop to check on him then. We'll bring you some wine to replace all this we just used," Joel assured her with a grin.

Mehida spread a gummy smile. "Then you may visit any time you like. Would you share my cheese and bread?"

"We would," Abidon responded. "In fact, we can add a bit of dried fish to the meal, and we'll leave some other meat with you."

"I'd like that. I haven't had meat for a time." Mehida studied the two young men. Hmm. *Maybe I could adopt these two. They would make good sons.*

The injured man didn't awaken during their meal. After Joel and Abidon took their leave, Mehida made a small amount of broth, using part of the mutton the men had left with her. She spooned a little into the injured man's mouth, stroking his throat to encourage him to swallow. Throughout the night, she repeated the process every two or three hours. In the morning, she changed the dressing and poured more wine on the wound.

Chapter 10

April AD 30

Sarah's feet dragged as she made her way back from the marketplace. If not for Tammy, she'd wish to be back in their house on the half-acre, landscaped lot in Wickenburg. Now here she was in ancient Tyre, Phoenicia, living in a one-room hovel, working as a cook for a man who would lose his job or be sued for sexual harassment in modern times. The trouble was that in modern America, Tamara lay in a small, grass-covered grave. Here, Sarah worried about Paulos's disappearance, but she had hope they'd find him. In the future, they had no hope Tammy would return.

How in the world did this switch happen? And why? She made a wry face. Maybe she'd lost her connection to reality and all this wasn't really happening. Maybe, even at that moment, she was lying in a psych ward at the Sunrise Medical Center in Peoria, Arizona. If so, did she want to wake up?

That answer was easy: No. Not at the expense of losing her little girl again. If this were a psychotic fugue, she'd rather live in the fugue than deal again with Tamara's death. So be it. Somehow, in this dream world—psychotic fugue or reality—they would find Paulos … and Mariah too.

Arriving at the villa, she first checked on Tamara, then began preparations for still another meal, a leg of lamb cooked with onions and garlic this time. She smiled. Even if she had to say so herself, she could cook a pretty yummy lamb.

As if staged, Hamath arrived and sniffed the air. "Whatever you've made smells delicious." He walked up close behind her, much too close for her comfort. She moved to the shelf with spices and tried to appear as though she were looking for one more ingredient.

He grasped her arm and turned her. "Why do you move away every time I draw near, Sarah?" He caressed her shoulders. "You act as though I were some repulsive lout rather than your very tolerant master."

"Tolerant?" Sarah asked. *No argument about the repulsive part.*

"Yes, tolerant." Hamath leaned closer. "Did you think I didn't know of your loud argument with Paulos or of your disappearance with my father-in-law's young slave for several hours? Do you prefer boys, my comely Sarah?"

Sarah glared at the master. "Benoni helped me look for Paulos. He wanted to help me because I bandaged his injured arm. Since a lone woman might not be safe on the streets at night, I agreed to take someone with me." At his lowering brows, she added a humble, "I hope this didn't offend you, sir," as she remembered to bow her head.

"Very well, Sarah." He backed up a half step. "However, now that you don't have a husband, you shall become my concubine, and you shall ask me if you may accompany any other man, however young, wherever you may want to go."

"My husband is not dead, master, only missing. I'm sure he'll come back to us. His daughter is precious to him. And since I'm still a married woman, I can't be your concubine."

The master stepped forward and reached again for her shoulders. "You may as well accept the facts, woman. Your husband must be dead. Even if he isn't dead, he's at least dead to you."

Sarah tried to dodge, but in the narrow confines of the kitchen, she found nowhere to run. He blocked her way out. She flattened herself against the wall, wondering what to do now. If she struck or fought him, he could have her stoned to death. If she ran, she could be returned to her master and beaten. If she submitted to him ... She shuddered. *God, help me!* The master's eyes gleamed as his body pressed hers to the wall.

She raised her voice. "My husband is not dead!" Just then, the mistress entered the enclosure.

Her voice dripped icicles. "Is there a problem, husband?"

He jumped back like he'd been hit with pepper spray. "Of course not, wife ... I'm just trying ... trying to make Sarah see the logic of her situation. Paulos is gone and probably dead."

"Her husband is dead? I haven't heard of his body being found, have you? No? I didn't think so. Leave the poor woman be. She has enough to worry about without your unwanted attention." The mistress propped her hands on her hips and pushed her face close to her husband's.

The master retreated from the kitchen, muttering something about the horses.

Good for you, mistress. You have more spine than I gave you credit for.

"Sarah, after our midday meal, I want you to come with me to the children's play room. The boys need instruction in the Greek language. You came to us from a Greek household, and you're an educated woman." The mistress's eyes narrowed as if daring contradiction. "You may teach the children between meals. Orphah and Tamara may stay with the boys while you're teaching. I'll double your pay."

"I'd be happy to, mistress," Sarah agreed. After this rescue, Sarah would have knelt and kissed her employer's feet, but she had turned and left the room.

Wait a minute. Did the mistress enter on the heels of a prayer? Sarah shook her head. Coincidence. Just a coincidence.

After the meal, she followed Dorcas down the hall. "Mistress, would you help me send word to Paulos's kin to see if perhaps he's gone to them? I have little to give you in return but the pittance that he earned on the streets before he disappeared. Maybe I could do some extra work in return, or you could hold what is owed from my wages."

The mistress smiled at her. "I'd be happy to provide help to find him. Despite my Hamath's questionable ways, I'm fond of him. I want to keep him for myself. If we find Paulos, Hamath will leave you alone, and I'll be rewarded for my efforts. You owe me nothing."

She paused. "Also, come to me if he gives you further trouble. He holds me in some regard, maybe because I come from a wealthy family. Most of our wealth came from my dowry, which was our purple dye company."

Sarah bowed her head. "You appeared at the right moment. Thank you."

The mistress nodded and led Sarah into an airy room with several glass windows and a doorway leading outside. The high windows reminded her of the frosted ones in the bathrooms in her Arizona house. Gideon, Orphah, and Tamara were playing with Keddy, who galloped after the stick they threw for him, skidding comically on the marble floor.

Sarah remembered her Canaanite parents worked for a Greek household, but both parents spoke Aramaic in their home. She also remembered she'd been fourteen when she married Paulos. *Fourteen? Married at fourteen? That's obscene!*

Why would that be so wicked?

She wished again that Paul ... or Paulos ... were there. As a Greek, he could teach the children without a problem. Even in the twenty-first century, Paul and his mother switched back and forth between Greek and English as the mood struck them. He taught Greek, French, Latin, and English at Arizona State University and could also speak Spanish and German fluently. He learned languages as quickly as Sarah learned a recipe.

I'd give my eyeteeth for a computer and access to the internet.

Sarah had taught Tamara the ABC song when she was almost three. At the same time, Paul had taught them both the Greek alphabet with a song. She could start these children with that alphabet.

Now if she could only find a teacher for herself.

Dorcas brought wax tablets, and Sarah found tail feathers dropped by the rooster. *Oh, for some paper and pencils.* She began to show the children how to make the letters. Tamara and Orphah were still too young to form perfect letters, but they proudly showed her their efforts. The boys made letters with more dexterity. She glanced up, startled, when Tamara began to hum the ABC song as she scribbled on her wax tablet.

When the time came for Sarah to begin the evening meal, she clapped her hands. The children looked up, startled. "You've done so well today! You've learned to pronounce and have drawn the letters all the way to zeta. Tomorrow afternoon we'll do some more, maybe even to *mu* or *nu*.

I have to go see Jonas in the morning. Maybe he'll help me with my own Greek lessons.

Sarah still needed to find out what Tamara knew about their other life. She hoped the child didn't talk about her knowledge to any others, although her tales could just be interpreted by adults as childish pretenses. After all, children invented play worlds in the twenty-first century—surely, they did now too.

After the evening meal was served and cleaned up, Sarah made her way home, leading Tamara by the hand. Once they were inside the house, Sarah knelt and hugged her. "I want to ask you about something, Tammy."

Tamara squeezed Sarah's neck. "'kay. What?"

"How do you know the ABC song?"

"You and Papa taught me, don't you 'member? I sang the song to Grandma. She was so s'prised!"

"That's right. How did you come here?" Would Tamara understand what she meant by "here"? Sarah lifted her daughter and carried her to her bed.

"This place is on the other side of a windy web that smells like flowers. But I can't find the windy web anymore. You and Papa are here, so here is okay. Do you know 'bout the windy web now? You didn't used to know. Papa doesn't know either. I asked him."

Sarah nodded. "I came through the windy web too, but not very long ago. Have you been here a long time?"

"Sometimes I think not very long, and sometimes I think since forever. Do you know where the windy web is? I thought maybe under my bed, but there isn't an 'under' there 'cause it's on the floor, and anyway, I looked one time when you lifted up the bed. I want to go see Grandma, but I don't want to go back to the hospital, even if Grandma's there. Even if Jesus is there too." Tamara sat down on her pallet and lay back on a small wooly lambskin pillow.

Sarah caught her breath. Where had Tamara learned about Jesus? Jesus hadn't been a topic of discussion in their household. They hadn't wanted to teach their daughter myths like religion, Santa Claus, or the Easter Bunny were real.

"What do you mean, 'Jesus'? Has someone been telling you about Jesus?"

"He did." Tamara hugged her doll and tucked her under the blanket.

"He who?"

"*Jesus* did," Tamara said. "You know, that man in the hospital room who said it would be okay to go away from the hospital with him. He was nice, and when he hugged me, I felt warm, 'stead of so freezy."

Sarah couldn't believe her ears. Tamara must have been hallucinating. Yes, that would explain it.

"We didn't see him, Tammy."

Tamara tilted her head to the side. "Don't you 'member? He lifted me up off the bed and held me when you and Papa and Grandma were crying. You picked up the old me and rocked me in the chair. Then Jesus took the new me out the door and through the windy web and laid me on this bed." She pointed to the pallet she slept on. "I felt lots better, just sleepy. He said he'd see me soon, then he went away. I haven't seen him again."

Did Tamara think this Paulos was her papa? He looked and sounded like Paul, but how could he be both places? But then, how could she and Tammy have been in both places? *I don't get it. Have I gone insane?*

Sarah hugged Tamara tight. "If Jesus said you'd see him again, then surely you will. Now it's time to go to sleep, sweetheart. Do you want me to tell you a story?"

"Where's Papa? I want to kiss him goodnight." Tammy raised her head and looked at the door as though she expected him to walk through.

Sarah shook her head. "I don't know, Tammy. He isn't here, and I don't know where he is. He must have taken a trip or something. I'm sure he'll come back." She brushed Tammy's hair out of her eyes.

"Maybe he's with Jesus," Tamara said.

Sarah cringed at the thought generated by the child's innocent words. "I don't know." She leaned over and hugged her daughter, kissing her forehead. Tammy felt a little warm, but maybe the excitement of the conversation made her seem so. She tucked the soft blanket up around Tamara's shoulders. "Night-night, sleep tight."

"'Night, Mama. Don't let the bedbugs bite." Tamara yawned, rolled over, and closed her eyes.

Sarah lowered the lamp flame and almost smiled. In their other world, bedbugs weren't all that common, but here, vermin in the beds were a fact of life, even in wealthy households.

Lying on her pallet in the darkness, she allowed her thoughts free rein. Was Jesus real? Had Tamara been hallucinating, or did she really see him? Maybe Jesus really did exist, at least historically, in this ancient world, because Benoni had seen him too. But why would he take Tamara through "the windy web that smells like flowers" and bring her here?

That event must have happened when Tammy died, because that's the only time Sarah could think of when she, Paul, and Halena had all been crying at the same time. *So—if Jesus really does exist, and if he really does care, and if he really is superhuman, would he be willing to help her now?* Sarah decided she had to at least ask. After all, if he didn't exist, nobody would know she spoke to him, and if he did exist? Maybe he would make Tammy's tumor go away. She took a deep breath and whispered a prayer. "Okay, Jesus, if you really are here, would you please make Tammy well? And please take care of my husband, wherever he is. I do love him, even though we've been at odds. Please help us find him, please. If he comes back, I promise I'll start the communication again—good communication, not just talking when we have to."

Tears stung the corners of her eyes. "And I'm sorry I didn't believe in you before. I thought you were a myth."

A sense of peace filled Sarah, and she fell asleep in an instant.

Anne Baxter Campbell

Chapter 11

April AD 30

The next morning, as soon as breakfast was finished, Sarah wrote notes to Paulos's brothers and sister. She told them what she knew about him—his disappearance, his broken leg, and that he might be in a cloth merchant's caravan. She gave the letters to the mistress, hoping his siblings could read Aramaic. She was able to write in Aramaic but was not at all proficient enough with their language to write a letter in Greek.

"Sarah," Dorcas said, "Tamara should join us for meals, at least until her father returns. Orphah and the boys enjoy her company."

"My thanks, mistress." Sarah bowed her head. "Sometimes she does get hungry waiting until I've finished."

The master had made no overt passes at her that morning, though he did give her a smarmy look during breakfast while his wife chided the children for arguing at the table. Sarah didn't plan to mention the look to Dorcas. Too much like grade-school tattling for such a petty thing.

As she cleaned up after breakfast, she heard a thump and a yell from outside. Darius came running to the kitchen. "Sarah, come quick! Gideon fell out of the tree, and he isn't moving."

Sarah dropped the pan she carried onto the work table. "Run, get your mother. I'll see what I can do."

She ran outside and found the boy lying on the ground under the tree, breathing but unconscious. Carefully she felt along his arms and legs for broken bones, looked for wounds, and checked his ears for blood. Finding a bump and cut on the back of his head, she sent Tammy to ask Martha for clean strips of cloth and a bit of wine. Grateful her bosses in the real world had insisted on first-aid training, she held his head still with one hand and gently patted his cheek with the other.

"Gideon, can you hear me?" she called in a loud voice. Gideon squinted his eyes open, blinked at the light, and whimpered. His hand moved to the bump on his head, then he sat up and began to cry.

Sarah breathed a sigh of relief and gathered the little boy into her arms, grateful the injury wasn't severe. "Shh," she murmured, rocking him. "You'll be all right. Your head will stop hurting soon."

When the mistress arrived, Sarah handed the child to his mother.

Sarah patted Gideon's back. "He's all right, but we need to make sure he stays awake for several hours. We can't let him take a nap today. Tamara's gone for some bandages for the cut."

Dorcas gazed at her in astonishment. "Are you also a healer, Sarah?"

Sarah shook her head. "I only know a little, mistress, although I know enough that if I'd been here when my husband fell, I could have set his leg better than that man who called himself a healer." *Or not. That was before the windy web.*

"Hamath sent for a healer." The mistress's lips tightened. "If only we'd been here instead of going to fetch the puppy for the children in Ornithoupolis, your poor husband wouldn't have had to suffer the ministrations of a man who didn't know what he should have about broken limbs. It's my fault. I should have sent for a real physician as soon as we returned. Or have had you reset the leg, had I known you were a healer."

"But by the time we returned, the limb had been set. His leg was so swollen we couldn't tell the job hadn't been done right. Anyway, he was in such pain no one wanted to cause him more."

"It may be too late to do anything about his leg now. If he is found—*when* he is found—we will send for my physician and try to make amends," Dorcas said. "Meanwhile, I can't stay here this morning. I have an appointment with someone who wants to sell a piece of land next to our dye production, a parcel I might want to buy. Please watch over Gideon."

By this time, Gideon had stopped whimpering and started to squirm. When Dorcas put him down, he ran off to play with Darius.

"Of course, Mistress." Sarah nodded. *There went the trip to the marketplace to see Jonas this morning.*

The next day was Saturday. After the morning meal, Sarah left for the marketplace, but Jonas's shop was closed up. A few others were as well. She shrugged. *Ah, well, there's always tomorrow.*

Vendors weren't the only ones needing days off. So far, the children were still busy with the alphabet, but they should have a day or two off during the week to just have fun instead of study, even though they enjoyed the lessons. Sarah gathered vegetables, fresh fish, fruit, and some ground grain for the next few meals and headed back home.

That evening after the meal, the mistress came to the kitchen. "I won't be here all day tomorrow, at least until the evening meal, but Martha will be here if you need anything."

"Thank you, mistress," Sarah said. "By the way, would it be all right with you if the children take one or two days a week off from study? I thought I might take them for walks or to the sea. I could teach them names of plants and to swim."

"That sounds good to me," the mistress agreed. "I'll also tell Hamath, so he won't object. And you won't need to ask him, which he could interpret as a favor that would put you in his debt."

Sarah smiled. Her employer knew her husband well. Still, Sarah was amazed how fond—and tolerant—the mistress was of the master, despite his lecherous tendencies. While she- was gone, Sarah could keep Martha near with a minimum of effort. All she needed to do was begin a conversation, and Martha would stay and chat as long as Sarah nodded occasionally.

By the time Joel and Abidon returned a few days later, the fever had subsided a little more. The man, still only semiconscious, opened his eyes when Joel prodded the skin next to the break, then with a frown, he closed his eyes again.

"You're caring for him well, old woman." Joel nodded.

"You could maybe call me Mehida." She tried to glare, but she couldn't keep from grinning. "I answer to that quicker than 'old woman.'"

Joel turned from his inspection and faced her. "Very well, Mehida. Keep giving him broth. There's some goat meat in our pack, and we'll leave it so you can make more. Does he talk to you at all?"

"No, except to tell me to stop when I pour wine on his leg. He opens his eyes for a moment, then closes them again. I make broth for him, and then I eat the meat and legumes. They're soft enough for me then."

"He needs sleep now. I'm encouraged that he opens his eyes, and the fever has lowered a little. I didn't think he would live when I first saw the wound. Do you know who he is yet?"

"No, he hasn't said much of anything. Maybe next week."

"Perhaps."

The men left, leaving Mehida a new skin of wine.

Mehida gazed at the young man lying asleep on her bed. *I'll adopt this one.*

She walked over to the bed and poked his arm until he opened his eyes, scowling.

"You're my son, and your name is Abner."

He closed his eyes again.

Another week went by and 'Abner' slowly improved. The fever disappeared, and he seemed more aware of his surroundings, even drinking the broth without Mehida's help. Whenever he opened his eyes, Mehida repeated the new name she'd given him and told him he was her son. His eyebrows lifted at the pronouncements, but he didn't argue.

Chapter 12

April AD 2008

Paul had called the sheriff's office every day for over a week, but the news never changed. Although Paul went to work daily, he functioned by rote. With so many people expressing their concern, he began to dread talking to anyone, particularly Maureen.

Am I ever glad I didn't go to that party with her. The cops would have been dead certain I made Sarah disappear. I feel guilty enough without adding that mess to my mind.

Maureen's sympathy was a couple of miles over the top. She made countless offers to console him, including a drink after work in the quiet of her apartment. He grew weary of dodging her.

One day, Paul decided to take the same route Sarah usually took between home and work. The police had certainly checked the road already, but he wanted to do it himself. He'd take his time and stop anywhere there was the least possibility she could've gone off the road. Maybe the car was hidden by brush or in a gully.

After his last morning class, he posted assignments on the board alongside a note explaining that he wouldn't be there that afternoon.

One of his fellow professors had the room next to his. "Michael, would you look in on my class once in a while this afternoon? I'm going to take off early."

"Sure, Paul. No problem."

As he walked to the parking lot, he went over the road in his mind, visualizing places where brush, gullies, or rocks could hide a car.

Paul drove slowly, irritating vast numbers of drivers behind him. Cars could easily pass him on the freeway, but on the Carefree Highway, they weren't so tolerant. A few of them made crude gestures as they drove past, but he didn't care. He wanted to be able to stop and take notes here and there.

When he got home, he called Sergeant Willis and related his ideas.

"We had the same thoughts, Paul, so we had a patrol car go along the same route you just took with the same goal in mind. The officer even got out of the car and checked for tire tracks in places where a car might have left the highway and be hidden from view."

"Oh." Paul's hopes deflated like last week's balloons. "I thought I might be coming up with new ideas that could help."

"Don't stop doing that. Just because we had the same idea doesn't mean you might not think of something we haven't. After all, you know her much better than we do."

"I feel pretty helpless. I don't know what to do, but I've got to do something. So far, nothing has brought me any closer to finding Sarah. I keep finding myself wondering what I could have done to change the past."

"I think somewhere in our notes, I read you've been in therapy. Have you been to see your therapist since your wife disappeared?"

"No, not yet, although I've thought about it several times. Maybe I should quit postponing."

"Seeing him can't hurt and might help."

"Maybe. Sounds like maybe you'd make a good therapist yourself, sergeant."

"Thanks, Paul, that's the nicest thing anyone said to me all day. Come to think—all week."

"Yeah. Well, I'm glad I made someone's day. Believe me, it's a first. I've been a dark storm cloud for a while now."

"I can't imagine anyone blames you."

"Thanks. I'll talk to you later, no doubt."

Paul sat slouched by the phone for several minutes. With a sigh, he picked up the phone and punched in his therapist's number.

"Hello, this is Paul Johnson. Does Dr. Howard have any openings next week?"

Several days passed before Sarah could go back to the marketplace to restock the larder and see Jonas. He was again missing from his shop, but a boy stood up from behind some bolts of cloth.

"Hello, mistress. May I help you select some fine materials this beautiful day?" His voice wavered between a manly bass and a youthful falsetto on the last word. His face reddened.

"Thank you, no," Sarah said. "I'm looking for Jonas. You resemble him. Are you related?"

"Yes, mistress. I'm his son, Dathan. My father's gone on a journey, but he'll be back next week. Shall I give him a message from you?"

"I'm glad to meet you, Dathan. I'm Sarah. No, no message. Your father and I have something in common, a missing spouse. He's been trying to help me find my husband. You must be proud of him. He's a kind and caring man."

Dathan nodded. "He's a good father. You know, then, that my mother was kidnapped and is somebody's slave … somewhere." He looked off in the distance. "I don't remember her very well. She disappeared so long ago, and I was young." His gazed drifted back to Sarah. "I remember her singing to me. She had a beautiful voice. *Abba's* sister, Miriam, lives with us now, and she has cared for us since my mother's been gone."

"I imagine your father's grateful for her help, and I think he must be pleased with his son too."

"If he's not, he pretends to be." Dathan grinned. "He let me tend his wares here this week for the first time on my own."

"Good for you! I'll come back next week to see him. I'm hoping he can help me with still one more thing. Good-bye, Dathan. It was good talking to you."

"Shalom, Sarah. God go with you." Dathan raised his hand in a wave, then bent back down behind a bolt of purple cloth.

Chapter 13

April AD 30

Two weeks had passed. Sarah often found herself wondering how Paul was doing "back" in the twenty-first century. Did he ever miss her or even think of her? She worried so much for Paulos. Was he alive or dead? She wondered, too, if Paulos and Paul were sort of two halves of a whole, like the first century Sarah and herself. She shook her head. *Do the two halves of me being married to Paul and Paulos make me a bigamist? How can I think of them both as my one husband? Confusing.*

Between meal preparations, Greek lessons, and dodging her master, Sarah's days were filled with almost more activity than she could keep up with. There hadn't been time to ask Jonas for help. She went to bed exhausted at night, rose again in the morning, and struggled through the next day. She thought her emotions were safely buried, but at times, something would remind her of Paulos, bringing tears to the surface again. She missed him more than she ever thought possible.

One moonless night, Sarah woke up, her heart pounding. She wasn't sure what the hour was, but she hadn't been asleep long. Then she heard the knocking sounds coming from below the window. Feeling her way to Tamara's side, she pulled the pallet away from the wall so her child wouldn't hurt herself.

When the seizure ended, Tammy lay limp on her bed. Sarah dampened some cloths to cool her daughter's hot skin. Finally, Tammy drifted back into a natural sleep.

The convulsions had progressed like this before. For the second time, Sarah decided to pray. *I hope two prayers in two weeks won't tax God's patience with me—or his abilities.*

"Please, God, please don't let her go through all this just to die again." She gazed out the window at the night sky. When Tamara had been sick before, the onset and retreat of each bout had been sudden. The chemo and radiation hadn't helped, and none of the antibiotics they gave her did any good. Her hair had just begun to grow back when she died.

In the morning, the sun beamed in the window, waking Sarah. She yawned and groggily got to her feet, wishing for one good night's sleep. When she approached Tamara's pallet, her sweet baby opened her eyes and smiled. How could she always be this cheerful?

"Good morning, sunshine. We need to go fix breakfast. Maybe the hens laid a few eggs for us. Want to help me find them?"

"Okay, as long as that mean ol' rooster doesn't chase me."

"I won't let him." Sarah promised. After combing her own hair and then Tamara's, they went out to battle the hens for their eggs, shooing the rooster with a stick when he got too close. Wandering free in the courtyard, the hens tended to lay eggs under the bushes, in the tall grass, or wherever else they felt like putting them.

Sarah smiled to herself. *Hmm—a little like an Easter egg hunt.* That's another thing she'd have to ask Tamara if she remembered.

Leaving alone the established nests with three eggs or more, they still found plenty for breakfast. When they had all they needed, Sarah entered the kitchen, leaving Tamara in the courtyard to play with Keddy.

Martha bustled into the room and announced, "There's a man here looking for you." Her face was lit with curiosity.

"Who is it?"

"His name is Jonas, the cloth vendor. Do you know him? I didn't know whether to let him in or not. He wouldn't say what he wanted, so he's waiting in front of the house. Should I let him in? I've always thought he was a good man. Do you think so?"

Sarah's heart skipped a beat. "Oh, maybe he has news of Paulos! If the master or mistress asks for me, tell them I'm just outside. Wait, maybe I need to find out what Jonas wants first. I might need to go with him." She hurried to the front door and stepped outside.

"Good morning, Jonas. Do you bring word of my husband?" Embarrassed at the eagerness in her voice, she ducked her head and brushed some imaginary dust from her tunic.

"Shalom, Sarah. No, I'm sorry. But I did hear something of the cloth merchant. I'm told he planned to travel north at least as far as Sidon. The traveler I spoke to didn't see anyone who was crippled with the merchant, but if Paulos rode on a camel or donkey they might not've noticed his injury."

Sarah nodded. She had been holding her breath; now she exhaled as her shoulders drooped.

"I understand. Well, thank you. Maybe other news will come in from Paulos's kin. Good-bye, Jonas." She turned to go back into the house, then remembered and whirled. "Oh, Jonas, are you proficient in Greek? Can you read and write as well as speak?"

He turned back to her. "Yes, I suppose. I have to be able to negotiate with the Greek-speaking travelers and merchants who come for my fabrics."

Sarah smiled. "Would you be willing to give me lessons? The mistress has me teaching their children, but my knowledge of Greek is basement ... I mean basic. I need to learn more to teach them beyond the little I know."

Jonas smiled and nodded his head. "I'd be happy to help, my friend. Maybe I could put together a list of words and meanings and some common phrases for you. Would that help?"

"Oh, yes! And if I can help you with anything, let me know."

"Indeed." Jonas nodded. He waved as he turned again to leave.

Sarah returned to the kitchen and began preparing the morning meal. She jumped when Martha walked up behind her. "What did Jonas want?"

"He has a lot of contacts with merchants and travelers, and he thinks Paulos left with a cloth merchant. When I spoke to him before, he didn't know which direction the merchant went. Today he said someone told him the merchant traveled north to Sidon."

"Ah." Martha nodded, making her jowls bounce. "My sister, Hannah, lives in Sidon. Her husband, Marcos, is a vendor. He sells cheese. I'll send word to them in case they might have seen Paulos. Wouldn't it be exciting to find he's such a short distance away? Sidon is only two days' travel from here, or one if you're a fast-walking, long-legged man or have a horse. Maybe the mistress would let you go bring him back, if he's there. I could do the cooking for a week if you would give directions to me."

Sarah certainly would be excited to find Paulos so close. If she only had a car, the four-day round trip could be trimmed to about three or four hours, including lots of time to search for him. Maybe Dorcas would grant her a week off to bring him home.

Sarah's spirits lifted a little, but she was afraid to hope too much. She wrote a message to send to Martha's brother-in-law, describing Paul and asking for a quick reply.

After the morning meal, Sarah hurried to the marketplace with Martha's message. "Good morning, Jonas and Dathan. Would you send this with one of your merchant friends to Sidon? The message needs to go to Marcos, a cheese vendor there."

"Shalom, Sarah. I would do that gladly. I have a list here for you." He handed her a small scroll with Greek words and phrases, complete with definitions.

Sarah noticed he kept the words and phrases simple. "You should be a teacher. I can see you know what's right for beginners."

Jonas chuckled. "I'm a rabbi too. I'm supposed to know how to teach. Most of my lessons are of Hebrew history and in the Aramaic language. However, the rest of the world speaks Greek, so I must also know that language."

"You're a Jew? Ah, that explains why you weren't here on the Saturday I looked for you." Sarah tucked a strand of hair back under her scarf.

"Yes, that's the Sabbath for Jews. There are a few of us here in Tyre."

"I have a question." Sarah glanced around and then back at Jonas. "Do you know of a Jew called Jesus?"

"I know a few. Jesus is a common name. I've heard of one Jesus who some Jews believe to be a great prophet or maybe even the Messiah, or the Christ as the Greeks say. Is that the one you mean?"

"Probably. What do you think of him?"

"I don't know yet what to think. I make my decisions based on personal experience, not on speculations from gossipers. Thus far, I have no personal knowledge of the man." He tipped an eyebrow at her. "How did you hear of him?"

"A young slave named Benoni was here with his master. The slave told me he'd seen Jesus in Samaria. Benoni went on endlessly about how wonderful Jesus the Messiah is. And oddly enough, my little girl, Tamara, says she's seen him. I don't know what to think about that bit of information."

"How did your daughter come to see him?"

"In the hosp—uh, I guess in her dreams, or maybe hallucinations. One time when she was very ill, and one time when she was sleeping." She had corrected herself quickly, but Jonas was quicker.

"In the 'hosp'?"

Sarah didn't know what to say, so she decided to tell the truth, at least to a point. She didn't think even Jonas would understand how she happened to have bounced from the twenty-first century to ... what? Thirty AD? "I started to say *hospital*, which is a place where sick people go. She was very ill."

Jonas tugged on his beard. "I don't think I've heard that term before. No matter. Children have many dreams and imaginings, although it's odd she'd dream about this Jesus. Do the other children speak of him ... or other adults ... or you?"

"No. The master's family has their own set of gods, and my own beliefs haven't ever been strong. Neither Paulos nor I ever discussed Jesus or any other religion with her."

"Odd. Odd about her dreams, I mean. You said Tamara was very ill. Did she recover all right?"

"I don't think so. She still has fevers and, um, convulsions." Sarah trusted Jonas, and she hoped their conversation wouldn't result in a flurry of exorcists descending on the villa.

He nodded. "Dathan had some fits when he had a hot fever once. A lot of people think they're caused by demon possessions, and I'm sure some are, but I tend to think the ones with fevers are because of the fever. Have you talked to a good physician?"

"Yes, a few, but they don't know what to do with her."

"You must be frightened. I wish I could help, but I know nothing about healing other than prayer, which of course, I'll do."

"Thank you, Jonas, but that won't be necessary. I've already prayed for her, and I wouldn't want to irritate God with too many requests for the same thing."

Jonas laughed. "I don't know whether to be amazed by your faith or blessed by your naïveté. Let me assure you, our mighty God is not angered by repeated requests. He's angered by rebellion, cruelty, or arrogance, but never by well-intentioned requests. I'm convinced he wants us to come to him every day with our needs as well as with our thanksgivings. He's all-powerful and everywhere, so he's able to hear us as though we are the only person in his presence. That's my experience with him, and that's my belief."

"Hmm," Sarah said, "that's an immense belief. I'll have to think about that for a while."

"Good. That's as it should be. Don't let others tell you what to believe. You should always study so you can make your own decisions. Others' beliefs, no matter how well meant, might not be well studied or accurate. Just because something is believed doesn't necessarily make the belief true."

A customer approached, and Sarah bid Jonas and Dathan a good day. She shopped for the food she'd need and made her way back home, deep in thought about Jonas's words.

How could she study enough to draw her own conclusions? She didn't have a Bible or access to any of the scrolls that would have the books of the Old Testament. Even if she did, she didn't know how to read Hebrew. She remembered a few of the old Bible stories from the Sunday school she'd attended before her mother died. Maybe Jonas could be a source again. This topic could use lots more discussion with someone who knew more than she did.

Chapter 14

Back from the morning shopping, Sarah went directly to the kitchen. The master waited for her, his chin jutted forward. "Where have you been?"

"I went to the marketplace. Even though I put food in the ice house, I must restock every two or three days or the food tastes bad. But I'm sure you know that."

"And seeing your friend, the cloth vendor? A visit from him this morning wasn't enough?" His upper lip curled over the word *friend*.

Sarah struggled to keep a straight face. "Jonas is indeed a friend. He has contacts with a lot of merchants, and he's been kind enough to help me try to find Paulos."

"With a little persuasion, I could be kind too." He smirked and stepped closer. "Paulos will never be found. I'm sure he's dead, as I've been trying to tell you. However, my kindness is without boundaries. As my concubine, you'd be more likely to receive my kindness. If Paulos were ever found, which is unlikely, of course I'd release you to be with him."

"I cannot be your concubine, sir. I'm a married woman and will continue to be a married woman until or unless I know Paulos is no longer living. But I don't think he's dead, and I believe with all my heart he'll return to us. I won't willingly choose to become an adulterous woman, and I'm sure you wouldn't choose to be an adulterer either. Would you?"

Before the master could lose the battle of wanting to appear honorable, Sarah quickly excused herself to take her purchases to the shaded dugout behind the courtyard.

As she crossed the yard, Sarah wondered how long she would have to wait for Paulos's siblings or Martha's sister to write back. *Why, oh why didn't they invent the telephone centuries ago?*

Two more weeks passed before Martha received a message from her sister. Hannah and her husband had asked several people in Sidon, but no one had seen a crippled man matching Paulos's description, either with the cloth merchant or otherwise. Sarah sighed heavily. But still, maybe Paulos's siblings would have better news.

She almost smiled. At least the master's frequent harassment kept her insisting Paulos was alive somewhere and he would come back. Her constant repetitions of this little speech helped her to continue believing it herself.

After finishing her morning chores, Sarah decided to go home to change her gravy-splattered tunic. As she shut the courtyard gate behind her, the master, out of breath and sweating, suddenly appeared at her side. "Wait, Sarah! I want to talk to you."

Where had he come from? The stables? She should have stayed in the house with Martha.

"Dorcas isn't here today, and I thought you and I might, well, talk for a while. In your house."

"I'd prefer to talk out here or in the courtyard, sir." Sarah backed toward the gate.

"I have something for your ears alone." He stepped closer and reached for her arms.

"I see no one around us, sir. You may speak here." Her stomach twisted into an anxious knot as she eluded his grip. Could anyone hear her scream from here?

"You never know where other ears might be—around a corner of your house, just inside the gate, in the stables. Someone could hear us." The master's face glowed red, and his eyes darted toward the supposed hiding places. "Let's go into your house."

Sarah squared her shoulders. "Sir, I have no wish to anger you, but I don't think your wife would want me to do that, nor would my husband. I won't enter my house alone with you, nor will I go anywhere else alone with you. If you force me to do so, I'll tell her."

The master straightened to his full height and looked down his nose at her. "Who do you think she would believe? You? Or me, her husband? And I keep telling you, your husband is no doubt dead."

Sarah eyed him with a steady gaze. "Do you really want to find out who your wife would believe ... sir?"

His eyes widened. "Woman, you are an impertinent and rebellious servant. You are dismissed. Get your belongings and go. I won't have you here under my employ for another moment!"

"Very well, sir." Sarah bowed her head. "I'll get my daughter and inform Martha of my dismissal, since she will have to prepare the meals until you find another cook." She turned and walked toward the gate.

"W-wait!" the master sputtered, "You ... uh, I ... um. No, let's just say you're ... uh, warned, um ... not to, uh ... treat me with such disrespect in the future."

"If you say so, sir." Sarah kept her eyes lowered, oh so respectfully, which was just as well. The taste of triumph put laughter in her throat that threatened to spill out. "Am I dismissed, sir, or shall I continue with my responsibilities?"

"No! I mean, no, you're not dismissed. Go about your duties. I'm leaving on my morning inspection of the dyes." Hamath turned and stomped off to the stables.

That was close. I think I'll spend the rest of the day with Martha. She hurried back to the courtyard. The gravy on her tunic would have to stay there for the time being.

Chapter 15

May AD 2008

A month had passed since Sarah disappeared. He and the police made almost daily contact, but the reports were all the same. Nothing. He continued his work, showed up at the campus, kept himself busy. The constant concern expressed by coworkers and students depressed him—too-often reminders Sarah hadn't been found. Especially Maureen. If he saw her before she saw him, he usually dodged into the men's room. Once he had even hidden in a broom closet.

While walking to his one o'clock class, his cell rang. He glanced at the display—Maricopa County Sheriff.

"Paul Johnson here."

"Hello, Mr. Johnson. This is Sergeant Willis.

"Hello, Sergeant. Any news today?"

"No, I'm sorry, Mr. Johnson. We'd like for you to drop by here today."

Hmm. She'd been calling him Paul. What now? "Sure. I have a class beginning in fifteen minutes. I could come by at about four. Would that be all right?"

Sergeant Willis spoke to someone else in the background. "Yes, sir, that would be acceptable."

"All right. See you then." Paul broke the connection, frowning at the phone.

After class, he retrieved his car from the faculty parking lot and drove to the Maricopa County Sheriff's Department, his innards in turmoil. He mentally shook himself as he pulled into the only shady parking spot he could find.

He asked at the information desk for Sergeant Beulah Willis. Within a minute, she came around the corner of the hallway. She looked a lot like he'd pictured—a tall, attractive black lady, maybe thirty or thirty-five years old, close to his height. She approached him, her face serious, unsmiling.

"You must be Paul. Please come with me." She led him into what had to be an interrogation room, complete with a two-way mirror.

Uh-oh. I hope this doesn't mean what it looks like.

Beulah smiled disarmingly, thirty-two white teeth promising good intentions. "Relax, Paul. We need the answers to a few more questions. We've been talking to Sarah's friends and relations, her therapist, and your mother. All of them agree Sarah was depressed. Under those conditions, very possibly a person might choose to run away and hide from the world. Is there a particular place she liked more than others?"

"She loves the Grand Canyon, Lake Powell, Arches, Monument Valley—places like that. But she doesn't carry much cash, so she'd need to use a credit or debit card. Lieutenant Jones took our card numbers to see if she was using them anywhere."

"We haven't seen any instances of her cards being used, only yours. You withdrew three hundred dollars yesterday with your debit card, isn't that right?"

"Yes, ma'am. We've done that for years. Whenever we run low on cash, we get a couple hundred out of a money machine and put all but what we want to carry into our safe at home. We were out of cash there, so I got some more." He exhaled. "Your next question is probably 'Could Sarah have taken cash from the safe,' and yes, she could have, but she didn't. I took the last hundred out last week. She hadn't taken any. She probably had a little cash on her, but not more than fifty or sixty dollars. She only used cash for lunches or odds and ends. Gas and groceries went on the card. And we haven't been out for dinner or a movie or the theater since our daughter died. Nor have we gone on any vacations. We used up most of our vacation time and savings while Tammy was so sick."

"Yes, we knew about your daughter. We have Tamara's illness and death in our records. I'm really sorry about your loss, sir. Now, do you have a passport?"

"Yes, I do. We went to Paris four years ago, sort of a delayed honeymoon." Paul thought about what a great time they had in that romantic city, and his eyes stung. He brought his feelings back under control with difficulty.

"I have to ask you to surrender the passport to us. Just until Mrs. Johnson is found, you understand."

Paul hesitated, then sighed and reached for his briefcase. "I've been carrying my passport for some time. Once in a while, I need a second form of identification. I really wasn't thinking about running. I guess this means I'm officially a person of interest."

"Yes, to be honest. You understand it's just procedure. We have to do this. Please don't leave town, or at least don't leave this part of Arizona. Restrict your travels to between home and work. We know you live in Wickenburg and work in Tempe." Beulah shifted uneasily in her chair.

"We'll also need to check your car and home more thoroughly. I could get a search warrant, but I'm hoping you will consent to the search without one. It'll look better in your file."

"Okay. The only thing I ask is that your people don't tear the house to pieces and leave me with a mess to clean up." He barked a short laugh. "Come to think, maybe cleaning up the mess would give me something to do with my time."

"I'll ask our crew to be considerate, sir."

"I guess I'd better find a lawyer, too."

"That would probably be wise."

"I'd like to go home now, sergeant … that is, if I'm not under arrest."

"No, you're not under arrest. I hope it won't come to that. I do have a few more questions, though. One is regarding your relationship with your wife."

"I wish I could tell you we were close, but over the past year or so, we grew apart, especially after Tammy got so sick. We used to be close. I wish we still were, if that counts for anything."

"I'm glad you told me about the distant relationship, because we've heard the same thing from others. The other question is about one of your coworkers, Maureen O'Malley. What's your relationship with her?"

"There is no relationship, other than coworker. I admit I thought she was attractive, but nothing ever developed."

"She appears to feel otherwise. She said you've been making advances toward her."

"What? No! Just the opposite. She's been for some time, well … flirtatious. Before Sarah went missing, I was flirting back, but only at work. I didn't go anywhere with her. Now she offers to console me at every opportunity. Our secretary could probably verify that for you."

Sergeant Willis lifted her eyebrows. "You must be flattered to have an attractive lady so obviously throwing herself at you."

"I felt flattered for a couple of weeks, but before long the attention became embarrassing." Paul took a deep breath. "I see you're wearing a wedding ring, Beulah. Would you feel flattered if one of your coworkers threw himself at you day after day?"

"Not particularly." She stared at her paperwork a moment. "Okay, that's all I need. Go home. I hope you will sleep well tonight, despite this conversation."

Chapter 16

May AD 2008

The lessons with the children progressed better than Sarah expected. Even the little girls could recite the alphabet and count to ten, and the boys had begun teasing each other using the short Greek phrases they learned. Every few days, she'd go to Jonas for more lessons. At the same time, she asked him about the Hebrew laws, prophets, and the psalms, which were his favorites.

Her thoughts returned so often to Paulos. Why hadn't they heard anything from his family? Surely, they would be concerned about him too. She could see why there'd been no word from his brother in Crete, so distant and accessible only by boat, but his brother in Barytas and sister in Ptolemais weren't so far away. The mistress might know if any messages had come to them, but she hadn't been around all day.

The next afternoon, she came into the room where the children received their lessons. "They seem to be making good progress, Sarah."

"The credit all belongs to them. They're eager students." Sarah paused. "Mistress, may I ask a question?"

"Of course."

"Have you received any messages for me from Paulos's kin?"

"No, I haven't." A crinkle brushed across the mistress's brow. "It's been some time since we sent those letters. I wonder if Hamath might have intercepted the replies. I'll ask him." She left the room with purpose in her steps.

Moments later, she was back with two small parchment scrolls in her hand. "This might be what you were waiting for, Sarah. Hamath isn't here, but these were behind a cabinet in our room, hidden in a hole in the wall where he often tries to keep things from me. I usually look at things there and put them back." She gave a sly grin. "I wouldn't want him to cease hiding things where I can find them." She handed Sarah the scrolls.

Sarah eagerly rolled them out and began to read. When she finished, she felt discouragement running through every muscle of her body and cell of her brain. "The scrolls are from one of Paulos's brothers and from his sister, but neither has seen him. Thank you, anyway, mistress, for showing them to me." She handed them back.

"You shouldn't give up hope, Sarah. There's one yet to hear from, isn't there?"

"I doubt any word from his brother in Crete will be different. How would Paulos get that far? He didn't have enough coins to pay passage on a ship to Crete. Maybe the master is right. I should accept that my husband won't be coming back." The words stabbed through her like a hot knife. She didn't realize how much she was counting on news that Paulos rested safely in the care of one of his siblings.

Dorcas slipped an arm around Sarah's shoulders. "I know you're upset. I realize people don't usually get to know their servants well, but I do try to be observant. I can't believe Paulos would deliberately leave you and Tamara."

Sarah shook her head. "We had an argument that morning, mistress. The master had agreed to get a physician to reset Paulos's leg, and when I told my husband, he became angry. I think he might have been frightened about the pain he'd have to go through, although I don't think he was so much afraid of the pain as afraid his leg would be reset by another incompetent healer. He also wondered if I had promised the master ... something in return. I didn't."

"A physician? Hamath said nothing to me about a physician."

"Paulos disappeared the day your parents arrived. The physician was scheduled to be here the next morning. When I told your husband Paulos hadn't come home the night before, he was furious. He said Paulos should never expect another favor from him."

Sparks shot through the mistress's eyes. "Hamath didn't send for a physician. I pay our accounts, and he would have had to tell me. He isn't home now, but we'll have a discussion when he returns. A serious discussion."

Sarah felt her stomach tighten. "Mistress, you surely don't think he would have Paulos killed?"

"No, I don't believe he would go that far," Dorcas replied. "Hamath is devious sometimes, but I can't see him going to that extreme. Besides, he'd have to pay for that, and I would have known."

Sarah bowed her head. "Mistress, there is something else. The master said I was to become his concubine if Paulos was ... was d-dead, and I don't want to be, even if ... he—"

Dorcas's eyes widened, and her jaw dropped. "His concubine? That will happen only if my own body is dead and cold. Not you or any other woman. I'll make that clear to him too. Despite his actions toward you, I don't think he wants to change wives."

"I don't want to become his concubine or his wife, mistress. I hope you believe me."

Dorcas patted Sarah's arm. "I believe you. The way you react when he's present tells me that much. You, I trust. Now, go prepare our evening meal, and I'll wait for Hamath's return."

Sarah could hear when Hamath came in. Dorcas was obviously reading him the riot act or whatever took the place of the riot act in this time. She couldn't hear his voice. Apparently, he spoke softly if at all, but Dorcas was loud and angry.

Sarah smiled. She almost felt sorry for him. Almost.

When she served dinner, the master was a quiet, well-behaved mouse. Not one single surreptitious glance did he cast in Sarah's direction, and his mouth moved only to chew. Dorcas's dark eyes smoldered, and her lips were set in a thin line. Even the children and the puppy were on extra good behavior, casting anxious eyes in the mistress's direction.

Hmm, I wonder if she has a touch of fiery Italian in her blood?

When the meal was over, the mistress signaled Sarah to her side. "I wish to speak with you, Sarah. Please come with me to the courtyard."

Sarah followed obediently.

When she arrived on the far side of the yard, Sarah heard a faint giggle from behind a bush. *A giggle? From the mistress?*

She snorted, holding her hand in front of her mouth to muffle the sound. "Oh, Sarah, did you see the look on Hamath's face? I haven't had such a time hiding my glee in years." She sobered. "I have some good news, but I also have some unpleasant information."

Sarah steeled herself. "What is it?"

"Hamath *was* behind Paulos's disappearance. He's probably alive, so Hamath tells me, which is the good news. But the discouraging part is that Hamath doesn't know where your husband is. He gave your husband to a slave master who planned to use a cripple to beg for him at the Jews' temple. He said the slaver is from Jerusalem. The merchant who took Paulos captive here was to carry him a mile or two outside the city to a camp where the slave monger waited."

Sarah's heart sank. Paulos was as good as lost forever. She didn't have the freedom to leave Tyre, let alone the money to travel or buy his freedom, and she couldn't leave her employment. Worse, with Tammy's eroding health, Sarah couldn't drag her across the countryside in search of Paulos.

"Oh, Sarah, don't despair." Dorcas put both hands on Sarah's shoulders. "All is not lost! You see, Hamath has 'volunteered' to go after Paulos himself. When he finds him, he will buy him back and they'll come home together. My husband leaves tomorrow on a fast horse. Our conversations tonight could be much happier than before our evening meal." Dorcas had a sly sparkle in her eyes. "He should return with Paulos within a month."

Sarah beamed. "Oh, mistress, you're wonderful. I'm forever in your debt."

She almost danced as she walked back to the kitchen. Tamara was still there, playing with some pans. Sarah picked her up and whirled her around, squeezing her until she squealed. "Oh, Tammy," she sang. "The master is going to go find your Papa."

Tamara shrieked with joy. "Papa's coming home? Is he going to be here tonight?"

"No, Tammy, but soon—a few days. We'll need to be patient, but not too long." Tammy began to squirm, and Sarah set her back on her feet.

"I'm going to go tell him 'thank you.'" Tamara ran into the hallway. Sarah made a move to stop her and then thought. Maybe it would be better that Tamara and Hamath both thought Dorcas had only told the good side of his change of heart. And who knew? Maybe a little girl's gratitude could soften the man's heart.

She waited for Tamara to return, and then they walked back to their house, Tamara chattering all the while about Papa's homecoming.

Mehida watched her patient daily for signs of recovery. He opened his eyes sometimes, but he didn't seem aware of his surroundings for a full month. Then one day, he rose on one elbow and croaked something unintelligible. She ran to his side.

"Yes, my son?" She squinted as she peered into his eyes, wishing he didn't look so blurry. "What is it you need, Abner?"

He coughed. "Where?"

"You are in the home of your mother, Mehida."

Paulos frowned. "Mother?"

Mehida nodded her head enthusiastically.

"Hungry," he rasped and attempted to clear his throat. "Thirsty."

"I have some bread, cheese, and milk. Honeyed wine too. We're out of meat. I used the last for broth yesterday." She brought the items to him on a platter and started to feed him, but he took the food and fed himself.

Mehida chortled with pleasure. "You are going to live after all, my son. You surely fooled those physicians."

He lay back down. "Sleep," he whispered, closing his eyes.

Paulos met Joel and Abidon the next day. He didn't remember them, but when Joel mentioned setting his leg, that memory surfaced all too clearly.

"I believe you're going to walk again, Abner," Joel said. "Another three or four weeks, maybe. I didn't think you'd live past that first day we saw you. Mehida and God have worked a miracle."

The physician had brought more meat, and the old woman promised Paulos a thick stew. She invited the men to share the meal too, but they had to travel on.

Paulos's muscles had stiffened, but they began to loosen as he moved them more. The swelling in his leg was going down. Gradually, he bent his limbs further. The first time he tried dangling them over the edge of the bed, though, he couldn't keep from crying out over the stabbing pains. Day by day, he increased the time of hanging his legs down, straightening and bending them.

His mind sharpened slowly. Adding to his confusion, Mehida kept calling him Abner and insisting he was her son.

"Mehida, you're not my mother," he told her one morning. "I'm grateful for your help, and I will pay you back if I can, but I'm not your son. My mother died years ago, and my name isn't Abner. It's Paulos."

Mehida pouted. "I need a son, and if your mother is dead, you could use a new mother."

Paulos chuckled. She sounded so reasonable.

"If you insist, I'll allow you to call yourself Paulos, although Abner is a much nicer name. Abner was my father's name."

Paulos raised his gaze to her face. "Why is it you need a son?"

"I have no living son and only one living daughter, but she ran off to Tyre or Sidon ... or maybe even Ptolemais ... with a fisherman named Ebenezer. I haven't seen her since."

"She ran away? Why?"

"Well, she didn't exactly run away, but Emma married someone who took her too far away to care for me in my old age. My only child, my beloved daughter, and she's gone from me. For all I know, she could also be dead. Now I'm getting old and feeble. Soon I'll need someone to take care of me. I've taken good care of you, haven't I?"

"Yes, Mehida, you have, but I'm only a servant. I live in a small one-room house provided by my master in Tyre. I have no place to take care of you, but maybe I could help you find your daughter." He looked down at the floor and scooted to the edge of the bed.

"No, no! You can't stand yet!" Mehida pushed him back. "You have to wait. Another full moon must pass before you can walk. If you walk now, your leg might break again."

Chapter 17

May AD 2008

Paul sighed. Getting a lawyer and going to see Dr. Howard hadn't helped his attitude much. The cops still followed him everywhere, and the cold ache in his heart only grew worse.

He should admit to himself they wouldn't find Sarah alive. He cringed at the thought, but he had to know. Maybe if there were a memorial service, he might stop expecting her to walk through the door. No, he couldn't arrange that without knowing for sure, and they had to find her to do that. Otherwise, the investigation would remain open until she could be declared legally dead. Still ... maybe she was okay, just lost. He couldn't—wouldn't!—believe she was gone forever.

In the Valley of the Sun, early May isn't as hot as later in the summer—eighties and nineties for the high, sixties and seventies at night. Paul rose early one cool Saturday morning thinking it would be a great day for a drive. He remembered Sergeant Willis's admonition to restrict driving to the Wickenburg-to-Tempe areas.

Bummer.

Paul decided to take another drive along Sarah's usual route to work and hike around. This time he'd wear comfortable shoes. He'd also take his walking stick, seeing that diamondbacks were often on the move this time of year, and they tended to be grouchy with critters other than rattlers of the opposite sex.

There were only a few places along the way where a gold Taurus could go off the road and be hidden. One location drew him, the place where the Agua Fria River passed under the Carefree Highway. The river wasn't flowing deep now, so he could at least look. There were several other small creeks and gullies, but they were less likely since were shallower, they only ran for brief periods after rainstorms, and then they went dry within a day or two. Since there'd been no rain in a week or so, he should be able to see a car, though he'd probably need to hike some distance down the river. If a car went into the Agua Fria when it was running as full as when she disappeared, the car could be carried downstream for a mile or more.

Paul made several stops along the way to the Agua Fria crossing, but just as he thought, he found no trace of wheel marks going off the her side of the highway near any of the gullies or creeks.

He pulled off the highway at the entrance to Lower Lake and parked in a wide spot by the road. He gathered the walking stick from the back seat and secured his water bottle and cell phone in holsters on his belt. He waited for several cars to pass before crossing to the south side of the highway.

This road's a lot busier than it used to be before they built the New Waddell Dam. I was barely a teenager when they finished construction twenty years ago. Now look at all the pickups pulling boats to Lake Pleasant and then towing them home again. Well, except for the lucky cusses who rent docking spaces for their houseboats or outboards.

Not ten steps off the highway, he was glad he had the stick. A Gila monster on the path turned, snapping its jaws at the stick Paul used to encourage it to leave the path. Paul jerked back in time. For usually slow-moving lizards, they could turn fast, and their bite could be extremely painful or even deadly. He waited until the eighteen-inch, black-and-orange critter ambled off the path, stopping to sun himself in a bare section of dirt.

The only snake he saw was a five-foot red racer. At first, the reptile looked like a section of heavy-duty electrical cord, but as he approached, it slithered away. Javalinas trotted away from the river when they saw him, and several jackrabbits took off, bounding high every few jumps. Normally all this wildlife would have made Paul smile, but not today. For about an hour, he hiked south along the Aqua Fria, but didn't see anything that resembled a car in the riverbed, other than one rusty fender, probably from an ancient pickup.

Discouraged and hot, he began the hike back to his car. He knelt to retie a loose shoelace when he was nearly back to the highway. That was when he saw the flash of light.

The sun glanced off something shiny under the bridge. He got as close as he could, but with the mud nearly as deep as the water, he found getting into a position to see anything clearly impossible. He would have to call the sheriff's office again. He pulled the cell out of its holster. *Hmm. Only one bar.* He shrugged and hiked up to the road.

This time, the cell showed three bars. He punched the buttons, hoping Sergeant Willis would answer, but a Lieutenant Tony-somebody took the call. Paul didn't catch the last name, and he was too excited to ask him to repeat it.

"Officer, I'm Paul Johnson. There's an ongoing investigation in your department to find my wife, Sarah, who's been missing since April 8. I've been hiking from State Highway 74 downstream on the Aqua Fria, and I think I might have seen something. I can't get out into the river, but there's something that might be a car caught in the culvert under the bridge."

"Wait just a minute, Mr. Johnson. I'll check your file. The computers are running a little slow this morning." After a pause, the Lieutenant continued. "Yes, I see the investigation. We'll send a team out. Could you wait there for them?"

"Yes. I'll be at the edge of the highway on the south side." Paul wiped his forehead and neck with a tissue and hoped they wouldn't be too long. The day was warming up fast.

Paul sat on the guardrail. A half hour later, a patrol car pulled up, and Paul led the two officers to the spot downstream from the bridge where he had caught sight of the mirror-like gleam. The sun wasn't in a position anymore for the reflection to be obvious, but using binoculars, they located what he saw.

"That could be something, Mr. Johnson. We'll get a team out here to check it out. I'm not sure when we will be able to get one set up … probably later today. You may as well go on home. We'll call you with our findings."

The officers led the way back to the patrol car where one of them radioed their office about the find. Paul returned to his car and drove home to wait.

Chapter 18

May AD 2008

The next morning, Sarah's stomach tightened as the master approached. Would he accuse her of tattling? Or back her into a corner again?

He stopped a good ten feet away and cleared his throat. "Sarah, Enoch and I will need food enough to last about a week and a skin of water apiece ... plus two skins of wine. Have all of it ready within the hour."

Sarah bowed her head. "It will be as you say."

An hour later, the servant Enoch tied the dried meat, fruit, and water skins on a pack mule. Before they left, Sarah lifted her gaze to Hamath. "Thank you, sir, for going after my husband."

Hamath glanced at her with narrowed eyes before mounting his horse, but he didn't answer.

After Hamath and Enoch left, Sarah made her way to the marketplace, carrying her basket in one hand and holding Tamara's hand in the other. Tammy didn't slow Sarah's progress much. In fact, sometimes she was hard put to keep up with the three-year-old, who didn't act at all sick today. *Adrenalin?*

At Jonas's shop, Tamara skipped in a circle around her mother. Sarah laughed as she pulled the child to a halt. "Jonas and Dathan, please allow me to introduce you to my little animated angel—my daughter, Tamara."

"Hello, Tamara." Jonas grinned, kneeling at her level. "Are you always such a happy girl?"

"My Papa's coming home, coming home, coming home!" Tamara sang.

"Oh, that is happy news." Jonas said, turning to Sarah with a question in his eyes.

"Yes," Sarah said, glancing at Tamara. "My mistress had a ... *discussion* with her husband yesterday. Apparently, the master might have contributed to Paulos's disappearance, and he sort of, uh, volunteered to go get him back."

"How, um ... nice of your master." Jonas grinned. "And how wonderful that Paulos will be returning. I rejoice for both of you. Does Hamath know where Paulos is?"

"Not exactly, but apparently he knows where the slave master is from. The mistress is confident Hamath will have Paulos back within the month." She picked up Tamara and hugged her. "We've been celebrating ever since we heard the good news last evening, haven't we, Tammy?"

"Yes! We're cebberlating!" she confirmed, bouncing up and down in her mother's arms.

Jonas and Dathan laughed.

"Wonderful! May his return be quick and safe," Jonas said. Customers began coming into his shop. Father and son turned to help them, waving goodbye as Sarah and Tamara wove their way through the early morning crowd to the food section of the busy marketplace.

By the time they returned home, the day was much warmer. Summer was in full swing, with very little rain. Today's temperature, she guessed, was close to eighty degrees, perfect swimming weather. After the midday meal, she gathered the excited children and led them to a sandy area of the beach. The children played nearly naked in the cool salt water.

Sarah removed her outer tunic, tied a knot in the bottom of the inner tunic between her legs so it wouldn't ride up, and she waded in.

One at a time, she showed the children how to float in the shallow water. Then she had them compete to see who could float the longest, making sure none of them floated out beyond where they could easily touch bottom. After about an hour, they dressed and walked back home, happy and smelling much better.

Sarah was glad her days would be busy over the next month. Waiting patiently until Paulos returned would be difficult. She worried he might live crippled and in pain for the rest of his life, but at least he would have a place to live where she could take care of him.

Enoch knew better than to talk to the master while he was in one of his moods. Despite Hamath's promise to Dorcas that he'd hurry to Jerusalem, once out of sight, he slowed their pace to a walk and pulled a wineskin from his cloak, muttering to himself. Enoch wondered if his master had been sipping on the wine earlier. He swayed unsteadily in the wooden saddle.

"It would serve her right if I never returned," Hamath growled, taking a generous swig from the skin. "There are more congenial women in this world."

Enoch cast a sideways glance at his master. Should he respond? *No.*

The man continued. "After all I've done for her, you'd think she'd show more gratitude. I married her, didn't I, and brought my family name to her? Oh, all right, she already had a good family name. Well, I keep her supplied in jewels and beautiful clothing, do I not? She was already rich, but I've treated her well. So what if I look at other women? All men do that."

Paying careful attention to the trees and rocks on the other side of the road, Enoch jumped when his employer addressed him.

"Tell me, Enoch, must wives be happy with all of their men's actions? Do they look at their husbands as though they're worms just because they gaze at another woman, or is it just that ill-tempered wife I married? She can freeze a man with a cold look."

"I'm not married, but I'm sure you're right, sir. I think most wives would object to their husbands gazing at other women with desire in their eyes."

"Of course, I'm right! Women! Dorcas tries my patience past what a normal husband should bear. It's the nature of men to look. I'd be less than a man if I didn't. That woman should rejoice that I'm her husband. When I get home, I'll beat her. That'll prove to her *I* am the man of my house. If I find Paulos, that will be just fine, and if I don't find him, so what? It's my home as much as it is hers."

"Of course, sir."

The master spurred his horse, and Enoch, leading the mule, had no choice but to follow as fast as he could. He hoped Hamath's anger abated before they ran their animals to death. The mule protested noisily, and water sloshed wildly in the large leather bags on either side of the pack saddle. The master glowered back at them, but he slowed to a walk.

I should have known he would. Enoch smiled to himself. *Hamath is fond of his animals, perhaps more than of his family.*

They made it as far as Ptolemais the first night. When they found an inn, Enoch took the horses and mule to the stable, making sure the horses would be fed grain and rubbed down properly. He then hauled the remaining food and wine to their room.

Hamath ordered a plate of food at the inn. Enoch could eat the likely stale bread and moldy cheese that waspish woman packed for them. After a good bit of wine with his meal, Hamath decided to stroll around the town. *There should be a willing wench somewhere, and there's no Dorcas around to narrow her eyes at me.* He spotted a tavern and entered, noticing a woman standing alone near the door. He approached, but arrived just a heartbeat too late—another man, much larger than Hamath, laid claim to her. He was no fool. Wandering past the couple to a table, he hoped the muscular newcomer thought that had been the original destination.

A serving wench brought him a cup of beer, giggling and dodging away as Hamath tried to put his arm around her waist. After several more attempts and many refills, he staggered out the door, wondering where the inn had gone. He squinted blurrily this way and that, but nothing looked familiar. Squatting next to the tavern wall, he dropped his head to his chest.

After eating his own meal, Enoch waited a couple of hours before searching for his master. He found Hamath sprawled next to the wall of the tavern. After helping him to his feet, Enoch half carried Hamath back to the inn.

"Thish ish a *mos'* unfrennly vil-village." The master hiccupped. "I bleeve I sh'd go t' bed now. Can you fine me a bed, Enoch, ol' fren?"

"Yes, sir. *This* way, sir," Enoch emphasized as his employer leaned in the direction of another tavern. He got his master to the inn and into bed without too much more difficulty. With a weary sigh, he lay on the floor by the door, wrapped himself in his cloak, and went to sleep.

Chapter 19

Enoch was awakened by his master's groans.

"Oh, my head. Where am I? How did I get here?"

"We are in Ptolemais, sir, at an inn. We arrived here yesterday." Enoch said, carefully avoiding the subject of the master's intoxication.

"Oh, that's right. I remember. I feel like I've been the road under an entire Roman legion."

"Shall I get you some breakfast, sir?" Enoch rose from the floor and ran fingers through his hair.

The master shuddered. "No. Maybe later." He groaned again. "I guess we should get on the road. Get our horses ready, Enoch."

"Yes, sir," Enoch said, ignoring his own growling stomach.

This day's ride was rougher than the day before, mostly uphill. The master didn't try to converse at all. Enoch didn't start any new topics either. Sometimes he was hard put to answer his master with respect. Hamath expected him to always be truthful, though not so truthful he insulted the master.

When they stopped at an inn in Araba, Enoch noticed his employer didn't look for trouble like he had the night before. Apparently, even he had his limits.

From Araba they rode south, traveling five more days. Hamath made no more attempts to contact prostitutes, and he avoided taverns as if they were poison.

At least we're in Jerusalem now. Enoch mused. *I hope there will be fewer places of temptation for him here.*

Once they found an inn close to the center of Jerusalem, Hamath and Enoch ate their fill, then remounted their horses to explore. Jerusalem had to be one of the largest cities in the world. Some of the homes were three and four stories tall. People filled the streets and marketplaces. Sometimes the crowds were so thick they had to dismount and walk their uneasy horses.

Enoch was grateful they hadn't arrived during a festival. The number of people could easily double during the Feast of Booths, the Passover, and the Feast of Weeks. The first two of those holy day celebrations were past and the next wouldn't begin for some time. *Wouldn't Hamath be surprised to find out I'm a Jew!*

At sunset of the first day, the master jerked a rag from his belt and impatiently wiped the sweat from his face. "I don't think we're going to find the slave trader today. We've asked every passerby willing to talk if they know this Bildad, but no one knows him. Or, at least they won't admit knowing him. We may as well go back to the inn."

As soon as the sun rose the next morning, they mounted their horses. They hadn't gone far when Hamath pulled his mount to a stop. "There's quite a crowd over there. Surely in a group that large, someone would know of Bildad."

They dismounted and walked to the edge of the crowd. Despite the distance between them and the speaker, Hamath could hear him clearly. The man had a powerful voice, yet Hamath felt like he spoke for his ears alone. *Remarkable.*

While the speaker talked, something strange began to pull at Hamath's heart. Tears slid down his face and into his beard. He wiped his face, hoping no one would notice, but everyone seemed as engrossed by the man as he was.

Hamath asked in a quiet voice, "Who is this man?"

Someone nearby answered in a choked voice, "He's called Jesus. Some say he's the Messiah; some say he's a prophet. Whatever he is, he speaks truth to the heart."

Silently, Hamath and Enoch led their horses away from the crowd.

Hamath turned. "I'm at odds with myself, Enoch. I know you're my servant, but I should never have treated you like a dirty stall in my stable rather than the good and loyal servant you've been. I'm sorry."

"There were times when I was less than loyal to you, sir. My thoughts haven't always been charitable."

Hamath's shoulders relaxed. "You're forgiven, Enoch. At least you kept your unkind thoughts inside and didn't treat people like camel dung. That's what I've been doing. I've been blind and foolish."

Gathering the reins, he mounted his horse. "Enoch, what's the Messiah? All I know is that this man gave me a message that turned me inside out."

"The Jews believe God will send a savior to free them. In Greek, he'd be called the Christ. Maybe this is the one who's been expected." Enoch cleared his throat. "I'm a Jew, but I'm afraid I haven't been a good one. I haven't been attending the Sabbath at the synagogue, and as a result, I'm not as familiar as I should be with the prophecies."

"All I know is that he somehow made me see myself, and I don't like what I see."

"Maybe that's a step on the right path. Maybe recognizing we've been less than perfect at one time or another—hah! many times over!—is a beginning."

"I'll try, Enoch. When we get home, I'll throw out those useless household gods." He looked up toward the sun. "Let's go. We still need to find Paulos."

Hamath hailed a passerby. "Shalom, friend. We are looking for a certain slave trader named Bildad. Do you know of him?"

"No, neighbor, I don't, but there's a slave who might give you better information. There is a chief of slaves at the Temple, one Petronius. He was a slave of the Romans and now belongs to a Jew. I think he could tell you where your slave monger might be found."

"Where is the temple? And may anyone go into it?"

The stranger pointed. "Take this road. It leads to the south gate where the Court of Gentiles is. If you're a Jew, you can go into the Court of Women, and if you're a priest, into the Court of Priests. Otherwise, stay in the Court of Gentiles."

"Thank you." Hamath led his horse, dodging beggars, tradesmen, and children on the busy street. He hailed a boy by the temple gate and gave him a silver coin to hold their horses.

Hamath and Enoch walked into the Court of Gentiles. Hamath stopped a man striding toward the next set of steps. "Do you know a slave called Petronius?

The man nodded. "Shalom, friend. Follow me." He led them back toward the entry and pointed toward a tall black man who stood with arms folded, talking to a vendor. "There," he said and turned again toward his original path.

Hamath's eyebrows raised in surprise. The tall, gray-haired, scarred slave wore a clean, white linen tunic and carried himself like a king. He looked more like a merchant than a slave, except for the hole through one earlobe, the symbol that proclaimed he had chosen to be a slave and stay with his master forever rather than to be freed.

"Are you Petronius?" Hamath asked.

"Yes. Do you need something, sir?"

"Do you know of a slave master called Bildad?"

Petronius's lip curled in contempt. "I know of him. That one is an evil man. I've heard rumors he kidnaps men, women, and children who have the misfortune to be away from the safety of their families. When he captures them, he treats them worse than dogs. He should be enslaved himself and treated as he treats these poor people."

Heat flooded Hamath's face as he recalled how he put Paulos into Bildad's hands. "Can you tell us where to find the man? We wish to rescue or buy one of my servants he, uh, took."

"When he's in the area, you can often find him at a tavern called the Edge on the outside of Jerusalem. Take the road leading to the Hippodrome, and you will find the tavern outside the city walls. I don't suggest you try to rescue anyone from him. You could end up as slaves yourselves. If you must, take some strong men with you or plenty of money. Or better, take both."

"Thank you, friend."

"God go with you. You will need him."

Chapter 20

The days dragged by on turtle feet. Sarah could see her mistress becoming impatient too. Dorcas stared out the door as though she could make Hamath appear with a visual command. When she wasn't busy, Sarah joined her in watching.

"Sarah, I have a request."

"Yes, mistress?"

"I have prayed to our household gods, but nothing happens. Do you have a god you pray to?"

"In a way, I do. I don't know really what I believe, if that sounds logical. But I have asked the God of the Jews to heal Tamara, and I've also asked him to bring Paulos back. It couldn't hurt, and I hope it might help."

"Then … would you be willing to submit a prayer or a sacrifice or whatever you do that Hamath will also return? I would deeply appreciate it."

"I will. I don't know how to do a sacrifice, but I will pray."

"Thank you." Dorcas nodded, with tears in her eyes.

Tamara's earlier energy had evaporated. Her seizures grew more frequent, usually less than a week apart, and sometimes three or four times a week. Each incident left Tamara tired and weak for longer than before. Even so, Sarah would never wish to go back to the twenty-first century. Those doctors hadn't found a cure either.

Sarah hadn't mentioned the episodes, not even to Dorcas. Other than Paulos and herself, Jonas was the only person who knew. Sarah's fears grew as Tamara's worsening health left her noticeably weaker. Tamara had said Jesus told her he would see her again, but Sarah feared Tamara would again see Jesus when he carried her away forever. Would she live to see her fourth birthday, only three months away?

Sarah was crossing the courtyard toward the cooking area to prepare the midday meal when the mistress stopped her. "Sarah, Tamara's obviously ill. She's thinner ... and you look thinner too. Are you eating enough? Would you like for me to send for a physician?"

Sarah glanced at her daughter, who'd had another bout the night before. "I'm tired, mistress, but not sick. Tamara had a fever last night, but she's better this morning. She's had several evenings when she hasn't felt well, once a week or more. I don't have money for a physician. And I'm afraid a physician might want to bleed her. She doesn't have any blood to spare. She's so small that bleeding could kill her."

"I know a wise and good physician here by the name of Nicolas." The mistress turned her gaze from Tammy to Sarah. "I don't think he always uses bloodletting to cure his patients. You are invaluable to me, Sarah, and your health is important. Even if I weren't fond of Tamara, I wouldn't want her to suffer ill health, because her illness would also affect you. I'll send for Nicolas immediately. Maybe he will be able to come after our midday meal."

"Thank you, mistress. You are too gracious."

"Nonsense. It only makes sense to take care of good servants. If you don't, they get sick or die." The mistress smiled. "Or worse, some wealthy family hires them away from you."

Sarah felt her stomach tighten. "I don't think he'll be able to tell what's wrong with her."

"Sarah, listen to my counsel. Tamara won't be hurt by this physician, and she might be helped. We have to give him a chance." Dorcas's firm voice halted any dispute.

Sarah sighed. "As you wish, mistress. Thank you."

One of the stable slaves webt after Nicolas, and Sarah walked to the outside cooking area. Despite her employer's recommendation, Sarah still worried he could do more harm than good. She fretted for the next two hours while completing her duties.

It was nearly time to prepare the evening meal when Nicolas arrived. The mistress brought him to the courtyard where Tamara sat with Orphah. The physician's graying hair indicated he might have some years of experience, and his soft brown eyes glowed with compassion as he gazed at Tammy. Sarah wiped her hands on a rag and joined them.

Nicolas knelt next to Tammy for a few minutes, smiling and teasing before asking if he could listen to her heart.

"Okay." Tamara tilted her head. "But where is your *steffiesoap*?"

It was the physician's turn to tilt his head. "What's a steffiesoap?"

"You know, the thing you put in your ears and on my chest to listen to my heart."

Nicolas shrugged as he glanced at Sarah, but she repeated the shrug. No way was she going to explain a stethoscope to him.

"Well, I must have forgotten to bring one today. I hope that's all right with you."

"I wanted to listen to my heart too, but I don't know how to do that without a steffiesoap. I guess it's all right, but how will you hear my heart?"

"Did you ever sit on your mama's lap with your ear on her chest? Do you remember hearing her heart beat?" At Tammy's nod, he continued. "That's how I'll listen to your heart. I can listen to you breathe that way too, if you're very quiet." She nodded, and he leaned over and placed his ear to Tamara's chest.

"Her heart rate and breathing are both a little fast, but not too bad," he said. "How often is she ill, and what happens when she is?"

Tamara looked up at the physician. "I get sick lots of nights. I get freezy, and I shake, and I feel all tired. And my head hurts, and sometimes I see two mamas."

Sarah sat on the ground next to her daughter. "I guess she wants to describe her own symptoms, sir, and she did that as well as I could have. She has these illnesses at least once a week." *I'm not about to tell this stranger—or Dorcas—that Tamara's shaking is a bit more than mere chills.*

"All right, little one. Now, can you walk over there to the fountain and back?"

Tammy only staggered a little in that short walk.

Nicolas nodded. "Very good. Thank you."

Nicolas stood. "If I understand, Dorcas, no one else here has had the same thing? Sometimes illnesses make the rounds of everyone in the sick one's vicinity."

Dorcas shook her head. "No, no one else."

Nicolas turned back to Sarah. "Does she also have fevers?"

"Usually."

Nicolas pursed his lips and frowned. "I don't like how pale she is, nor those dark circles under her eyes. It might be helpful if you'd call me the next time an illness occurs. I'm afraid I might know what's causing this, but I'd like to talk to some of my physician friends before I say anything. I've no suggestions for a cure for her right now. I'm sorry."

Sarah nodded. "I understand." At least he didn't suggest bleeding her, or toad eyes and lizard tongues or whatever passed for aspirin in these times.

As though reading her mind, Nicolas gave Sarah a few pieces of wood. "This is willow bark. Usually, the bark will help lower a fever and relieve pain. It won't cure her but should help. There is a willow stand beside the river on the mainland, and I can always get more. The leaves will also work, if you want to get some yourself. I've found the bark keeps longer, but fresh leaves might be more palatable. She can chew them, or you can make a tea from the bark or leaves. Drinking might be easier for her. Other than this, I don't have any other suggestions."

"Thank you, Mr. Nickle." Tamara patted the physician's hand.

"Yes, thank you." Sarah lifted Tamara into her arms.

"Please send for me if you need me again. Dorcas said you would object, but she's a wise employer. Listen to her. In fact, I'd like to study Tamara further. I won't ask for more compensation from you or from Dorcas." Nicolas made his farewells, giving Tammy an extra smile and a squeeze of her hand.

Sarah breathed a quiet sigh of relief as he left but still felt a little disappointed.

Chapter 21

Hamath was glad to avoid the notorious tavern that evening, but early the next morning after breaking their fast, he and Enoch mounted their horses and rode. They didn't have friends to take with them as Petronius advised, but Hamath was certain he had enough to buy Paulos. Bildad loved money, or he wouldn't kidnap men, women, and children to use as slaves.

They found the tavern where Petronius said, a squalid, ramshackle rock structure with the sour smell of urine and vomit hanging in a noxious miasma around the area. From the shabby appearance of three men who exited as they arrived, this wasn't a hangout for the wealthy—at least not the legally wealthy. Hamath left Enoch to guard the horses.

After Hamath's eyes adjusted to the dim interior, he asked the first person he saw for the tavern owner.

"Who wants him?" The man's voice grated as though drug over a rough, dry wadi.

"Hamath of Tyre. I'd like to talk to him."

"I'm the tavern master. Tell me what it is you want, and perhaps for a coin I might provide the answer ... if I feel like it." His smile—if one could call it that—more closely resembled an oily, gap-toothed grimace.

"I'm looking for the slave master called Bildad. I wish to buy a slave from him."

"Bildad?"

Hamath dug a silver shekel from the purse on his belt and held it up.

"Oh, *that* Bildad. You're too early for him. That one doesn't come here until the sun is well past its zenith. For another coin, I might give him your message."

Hamath pulled another shekel from the bag. "He can find me at the inn of Bar Judas, south of the temple." He walked out the door, holding his breath until he was far enough away to inhale somewhat cleaner air.

"I'd keep my back to the wall in that place," Enoch commented.

"Better yet, don't even go in there. Smells worse inside than out. The tavern master might be the first to place a knife in your back if you don't pay your bill, or if he thought you might have a few coins worth stealing."

On returning to the inn, Enoch and his employer found a table in the great room and ordered a platter of food and a skin of wine. This was the first time in Enoch's life that he had eaten at the same table with his master, and he wasn't sure how to act. The man chatted with him as he would an old friend. Enoch wondered more than once if this was the same one he'd left Tyre with.

After taking a swallow of the watered wine, Hamath said, "I hoped we wouldn't have to go back to that tavern, but we probably don't have a choice. I don't know any other way to find the slave monger. Unless ... Do you have any ideas?"

"No, sir." Enoch shook his head, still unsure if this change in the master would last past his next drink. "That would probably be the only way to find him—the way you said, that is."

"Not tonight. Tomorrow, then, after the sixth hour. With the sun high above us, we'll have to find shade, and we'll only stay until the eleventh hour. That should give us plenty of time to be away from there before dark. We'll do this every day until we make contact with him.

"As you wish, sir."

The next day, they returned to the tavern after the midday meal. After tying the horses to some tamarisk trees across the road, they sat down on a handy log in the sparse shade. They were prepared for a long wait, but not long after they arrived, a large man showed up, riding in a large, mule-pulled wagon. A dozen rough-looking men accompanied him, some in the wagon and some on foot.

Hamath's stomach tightened. *This doesn't look good.*

The leader wore a robe stained with grease and dirt. His scraggly, graying hair and beard nearly hid his sharp black eyes, small and set close together. His long nose jutted out, bulbous and red-veined.

Hamath rose and walked across the road, stepping in front of the large man before he could enter the tavern. "Are you Bildad?"

"Maybe. Then again, maybe not. Who would you be?"

"I'm Hamath of Tyre. I sent a man to you, one Paulos, a man with a broken leg. I want him back."

"You want him back? Why?"

Hamath swallowed. "Uh ... His wife and child miss him."

"His wife and child miss him." Bildad scoffed. "How touching. Go find his bones beside the road. That cripple you gave me didn't last long enough to be worth my trouble."

Hamath felt the blood drain from his face. "He's dead?"

"He died when we were only a couple of days out of town. You swindled me, Hamath of Tyre."

"Swindled you? I *gave* him to you. You weren't out one shekel."

"Not out one shekel? I fed him, watered him, and medicated him. And still he died." He offered a malevolent smile. "You should pay me for my loss, but it would be better luck if I had a slave to replace the lost one. You're soft now, but give me a month, and I'll put muscle on you." He nodded to his men, who seized Hamath's arms.

Enoch sprang up from the log. Drawing his short sword, he ran across the road. "Stop! Let him go!"

"No! Enoch, go back. Get help; go tell—"

One of the thugs struck Hamath in the stomach with the butt of his sword, dropping him to his knees. Gasping and gagging, he could only watch as the man turned to meet Enoch, swinging his blade in a deadly arc. The scar-faced swordsman wiped his bloody sword on Enoch's twitching body. He turned back to the slave master. "We'll have no more trouble from this one."

"Chilead, you idiot!" Bildad backhanded the swordsman, giving him yet another scar across his face from the elaborate ruby ring on the monger's right hand. "We could have had yet another slave, one who actually looked accustomed to working."

"One day you'll go too far, Bildad," Chilead snarled, wiping blood from his cheek.

"If you don't like my company—or my coins—there is nothing to keep you by my side. You are free to go at any time. Unlike this new slave." Bildad grinned, pushing Hamath with his foot. He kissed his ring with thick, puckered lips.

Chilead turned his back and stalked over to the tavern, kicking the door open.

The other men trussed Hamath and threw him over the back of his horse. One pulled the purse from Hamath's girdle and another from Enoch's body, laughing that now they had the price of an evening of eating and drinking for the lot of them. The men walked into the tavern with Bildad, ignoring Enoch's body, now attracting flies in the late afternoon sun. Hamath received a sharp blow to the head from the man who took his bag of coins. His world quickly faded from a gray mist to blackness.

Chapter 22

Darkness surrounded Hamath. *Am I in Hades?*

He tried to sit up, groaning as he realized his hands were tied behind his back and a collar encircled his neck. *I must not be dead, unless in Hades I would be bound. And my head; oh, my head.* He had been stripped to his inner tunic. He was secured by a rope run through a metal ring on the leather collar around his neck and tied to a tree. He stretched as far as he could reach, but the collar and the ropes held.

"Enoch. Are you there, Enoch?" he whispered. Then he remembered ... Enoch was dead.

Suddenly, a lamp lit up the darkness and a loud crack broke the silence. Hamath yelped at a sharp sting on his arm. Hamath yelped as the whip cracked again, this time connecting with his back, tearing the thin linen of his tunic.

"You speak only when spoken to, slave." A man with a whip stood about ten feet away.

"There's been a mistake. I'm not a slave. I'm Hamath of Tyre, and—argh!" The whip cut him again.

"You used to be Hamath of Tyre. You are now the slave of Bildad. He may give you a different name if he wishes or leave you without one."

Hamath opened his mouth to protest and received another cut of the whip. He gritted his teeth against another groan and lay on his side, silently fearing the lash would fall again. The man with the whip nodded and sat down by a tree, darkening the lamp by his side.

Hamath heard quiet voices coming from a rock building to his left. He strained to hear, but could discern nothing other than unintelligible murmurs. His discomfort kept him from sleep, so he lay still, thinking about the words of Jesus. The more he thought, the more miserable he became. He'd betrayed everyone who had ever loved or served him and made enemies of everyone else. Worse, Enoch died defending him ... or trying to. Otherwise, his servant would surely have been taken into slavery too. He would have responded when Hamath called his name, even if it meant getting whipped. The last thing he remembered clearly was someone hitting him in the stomach as Enoch rushed across the road. There'd been blood. A lot of blood.

Shame swept over Hamath. He'd caused so much trouble. All this happened because he betrayed Paulos into slavery. Now Hamath was a captive, or more likely, a slave himself. Both Enoch and Paulos were dead. How could Jesus forgive him for making such a mess of not only his own life but also the lives of so many others? Somehow, he had to get free and at least let Sarah know what happened. And apologize to her, acknowledging that her husband's death was his fault.

Enoch wasn't married, and his parents were already gone, but that didn't make Hamath feel any better about Enoch's death than

Paulos's death. And Dorcas—he'd beg her forgiveness too. Would she want him back? He not only couldn't bring Paulos back, but he had lost Enoch and all their coin as well. He deserved exactly what he'd gotten.

The next morning, Chilead kicked him awake. "On your feet, slave," he growled. "We need firewood."

Hamath struggled to rise, no easy task with his hands tied behind his back. On his knees, he decided maybe he should try to convince this Chilead. "There's been a mistake."

Chilead kicked him in the stomach, knocking him down. He gasped for breath.

"I said I need some firewood. If I want conversation, I'll talk to one of my companions, not to a slave."

Chilead carelessly cut the bonds, nicking Hamath's thumb, which bled freely into the dirt at his feet. He clenched his teeth and knelt in subdued silence. Chilead untied the rope that led to his collar and jerked him to his feet.

"That way," Chilead said, pointing toward the nearby shrubs with a tilt of his head.

Hamath wondered how he could get free. The whip master from the night before wasn't a big man, but the whip made up for his lack of stature. Chilead, however, was huge, with most of his bulk being thick, muscular arms, a broad chest, and legs like tree trunks. Still, Hamath had to think of a way. He would keep eyes and ears open.

That same night, Hamath's captors forgot to tie his hands. He smirked, careful not to let his captors know his jubilation. All he needed was a sharp rock to cut the rope to his collar. When he was sure the guards were asleep, he felt around in the dark. *Ah, there's a*

rock with rough edges. And a rounded rock. Almost as though they were placed here just for me. He pulled the rope in front of him, placed it firmly on the rounded rock, and began to saw with the rough rock. When he finished, he rose and took off through the tall brush.

The sound of laughter rang behind him.

It wasn't far before Hamath found himself surrounded by grinning faces.

"Thought you'd get away so easily, slave?" Bildad taunted. "Instead, you will provide our sport for the evening."

Each of the men held a short whip with multiple leather tails, knotted at the ends. They walked with deliberate steps closer to him, slapping their whips on their hands. One after another, each man took a turn, striking him on every available surface—face, shoulders, back, arms, legs, anywhere and everywhere. Hamath sank to the ground and curled into a ball, crying out as the knots cut into his flesh again and again, until he lost consciousness.

When he woke, Hamath lay in the large, barn-like shed he'd seen the previous night. One of the slaves, a small, brown-skinned man with a withered arm, dressed Hamath's wounds. Hamath tried to draw the other slave into a whispered conversation as he rubbed salve over the cuts, but the man shook his head, rolling wide eyes toward where the whip master watched. Hamath understood.

The slave held a smelly brew to his lips. Hamath gritted his teeth at the pain radiating from every part of his frame and turned his face away. The slave held the cup again to his mouth, glancing sideways at the whip master. Hamath groaned. He swallowed the fowl-tasting liquid, his first "meal" since his capture. He didn't care. Every inch of his body hurt too much to be hungry. He pulled a dirty, itchy piece of old linen over him and tried to sleep on the straw, hoping Bildad wouldn't expect him to work this day.

The next morning, Hamath felt well enough to eat the thin gruel provided to the slaves. He even managed to sit up as he ate. He suspected he had better get well fast or be prepared to suffer further under the whip. He didn't know what his back looked like, but the pieces of skin that hung off his arms made him look like a shedding camel. However, scabs had formed and looked only a little red. He guessed Bildad didn't want to kill him, just terrorize him.

People came and went at the slave encampment, sometimes bringing slaves in, sometimes taking some out. Hamath wasn't sure what was going on, but from the snatches of conversation overheard between Chilead and the strangers, he gathered that Bildad's slaves were being rented out. Or maybe sold.

Before long, Hamath noticed that the slaves had a method of communication, a shrug or a wave of a certain number of fingers when the whip master wasn't watching. A gaze might be cast this way or that, a nod or a shake of the head, even an occasional toe in the dust, quickly scuffed out if the whip master should look in their direction. Hamath wished he could learn the language. Maybe if he paid close attention....

Over the next weeks, Hamath worked every day, often went hungry, and was beaten if he didn't respond the way they wanted. He learned a little of the slaves' hidden language, enough to discover some of them had been there for years, and most of them had been kidnapped. There were enough slaves in the compound to break free if they would unite, but fear, more than the bonds, held them captive. Hamath learned that several of the men had also been treated to the "sport" of the men with the lashes.

Not the women, though. While the men's value wouldn't be reduced by whip marks, the women were expected to be spotless, particularly the pretty ones, and most of the women in the camp fell into that category. A few weeks before, Hamath would have been all too willing to rent one of these lovely females for a few days. Now his heart melted in sympathy for those who had no choice but to submit. Some women had small children, no doubt born in the camp.

The children didn't play. Their mothers kept them quiet, or tried to. If they didn't, Chilead or one of the others slapped both mothers and children until they were silenced, often knocked out by a man's heavy hand. It made Hamath wonder how many of the little ones died that way. He would want to kill anyone who treated his children like that, and wished he could batter these captors like they did these small victims.

He was sure most of the other men felt the same way. Nearly all of them were held back in fetters. The mothers were restrained too, and most children had learned to be quiet no matter what. The cruelty Hamath saw here was beyond anything he had ever seen or even heard of.

Chapter 23

June AD 30

More than a month passed, and Sarah hadn't heard anything about either Paul or the master. Dorcas had said nothing, but Sarah could see worry lines around her eyes and mouth. She knew the same lines must be visible on her own face. Despite her own mistrust and dislike of the master, Sarah couldn't help but feel compassion for the mistress.

Tammy pulled on the edge of her mother's tunic. "Is today the day, Mama?"

"I don't know, sweetie. Let's just keep going through the day till we find out."

Tamara had gone almost a week now with no convulsions, and she looked more rested. She was still pale, but the dark circles under her eyes weren't as bad. Even so, Sarah couldn't help but remember the course this disease took before. She could almost feel it building to the same conclusion.

She had to enjoy the time with Tamara now, because it looked like the outcome could be no different than before. Sarah didn't think

God would continue to accept constant prayers for Tammy. It was too much to ask of him to listen just to her when there were so many others calling for his help. He must sometimes feel overwhelmed with all the prayer requests he received. Jonas didn't think so, but Sarah didn't see how it could be otherwise.

As though her thoughts had brought it on, that evening Tamara had another convulsion, and Sarah placed cool, wet cloths on the child's head and body. When Tammy woke from the fit, Sarah gave her Nicolas's willow bark to chew on and then ran to Martha's quarters. "Would you please ask Dorcas to send for Nicolas? He said we should the next time Tamara got sick … and she is."

"Of course. Go back to Tamara. I'll find the mistress." Martha turned and ran toward the house.

Sarah hoped Tamara wouldn't have another seizure, but the child was already quaking by the time Sarah returned. Frantic, Sarah feared Tammy might choke on the bark, but then she found the bit next to the pallet. As the seizure ended, Sarah placed more cool cloths on her, trading one set for another when Tamara's body heat warmed each set. By the time Nicolas arrived, her fever had begun to subside.

Again, Nicolas listened to Tamara's chest, looked into her eyes and ears, and felt the heat of her skin. "Does your head hurt, Tamara?" he asked.

"Little bit," she said, her voice faint.

"Does anything else hurt?"

"No." Her eyes drooped.

"I want you to open your eyes for just a moment more, little one."

Tammy squinted at him. "'kay."

The physician's eyebrow rose. "Kay? What does that mean? Never mind, it doesn't matter." He held up a finger. "Can you see this?"

She nodded just a smidgen.

"How many?"

"Two."

"Do you always see two of things?"

"Most times. Can I close my eyes now?"

"Yes. Sleep, child." Nicolas stood and turned to Sarah. "Would you come outside with me for a moment?"

Once outside, Nicolas heaved a big sigh. "I don't have a good report for you. I fear your little girl might have a lump growing inside her head. I don't know anything more we can do for her. If she were older and stronger, I might open her head and take out the bad part, but I don't think she's strong enough. I'll ask among other physicians to see if any of them know something that might help. You are doing as much as I could do, cooling her when the fevers hit and giving her willow bark to chew."

"It does seem to help a little."

"Sometimes high fevers are accompanied by fits. If that happens, don't let her chew the bark or leaves because she could choke. Instead, make a tea by boiling the bark and let her drink that . She could have a demon, but I'm not one who can help with that. Very few can, and no one I know of in Tyre."

Sarah nodded. This was the first century. Not many in the twenty-first century believed in demons, but she knew she couldn't convince Nicolas of that.

"Thank you, physician. I know there isn't much you or anyone can do, but I appreciate your honesty and help."

"I wish I could help more. When the pain gets worse—and it will—there are some stronger medicines that will make her sleep. Send for me when that happens. I'm sorry." With sad eyes and a consoling pat to her shoulder, Nicolas left.

Sarah walked back into the house. Tamara was already asleep. Sarah lay down on her own pallet and closed her eyes, but sleep didn't come. Her worries kept creeping in and pushing sleep out of her head. Finally, in the wee hours of the morning, her eyes closed in slumber.

Chapter 24

June AD 2008

A few days after seeing the reflection under the bridge, Paul finally got a call from Lieutenant Jones at the sheriff's office.

"Hello, Lieutenant. What did you find out? Was it Sarah's car?"

"Yes, it was, and thank you for your, uh, detective work. We'd like to come out to your house and talk to you about it."

Paul's breath caught. *At last!* "Sure, come ahead. I'm not going anywhere." Excitement mixed with dread filled his mind.

"Good. We'll be there in a few minutes."

True to his word, two officers arrived within a couple of minutes. They must have waited to call until they'd pulled up by his driveway.

"Coffee, officers?" Paul smiled nervously at Lieutenant Jones. "This time I do have milk."

Jones shook his head. "We'd like for you to come with us to headquarters."

Paul's back stiffened. *Uh-oh.*

"Sure. Was the car hers?"

"The vehicle is your wife's, but she wasn't in it. We'd like to talk to you about that."

"Are you kidding me? She always used her seat belt. She had to be in it." *Stupid, Johnson. They wouldn't be kidding about this. Still, if she wasn't in the car, maybe she was able to get out.*

"No, sir, we're not kidding," Lieutenant Jones sounded as if his politeness was being stretched to the breaking point. "Please come with us."

He took Paul's arm, none too gently, and headed for the car. The other officer moved to Paul's other side. Paul shook off Jones's hand but went with them peacefully. He wasn't sure whether he was angry or scared or both. His heart thumped like a hovering helicopter.

They made the long ride in silence. Paul in the back seat, separated from the officers by a closed window.

When they got to the downtown Phoenix office, they walked silently into the building. Paul forgot to remove the spare change and keys from his pocket and had to walk through the metal detector twice. The officers then led him to an interrogation room and asked him to sit down. The second officer, Sergeant Marklet, went after coffee.

Paul broke the silence. "I don't understand what's going on. I thought if I could find the car maybe I'd get out from under suspicion. I don't understand either where Sarah would be. She always wore her seat belt, so she must've gotten out of the car. Would you tell me if you found any trace of her at all?"

"The only thing we found was her purse inside the console. Both front doors and one back door were gone. The vehicle was pretty banged up. I'm amazed you could see the car under the bridge, because most of the vehicle was underwater or covered with mud and brush. How did you know the car was there, Mr. Johnson?"

"I didn't. I just thought the Agua Fria would be the most likely place where her car could be hidden from the highway. The river had been running full at the time she disappeared. I hiked downstream for maybe two or three miles and came back. I was nearly to the highway when I saw the sun reflecting off what could have been a mirror. The river was still running too high to wade, so I called your office."

"Doesn't it sound to you as though it was a little convenient that you knew just where to look? Because I've got to tell you, that's what it sounds like to me," Lieutenant Jones said, taking a cup of coffee from Sergeant Marklet.

The sergeant handed a second cup to Paul, who, taking a sip, cringed at the bitter taste of old coffee.

"Man, how many days has it been since this stuff was made?" He pushed the Styrofoam cup away. "I'll pass on the coffee."

"I am so sorry, sir; we don't have a Starbucks here," Marklet said sarcastically. He dumped the coffee into a trash can.

Paul flushed. "Sorry, sergeant; I didn't mean to sound ungrateful." He turned to Lieutenant Jones. "I didn't know anything ahead of time. I just saw the light reflecting off what looked like a mirror. Only thing is, I thought the car would be downstream from the road, not under the bridge. She must have gone off on the left side of the road."

"Yes, she did. There are no skid marks, although we did find where she went off the road quite a way back from the river. It was obvious she didn't use her brakes, and there's no apparent reason the car would go off the road there. All of those things make me think she was already dead."

"She had been taking sleeping pills—Ambien, I think—most nights since our little girl died. If she got up early enough, I suppose they could still make her go to sleep on the road. I didn't hear her leave, so I don't know what time that was."

"You didn't hear her get up, get dressed, open the garage door? Nothing?" Jones sounded skeptical.

"I'm a heavy sleeper."

"Well, here's what I think happened, Mr. Johnson. I think you took her for a ride. Or maybe you followed her and nudged her car off the road. I think your wife was getting in your way. You had a bit of a thing going with that cute redheaded professor, didn't you?"

Paul jerked his head up. "No, not a chance! There's no way I'd hurt my wife. And maybe Maureen would have liked to have a *thing* going, but it never happened. It hasn't happened since, either. I think she's given up now. I hope so."

"The way I figure, you nudged your wife's car off the road with your car. Don't think I don't remember that dent in your bumper. Maybe you'd already killed her, then just pushed her car off the road with yours. We haven't figured that out yet, but you can bet when we do, you'll spend some time in Arpaio's tent city and probably the state pen."

Paul's shoulders slumped. "This is crazy! I keep telling you I'd never deliberately harm Sarah. Or anyone else for that matter. I don't know how to convince you otherwise, Lieutenant. You'll think what you want to, no matter what I say."

"Your wife's friends seem to think the two of you were having problems. You can see how we might be thinking less than positive thoughts about you."

Paul stared at the table. "Yes, sir. I'm afraid the best description of the relationship with my wife would be 'distant,' but there isn't any animosity. We just can't carry on a conversation anymore, and truthfully, I guess we just stopped trying. It's not something I'm proud of. I wish we could do the whole thing over."

"Sure you do," Jones said. "As for this Maureen you say is chasing you, she tells a different story."

"Yeah, so I heard, but it's not true."

They continued to question Paul about his activities around the date of Sarah's disappearance for several hours, going over and over the same things from every possible angle.

The lieutenant heaved a sigh and ran his hands through his thinning hair. "Sergeant Marklet will take you back home now, but don't go anywhere other than to work. Meanwhile, we're dragging the river downstream from the car. You'd better hope we find her body. It might not go well with you if we don't. In fact, it might not go so well for you even if we do."

When he got home, Paul noticed an unfamiliar car parked across the street. Two men sat in the car staring toward his house. *Hmm. Bet that's a stakeout.* He shook his head. *They could get really bored watching me.*

On Monday morning when Paul left for work, a different car pulled out, not making any secret of the fact they were tailing him. They trailed him all the way to the campus, and an officer followed him wherever he went on foot. They followed him to his classes, to lunch, and then back home again. Other than being embarrassed, Paul wasn't inconvenienced. His coworkers gave him the fisheye, though. Even Maureen avoided him. The only person who didn't avoid him was Evelyn, the secretary.

When he stopped by her office to collect his messages, she asked, "Paul, who is that man—or rather those men—who have been hanging around?" One was here on Monday, a different one on Tuesday and Wednesday, and now the first one's back."

"They're from the sheriff's office. You might have read in the paper they got Sarah's car out of the Agua Fria. The police think I'm responsible. Trouble is, it could be months before they find her body, if there is a body. I still wonder if she might've gotten out of the river and someone picked her up." Paul sighed. "I know it's a stretch, but people sometimes lose their memories, don't they? I mean, maybe she's wandering around with some homeless people, wondering who she is."

"Paul, sit down." He did. Evelyn got up from her desk and shut the door. In her sixties, Evelyn was a mother figure for everyone in the office, and Paul knew he was probably in for a lecture, gentle though it might be.

"You know the chances of her getting out of that river were pretty remote. Paul, these are hard words to hear, I know, but you need to accept the probability that she won't be coming back. I won't tell you to pick yourself up and go forward with your life, because I know you need time. But listen to me—Sarah is no longer with us. I think you know that, deep down."

Paul groaned. "I guess, logically, I should realize that, but my heart doesn't agree. I can't believe I won't ever see her again. Maybe it's only because I want so much to have a chance to start over; maybe it's because I have this yearning for us to be together again."

"You might someday, Paul, but I don't think it will be in this world."

"I don't believe in an afterlife, Evelyn. I sometimes envy you your belief, but I don't subscribe to it."

She shook her head, a wry expression pulling her mouth to the side. "Don't tell me you're one of those people who think the universe happened by accident."

"Well, it's either that or some being or beings caused the Big Bang and then stood aside to see what would happen. I'd rather believe that there's no God than believe there's a God who allows all the hate and cruelty in this world ... or who just sat there and watched Tamara die."

"Hmm. You wish God had created puppets who have no choice but to obey him? That no one ever got sick or died? That's the only way no evil or sorrow would exist in this world."

"Well, maybe not puppets, but if he exists, he shouldn't let bad things happen to children. Tamara did nothing to earn the misery she went through before she died, nor did she deserve to die."

"Do you see dying as punishment for something?"

He had to think about that for a couple of seconds. "No, not usually. Dying happens to everyone, but my view of life and death is that when you're dead, you're dead. No heaven, no hell, no reincarnation, nothing. Tamara was just a baby. She will never experience the joys of childhood or falling in love or having her own children. Sarah and I will never see her grow up, and we won't see the grandchildren she might have given us. And speaking of Sarah, the chances appear slim that I'll see her again, either. Everyone I've loved has been taken from me. What did I do to deserve that?"

Evelyn shook her head. "I don't see death as punishment either, but as the spirit's—or soul's, if you prefer—release from a body that no longer has the ability to live. There's a lot of good in this world, Paul, including Tamara. Have you counted the blessings of having her in your life while she was here? That child was an angel in disguise, if ever there was one."

Paul snorted. "Yeah, 'too good for this world' is the phrase used by some of our friends. If that's not an overused bit of hypocrisy, I never heard one."

Evelyn winced. "I agree. Every once in a while, though, I hear a child giggle and think of Tammy. She had the most infectious laugh ever. Even if they don't know the right words to give comfort, there are a lot of good people in this world, Paul. It may be hard for you to see that now, but they're out there."

"Yeah, you're right. I know a few." Paul stood. "You're one of them, Evie. Now, I've got to get to my class, or my students are going to think the police have already hauled me off."

Paul left Evelyn's office, his heart cold and heavy. He knew her intention wasn't to make him feel this way. She was about as good-hearted as they came.

What I told her was true. I have this unshakable feeling that Sarah is somewhere waiting for me, and that feeling keeps growing, despite all the logic in the world.

June AD 30

The day came when Paulos tried standing for the first time since his leg had been set.

"It's still too soon," Mehida fretted.

"Joel said this week would probably be all right. I don't want to wait any longer, Mehida. You made crutches for me. Would you bring them? Please?"

He chuckled when she brought him only one. "I'll need two." He waved the one crutch at her. "Otherwise, I'll have to put some weight on this leg, and you'll be chiding me."

She made an O with her mouth, then scurried out the door and produced the other crutch. "I forgot about this one."

An old tree stump stool sat on the floor near the bed. Gingerly, he put his good leg down and added his weight, a little at a time. Balancing with the makeshift crutches, he eased the uninjured leg to the floor. Dizziness threatened to overcome him, and he leaned on the bed, frowning in concentration, breathing deeply. When the vertigo passed, he cautiously hobbled across the uneven stone floor.

Mehida opened the door, and he passed through, inhaling fresh air for the first time in two months, savoring the smells of the forest and the yard. He stood in wonder for several minutes, gazing at the beauty of the day and laughing at the antics of some young kids gathered around the nanny goats.

However, his weakened body could only stand so much in this first excursion. Reluctantly, he turned and went back into the house to find that in the short time he had been outside, Mehida had put fresh straw and a clean linen blanket on the bed.

He crossed the floor and hugged her. "Thank you, Mehida. Thank you for saving my life. You have been as good a mother as my own."

Mehida burst into tears. "And I love you as a son, Abner."

"Paulos," he corrected, smiling as he did so.

"Abner is a better name. Paulos sounds like a gentile's name."

Chapter 25

June AD 30

One morning when Sarah went to wake Tamara, the child's eyes popped open wide before her mother could say anything.

"Is Papa home yet?"

"No, not yet," Sarah replied.

"He'll be home very soon. Jesus told me."

"Jesus was here? I didn't see him."

"He was in my dream." Tamara bounced with excitement as she pulled her tunic over her head.

"Oh." Sarah tried to put some excitement into her voice.

"He said to tell you not to worry," Tamara added.

Sarah started. Was this in answer to her anxieties last night? Did that mean don't worry about Paulos, or don't worry about Tamara, or both?

"Mama, when is 'soon?'"

Sarah smiled. "If you can tell me what 'soon' means, you're way ahead of me. And I'll try to stop worrying, but mamas have to worry all the time about something, right? Shall we see if we can talk the chickens into giving us some more eggs?" She held her hand out to her daughter.

"'Kay," Tamara said, holding her mama's hand. "Is that grouchy old rooster going to chase me again?"

"If he does, we might invite him for dinner."

"Yum!" Tamara giggled.

In the courtyard, they searched the bushes and found enough eggs to feed the whole family and the servants as well. Sarah didn't worry about taking too many. There were plenty of chicks this year, almost half-grown now, and next year there would be more. The boss rooster, more interested in looking for bugs for breakfast, ignored the humans in his section of the yard.

When they walked into the cooking area, the mistress stood waiting for them. She knelt in front of Tamara. "How are you, little one? Do you feel better this morning?"

"I'm all better," Tammy said. "Jesus said my papa is coming soon. Have you seen him yet?"

"Jesus?" the mistress asked, glancing at Sarah.

"He's a nice man. Sometimes he holds me when I'm sick, and in my dream this morning, he said Papa is coming home soon."

Dorcas nodded. "Dreams are very nice, aren't they? Well, I hope your friend is right." She winked at Sarah. "It would be wonderful if your papa came home soon. "I need to go wake the children. I'm getting hungry. I'll go so you can get our breakfast ready."

Sarah scrambled the eggs with butter, onions, and a little garlic.

The mistress mm'd. "Sarah, you're the best cook in Phoenicia."

Sarah smiled as she picked up the remains of the meal and started back to clean up the kitchen.

Suddenly, Martha burst through the door. "I'm sorry to interrupt your meal, mistress," she said to Dorcas, "but you must come quickly. You too, Sarah, and bring Tamara!" She hustled back to the open door.

Chapter 26

Paulos had begun putting some weight on his bad leg, although still not all.

"Mehida, it's time I began making my way back home. My daughter must be anxious about me. Or worse, maybe even forgetting me. Maybe my wife too. I don't want my family to forget me or believe I am dead."

"No, you can't go," wailed Mehida. "You can't leave me. I'm your mother now."

Paul smiled. "I wasn't planning to leave you, Mehida. You could come with me. We can look for your daughter."

"No, no! I can't leave my home. Robbers might come and steal all I have."

"What do you have?" Paul asked, bewildered. "We can lead your goats. A house, a bed, a table, a garden? Are they such treasures that you can't live without them?"

Mehida narrowed her eyes and glanced around. "I have more than you think. I have my goats, yes, but I also have a small treasure here. How do you think I buy our bread and wine? Did you think perhaps I sold my beautiful young body for food?" She laughed her old cackle, and Paul had to chuckle with her.

"No, son. I can't leave here," she said, her smile disappearing. Her rheumy old eyes began tearing up. "This is my home. This has been my home since my husband wed me forty years ago. This is the place where our sons and daughters were born and where my husband and all our children but one are buried. I can't leave them."

"Then this is my promise to you: I'll find your daughter and remind her you'll have need of her one day, and I'll send a coin to you when I can. If I can't find her, I'll somehow make sure someone will take care of you when you can't take care of yourself."

"I have no need of the coins," Mehida assured him. "I have enough to last me the rest of my days. My husband was a successful merchant. I live in this poor house with few furnishings because I choose to live simply, and because few thieves would believe I have anything to steal. People think I'm a little odd, and maybe they're right, but no one bothers me."

"Nevertheless, I owe you my life. I promise there will be someone to care for you when you can't care for yourself."

Paulos's brow furrowed. What was that he smelled—flowers? Where were the flowers?

Mehida's face was a picture of amazement as her form flickered and faded from view.

Chapter 27

June AD 2008

Paul's conversation with Evelyn stuck in his head. How could she be so certain about prayer? He should talk to her again. He mused on the topic as he left the campus headed for home. In the rearview mirror, he noticed a police car following close behind. When had they shown up again?

The previous evening, the Sheriff's Department had left a message on his answering machine, plus one on his cell. They obviously wanted to talk to him again, but Paul didn't call back. He wasn't in any hurry to hear what they had to say anymore. They'd either arrest him or they wouldn't. But then, they hadn't followed him every day or watched his house every night for a while. Either they got bored, or they didn't have enough people to spare. And now here they were again.

Paul drove on the I-101 Loop freeway, approaching the Arizona 60 Highway. Twice, the truck ahead in the left lane meandered into the emergency lane, nearly connecting with the concrete dividers before jerking back into traffic. He waited awhile for the driver to pull over to the lane he should be in, but the trucker hugged the left, sometimes speeding up or slowing down. *Why doesn't he get off the road and take a nap?*

Another truck on the right kept a steady speed, but somehow stayed parallel with the other truck. Traffic was piling up behind them, so Paul started to pass in the center lane. He was about halfway past the two when the truck on his left drifted into his lane, forcing Paul to slam on his brakes.

The crunch of metal on metal was deafening, and the pain unbearable. Both truck drivers jerked their vehicles away, but too late. Paul's car came to rest in the center of the freeway, three other cars sliding into his and more into them from behind.

The pain stopped, and Paul opened his eyes. *What's this?*

He floated above the accident, looking down at the mess below. A county police car was one of the casualties, but the policemen got out of the car uninjured. One officer was talking into his shoulder mike. He ran forward to Paul's car and looked inside, then pulled back, shaking his head. Paul could hear him talking to someone.

"It doesn't look good," the officer said. "I don't see how he could survive this."

The voice from the officer's speaker blared. "Yeah, too bad. Jones tried to call him to let him know he was cleared, but he didn't answer or return our calls."

"He was cleared?"

"Uh-huh. The guys found her body. I guess the M.E. could tell she died from drowning. Lots of barbiturates in her system. She must have gone to sleep. The lieutenant wanted to pursue it still, but the DA's office said, 'No evidence, no case.'"

Huh! I'm cleared!

An ambulance arrived in short order. Paul wondered how it got there so quickly.

"They were already close by, on Peoria approaching 101, in fact."

With a start, Paul noticed a man standing beside him. Dressed in a glowing white robe, the man himself also seemed to glow.

"Who are you? What's going on? Why am I up here?"

"So many questions. I have one for you. Do you want to see Sarah?"

"Her body? No. I don't think I could take it."

"No. See her, alive and well."

Paul nodded. "Yes, sir, more than life."

"You have a choice. You may go back to the car or you may go to Sarah and Tamara."

Paul knew he was signing his own death warrant, but he answered without hesitation. "I choose Sarah and Tamara."

"Then come with me, Paulos Anthony Johnson." The man extended his arm.

Paul reached for the outstretched hand without hesitation. When their hands connected, a howling wind whipped around him. The one who held him was like an unmovable rock in the middle of a killer storm, pulling him through what seemed like a scented spider's web.

Chapter 28

June AD 30

The next thing he knew, Paul was standing on a dirt road, wearing a brown robe. Dozens of people stared at him. He reached his hands up to rub his eyes and discovered he had a beard. *What?*

Some of the people turned and ran away from him, toward the town. Some gathered around him, speaking in a language he hadn't heard before. Oh, wait, maybe he had. He began to understand what they were saying.

"Aren't you Paulos?"

"Where are your walking sticks?"

"Where did you come from?"

"How are you standing without your sticks?"

"How did you get through the gate?"

Paul didn't know how to answer any of the questions, so he just stood there, bewildered. This didn't look like any version of heaven or hell he'd ever heard of. And didn't the man say Sarah and Tamara would be wherever this was? Where were they? Most of the people were shorter than he, and he could easily see over their heads.

A little girl in the same strange clothing pulled away from a woman who looked like—wow!—like Sarah! The little girl screamed "It's my papa! It's my papa!" as she ran toward him.

Paul began running too, pushing past the people in his way. When he reached the child, he stared for a moment, unbelieving, then picked her up and hugged her so tight she squealed. He shut his eyes. If this was a hallucination, he hoped it would last forever. When he opened his eyes, Sarah had almost reached him. She was crying, holding her arms out to him. With heart and eyes overflowing, he pulled her to his side and held her tight.

Sarah's tears flowed, a huge smile stretching her face. Paul's eyes were moist too, his mouth working as though he wanted to speak, but couldn't.

People gathered around them, asking Paul repeatedly how his leg had been straightened and how he had gotten through the closed gate. Paul, however, stood speechless as he held his wife and daughter, eyes squeezed shut, tears rolling down his face. His Adam's apple bobbed, and he shook his head, clearing his throat over and over.

When the mistress reached them, she was scowling. "Paulos, where is *Hamath?*"

There was a long pause. Paul opened his eyes and his brows rose as he turned his eyes on her. "Uhhh ... Hamath?"

"Yes. I sent Hamath to find you. He didn't come back with you?"

"I'm sorry, ma'am. I haven't seen ... Hamath. I came here alone. Sort of alone." He cast a quick glance skyward.

Dorcas stared at Paulos. After a long pause, she asked, "You haven't seen him at all?"

"No, ma'am, I'm sorry. I've never, uh ... haven't seen him, not since I, uh, left here."

At this point, Tamara spoke up. "Papa, is your leg all better?"

Paul's brow furrowed. "Of course, Tammy, why wouldn't it be all better?" Then his eyes widened at some inner thought. "Oh ... yes, it has healed up. Some good doctors ... ah, physicians ... and an old lady helped me."

Sarah beamed, understanding his bafflement. In English, she whispered in his ear, so that only Tamara and he could hear, "Did you come through the windy web?"

He cocked an eyebrow, then grinned and nodded. Tamara's eyes widened, and she started to say something, but Sarah held her finger to her lips.

Martha's eyes brimmed with a hundred questions, but when at the mistress's scowl and tapping foot, caution must have taken priority over curiosity because she remained agitatedly quiet. Dorcas glared at them like they were withholding something vital from her, and Sarah could see the storm clouds gathering in her eyes.

"Please, mistress, may we go home? Perhaps we can explain all this when we get away from the crowd."

Dorcas nodded, her lips a tight, thin line, the storm held in check for the time being.

Sarah turned to Jonas. "Thank you so much, my friend, for sending Martha to get us when Paulos appeared. If you have time now, would you like to come with us?"

Jonas shook his head. "I can't come with you this morning. Perhaps you and Paulos could come back here later, or I could come to your house after I close my shop this afternoon."

Sarah thought for a moment. "I might come back later this morning or after the midday meal. If the mistress agrees, Paulos could come with me. We could try then to explain to you what just happened."

The crowd pressed closer around Paul, now shouting their questions. He shook his head and promised an explanation later.

Sarah wondered how they could explain this away, but for now, she couldn't think about anything other than that Paul or Paulos—or both—was unaccountably here and whole.

With some effort, they pushed through the circle of curious citizens and made their way to Dorcas's house. When they arrived, they shut the door, and the mistress sat down at the table. Silently, she motioned for all of them to sit. Paul sat, still holding Tamara. She clung to him like a baby possum to its mama.

"Now, Paulos or Sarah—I don't care which—I want to know what has happened. How was your leg straightened, Paulos? How did you get back here? And what did you do with my husband?"

Where should she begin? And how could they make Dorcas understand? "Mistress, you will find this tale hard to believe. We will tell you what we know, but believe me, it's as hard for us to understand as it will be for you." She took a deep breath and blew it out through pursed lips. "Paulos, Tamara, and I come from a different time, hundreds of years in the future."

Dorcas's mouth turned down even more.

"I know. It sounds as impossible to us as it does to you. Please bear with us." Sarah continued. "In our own time, Tamara died of a tumor in her head. She had a lot of fevers—just like she's been having here."

Paul's eyes widened, but he remained silent while Sarah went on with her explanation. He held Tamara even tighter.

"Apparently, when Tamara died in that future time, she arrived here, except somehow she had already been here. This is where the explanation becomes thorny. I don't have any idea how this happened." Sarah cleared her throat.

"Six months later, I came too, joining—or becoming?⊠the Sarah you have known for so long. If you will remember back a couple of months ago, I might have been acting a little strange. That's because when I arrived, my memory of my future time was stronger than the remembrance of this time. However, as situations occurred, a 'memory' would pop up in my head."

"Yes, I remember," Dorcas said. "I wondered why you acted differently then. You seemed to ... to be *educated*, for lack of a better term. Suddenly you knew how to read and write."

Sarah nodded. "In this future time, Paulos had broken his leg in a fall from the roof of our house, but our physicians then have more education than now. His leg was set right and it healed, so he wasn't crippled. When I arrived, Paulos had no knowledge of the future time, but when he arrived here today, he sounded like he was going through the same delayed information reactions that I had. That's what I asked him when I whispered in his ear out by the gate.

"Now, love, it's your turn. You need to tell us what happened to you before you came here."

Paul rubbed his forehead with his free hand. "I'm not sure what happened. It's all more than a little confusing to me too. I guess at the time Sarah arrived here, she disappeared from home—I mean our home there. At first, I thought she had gone to work early— she worked for a construction firm—and I didn't become concerned until she didn't come home that evening."

"Construction firm?"

"Oh, right … That's a group of people who build things. So first I called her office, but no one was there. Then I called a friend of hers from the office—Betty." He looked at Sarah. "But she hadn't seen or heard from Sarah that day. At that point, I got really worried and called the police to report her missing."

Dorcas interrupted. "Wait! You say you called her office and a friend. I don't know how you *call* an office, and was the friend close enough to hear?"

"In this future time, there are ways to talk to people who are a great distance away with a device called a telephone. It's more complicated than I know how to explain, but sound makes a vibration. Here, let me show you with this tableware." He picked up a knife and a long-handled metal spoon lying on the table and handed Dorcas the spoon.

"Now place the spoon next to your ear—no, just one end of it, not the middle." Paul barely tapped the other end of the spoon with the knife. "You could hear the sound of the knife striking the spoon as though the spoon were struck right next to your ear, couldn't you? And feel the vibration?"

Again, Dorcas nodded.

"Well, people smarter than I am in the future figured out how to send this vibration through a wire—a very thin piece of metal like a string on a harp or lute—long distances so that it made the same sound where other people were waiting for the sound. So, what I meant by calling her office was that I tried to telephone to the place where she works—worked—but no one was there to answer the telephone, so I called the police. And then I called friends and relatives who might know where Sarah was."

Dorcas threw up her hands. "That's not believable, but let the explanation stand for the time being. Now, would you please tell me what or who is a 'police'?"

"All right. In our time, there are people hired by the cities, states, and countries to enforce laws and to find missing persons. They're called police. Like guards and soldiers. The police said usually people who are missing show up somewhere within twenty-four hours, but they would put the information into their system so police all over the area would be watching for her. She didn't show up, so I called them back the next morning. I didn't know if she had disappeared on her own, which would be unlike Sarah, or if she had been kidnapped, or if she had been mugged and killed."

"Into their system? Mugged?"

"The police have a way to tell other police things they need to know, sort of like on a telephone. If a person is mugged, that means they have been robbed or hurt by thieves," Paul said. His face reddened, then he continued. "Sarah and I had drifted apart in the months before. We seldom talked. We didn't have much in common any more. Our only child, Tamara, had died, and both of us were in therapy."

Again, Dorcas interrupted. "Therapy?"

"In this future time, some special physicians try to heal troubled minds, and the process is called therapy. But the police focused on the idea that we hadn't been getting along as well as married couples should. When they couldn't find Sarah, they began questioning me. I became their main suspect in her disappearance."

Sarah straightened. "How could they think that? I could have told them ... but then, I guess I wasn't there to tell them, was I?"

"They thought you would hurt Sarah?" This time the interruption came from Martha.

"Yes. No amount of convincing from our friends or from my mother about my sterling character seemed to dissuade them."

"Explain *sterling*, sweetheart."

"Oh, yes, well, I guess that means without flaws. In other words, my friends and mother were convinced I'd never hurt anyone, let alone my wife. The police weren't persuaded. They searched the house from top to bottom, turned my car inside out, and they were unable to locate her car. I found it, but she wasn't in it ... uh, how do I explain cars?" he asked Sarah when Dorcas and Martha looked lost.

Sarah laughed. "I'm not sure either. The nearest description I can come up with is that a car is a little like an enclosed wagon or chariot and has a method of moving that doesn't rely on horses, donkeys, camels, oxen, or people. It goes much, much faster than any beasts can." She shrugged. "I'm sorry I can't describe it better. It's as though you tried to describe making purple dye to someone who had never seen the sea or a mollusk before."

Dorcas gave a tight-lipped smile. "This sounds more and more like a child's imaginative story. If I appear confused, that's why. I think I believe you, but even if this is all a convoluted lie, it makes for a good story. Please continue."

Tamara spoke up. "It is all true, mistress, honest! Cars are really and truly. 'Cept I didn't die. Jesus just carried me through the windy web. The windy web that smells like flowers."

"Jesus," Dorcas said. "Wasn't that the man who told you your papa was coming home?"

"Yes, that's the one." Tamara nodded.

"Jesus told you I was coming?" Paul's eyebrows felt like they jumped above his hairline.

"Yes. He knows everything," Tamara replied.

"That's amazing," Paul said, looking at Tamara. He opened his mouth to ask her more about Jesus, but that could wait. He shrugged, then continued telling them what had happened. "The police questioned me on several different days. I think they wanted to arrest me, but they couldn't find any evidence that I'd done harm to Sarah. They watched me, though. They put a tail on me."

"They did *what*?" Martha's eyes were as wide as they would go.

Sarah and Paul looked at each other and laughed.

"That means they had a policeman follow me, like the tail on a dog follows him everywhere. However, now I must be dead there, because I was driving on the freeway and a trucker on my left didn't see me. He swerved into my lane and pushed me into another truck in the lane on my right."

"Trucker? Lane? Freeway?" Dorcas rubbed her forehead. "This is getting so confusing."

"A trucker is someone who drives a truck—a very large vehicle, some almost as long as this house."

Now it was Dorcas's turn for raised eyebrows. "Impossible!"

"In that future time, there are busy, wide roads called freeways, and vehicles like trucks and cars are supposed to be careful not to hit other vehicles that travel next to them in lanes—parallel roads within the wide road. The vehicles go faster than any chariot you ever saw, mistress, and if one hits you, it's disastrous, often fatal.

"I found myself looking down on my ruined car, and a man in a shining white robe stood next to me." Tears filled Paul's eyes. "He said, 'Paul, would you rather go back inside that car, or would you rather go to Tamara and Sarah?' Well, that was a no-brainer—I mean, easy to decide. I chose to go to Tamara and Sarah. The man in white took my hand as though he were taking the hand of a child. I smelled flowers and felt this ripping sensation and enough wind to blow over a stout tree. Suddenly, there I was, standing inside this gate, with people staring at me like I had arrived from the moon. You know what happened after that."

He paused and frowned. "I have another memory too, one of being with an old woman named Mehida who kept calling me her son. I think she saved my life. I seem to have two sets of life memories that are beginning to meld into one."

There was a long silence while everyone absorbed what they'd been told. Finally, Dorcas spoke up. "And no Hamath." Her voice was flat, dispirited. "And I told him not to come back without Paulos. Whatever shall I do now?"

Chapter 29

As Sarah prepared the midday meal, she couldn't help but hum and smile. At the same time, she sympathized with her mistress. The poor woman—her eyes red and puffy, her lips in a constant tight line—wandered around the house, stopping occasionally to stare out the door but seldom speaking.

She entered the cooking area, glancing around before she spoke. "Sarah, you weren't a servant in your other life, were you? Nor Paulos, either?"

"No, mistress. But we both had employers, which is similar."

"Do you resent being servants here?"

"Oh, no, mistress, I don't, especially not in working for you. And I'm sure Paulos agrees."

"But there are no ... ah, cars, did you call them? ... here, nor can you talk to people far away. Do you miss having those cars and talking things? I suppose there are other amazing things that are not here as well. Would you tell me more about this future time?"

"Yes, I have missed cars and telephones and other things sometimes, especially when I was so frantic about Paulos's disappearance and wanting to find him. I can tell you more later." Sarah turned to the fireplace to stir a pot, and suddenly thought about what would happen if all these stories should get around to the servants or to the rest of Tyre. "Mistress, if you talk about any of this to your friends, they might think you were drunk or crazy for believing such a fantastic story."

The mistress nodded. "I can understand how they would be skeptical. I have no intention of spreading this news. I find it too astonishing."

Sarah smiled. "I do too. For the first few days, I was sure I had to be dreaming, but the other side of me would argue that this was not a dream. With Tamara here, I didn't want to wake up. I don't think it's a dream anymore, and I don't want it to end." She smiled wider, and then she brought her hand to her mouth. "Oh, no. I just thought of something. Is Martha still here? I hope she has not gone to the marketplace or talked to the other servants about this."

"That's a good thought, Sarah. I'll go find her now." The mistress turned to go, then she spun back around. "Perhaps this afternoon or tomorrow, you'll tell me more about this future time?

"Whenever you'd like, mistress."

Just then, Paulos walked in. "I'm remembering more about my life here, Dorcas—I mean, mistress. I'm your servant—a handyman, correct?"

She looked a little confused. "If you mean a person who performs a wide variety of repairs and building, yes."

"Well, I noticed the gate in the back of this courtyard is pulling away from the wall at the top. Maybe that should be my first item of work."

"Perhaps," the mistress said. "What did you do in your other life?"

"I was a counselor and professor—a teacher," he said. "I taught languages, and I counseled students who were having problems or had questions."

"Ah, how perfect. Sarah has been picking up lessons from Jonas."

Sarah's eyes darted her way, and the mistress smiled at her. "Yes, Sarah, I knew. You were doing it for the children, so I didn't mind."

She looked back at Paul. "The children are getting beyond what Sarah can teach. She's been schooling them in Greek."

Sarah blushed.

Dorcas laughed. "No matter, Sarah, the point is you have been teaching them and doing the task well."

"I kept wishing Paulos were here," Sarah admitted. "I stumbled along, with Jonas's help, of course. Speaking of Jonas, mistress, I thought he might be a good resource to find Hamath. Jonas has many contacts among the merchants, so we could probably send word across all of Phoenicia, Samaria, Egypt, Judea, and perhaps beyond even those countries. I'd like to take Paulos with me to see him, too. We might be able to put to rest some of the gossip about his return."

"Jonas might be a good resource, and yes, take Paulos along," the mistress said. "Meanwhile, please tell him where you are with the children's lessons while you fix our meal. I'll go find Martha and make sure she doesn't spread these stories to all her friends."

Dorcas found Martha sitting on a bench in the courtyard, her mouth pursed, her eyebrows pressed together, and her arms folded across her chest. Dorcas chuckled. She would wager it was a little late to find Martha before she started spreading the news.

"Martha, I must caution you not to talk to your friends about this story of Paulos and Sarah. In the worst case, you could be responsible for their arrest. But even if that doesn't happen, your friends might think you are having visions, if not possessed by a demon."

"Yes, mistress." Martha flushed. "That's exactly what happened. They think that I've been drinking too much wine or that Paulos and Sarah have been teasing me with some fantastic story. I've been humiliated this morning, and I'll speak no more about it."

"Exactly, Martha. Because, if you can't cease speaking of this to others, I might have to have to dismiss you. I don't want to do that." Dorcas knew Martha well. Her lips overflowed with her every thought.

Martha blanched. "Oh, no, mistress! I swear I'll never say another word!"

"Good. Because you're an excellent housekeeper. I'd be sorry to lose you. I'm quite fond of you, you know. You're among my favorite servants."

A little sweetening with the scolding never hurt.

Paul and Sarah swung Tamara between them as they walked to the marketplace. They found Jonas at his shop, negotiating the cost of cloth with an argumentative matron. Dathan was there again, and his gaze fixed on Paul, a dozen questions in his eyes.

"Hello, Dathan," Sarah said. "This is my husband, Paulos."

"Shalom, Sarah and Paulos. Yes, I know Paulos." Dathan turned to Paul. "Your leg ... it doesn't hurt you anymore?"

"No, it feels much better now," Paul said. To change the boy's focus, he added, "You must have grown a foot—I mean, half a cubit—since I last saw you."

Dathan's cheeks reddened, and he ducked his head and grinned. "Perhaps a little."

Jonas joined them. "Ah, my friends Sarah and Tamara, it's good to have your husband and papa back, is it not?"

"That may be the understatement of the year, Jonas. We came to thank you for your efforts to find Paulos, and for all those lessons in Greek you prepared for me ... and now to seek your help one more time. Not with the Greek lessons. My husband is fluent in Greek, so we won't need your help with that anymore, nor with contacting his siblings. We sent word to them that he'd returned."

Tamara held her hands up to Paul. He lifted her and hugged her close.

"My siblings?" Paul repeated. "Oh, my brothers and sister. You sent word to them of my, uh, absence?"

"The mistress did. She hadn't heard from your brother on Cyprus, but she did hear from your brother and sister in Berytus and Ptolemais."

Jonas rubbed his forehead. "I'm happy to see your leg has improved so. You were in such agony the last time I saw you. Did you find a good physician wherever it was you went?"

Paul nodded. "It was painful for a time, but now it feels almost like new. Hardly a twinge anymore."

"So, now we need help finding the mistress's husband," Sarah said.

Jonas's eyebrows lifted as he gave a barely perceptible shrug. "And now you wish to find Hamath. I would think it might be well for that one to remain lost."

Sarah laughed. "Well, if it were up to me, yes; but the mistress is fond of him and wants him to come home."

"Very well," Jonas nodded. "When caravans are about to leave the gate, we will send word with them that Hamath's presence is urgently requested at the house of Dorcas. That should get his attention, if the word gets to him. Do you know where he was going?"

"He was going to Jerusalem. Dorcas says the slave owner who kidnapped my husband lives there. Do you know anything different, Paulos?"

Paul glanced skyward. Tamara provided a little distraction as she squirmed to get down again. "I was out of my mind with fever and pain. I don't really know the direction they took, but when Bildad moved me from one caravan to the other, I'm pretty sure we traveled south.

"When they threw me over the camel's back, my leg broke again. They weren't gentle, and the bone showed through the skin. I think Bildad left me for dead a few days later. An old woman called Mehida found me."

Paul's memory kicked in with more. "She tried to drag me to her hut, but I was too heavy. I couldn't get up and walk. Some travelers came along, a physician and his apprentice. I guess they carried me to her house and reset my leg. That's all I remember for some time. I lost consciousness when they set it. I didn't wake up for several days, and I didn't feel human for several weeks."

"It must have been a terrible experience." Jonas's eyes were full of sympathy.

Sarah touched Paul's arm, and he turned toward her. "Jonas's wife, Mariah, was abducted by thieves who sold her to a slave master, or maybe the slave master was the kidnapper. Jonas has never given up hope that she might be found. It's been ten years since she disappeared, but maybe this Bildad is the same one who took her."

"What did your wife look like, Jonas?" Paul asked. "I didn't hear any names, but there were a few women with the slave caravan."

"She's a small woman, about to my shoulder. She has blue eyes and brown hair, a little darker than Sarah's. Also, she has a red birthmark on her left temple, shaped a little like a flying bird. Sometimes I called her my little sparrow."

Dathan looked up from sorting bolts of cloth, his eyes wide and sparkling. "Abba, I remember the birthmark. Ima told me a story about a bird that got lost and then found its way to live with her."

"Yes, I remember that. You touched the birthmark and asked her why she had a sparrow, but you and I didn't." Jonas's eyes looked moist as he ruffled Dathan's hair.

Paul shook his head. "I don't remember any woman who looked like that. I'm sorry. I wish I could help, especially after all you did for Sarah."

"Putting the Greek lessons together has been no trouble," said Jonas. "Doing so broke up the monotony of the days. Sarah has been a good friend, and Tamara is an entertaining child. I enjoy the times she comes with Sarah. When she thought you'd be home soon, she jumped up and down with such joy I mistook her for a wild hare." His eyes twinkled at Tamara, who wrinkled her nose in imitation of a rabbit.

"Yes, she does get a little enthusiastic, doesn't she?" The proud papa smiled down at his daughter, who had begun peeking around the bolts of cloth at Dathan.

Paul returned his attention to Jonas. "You know, this slave master could have been the same one who abducted your wife. From the brief time I was with them, I got the impression their operation wasn't entirely on the up-and-up—I mean legal—and I think they've been abducting people for a long time. Also, this slaver seemed to be overly superstitious. I wonder what he would do if a 'ghost' materialized in his camp."

"Why would a ghost appear to them?" Jonas asked.

"As far as they knew, I was either already dead or wouldn't live through the night. If not for the old woman who rescued me, I would have died. The man must operate in this area, picking up slaves and taking them back to Jerusalem. Maybe we could find out when he will return. I can cover myself with oil to make me look shiny and ask him about your wife and the other missing people."

Jonas grasped Paul's arm. "I wouldn't want you to put yourself into danger, my friend. I'll see if some of the merchants know anything about this slave trader. The cloth merchant must know something, since he helped them abduct you, but he's not here. That, and he was too willing to take you. He probably wouldn't be the best one to ask anyway."

Paul pinched his lips. "With some help, I don't think there would be much danger. Bildad and his companions should be so frightened they won't feel much like attacking."

"Speaking of ghosts, there is a curious rumor going around. The local people who were here early this morning swear you appeared out of nowhere. According to them, you didn't come through the gate. Have you anything to add to this?"

"The sun might have been in their eyes. I assure you, I'm not a ghost!" Paul laughed, but sounded phony, even to himself. "Maybe a trick of the combined fog and sunlight."

"Perhaps," said Jonas, his eyes narrowing. "Perhaps."

He turned to his son. "Dathan, I left my measuring stick at home. Would you please go get it?"

Dathan had been following the discussion with avid interest. He left with a scowl on his face.

"Now, my friend Paulos, the fog wasn't that thick this morning. I confess I'm probably more curious than my son and the crowd combined. Are you a magician?"

Sarah laughed. "I was afraid that wouldn't be an adequate explanation for you, Jonas. You are much too observant."

Paul glanced at Sarah, and she nodded. "If anyone will understand, Jonas will, and he's not one to share what he knows with every stranger within hearing."

Paul sighed. "I hope you won't be calling for the guards to haul me off to the nearest prison or decide that I've gone insane, but I think a man called Jesus put me here. I don't know how or even why. All I know for sure is a guy in a bright white robe gave me the choice of dying—or at least being a lifelong cripple—or coming here to Tamara and Sarah. The choice wasn't difficult. More than anything, I wanted to be with Tamara and Sarah again, scarred and mangled or not. Tamara says the man was Jesus."

"What happened then?"

"The next thing I knew, I was standing inside the gate and people were staring at me. They must have been shocked. I know I was."

"What about the story about the old woman? Was that true, or were you perhaps not rescued by her after all?"

"That story's true. The slaver left me for dead, and she nursed me back to health. Then I was suddenly here, without having traveled a step, thanks to the man in white."

"That's quite a story, Paulos," Jonas said. "I've been hearing some astounding tales about Jesus of Nazareth, but discarding them as just that—tales. Maybe I should listen to them with closer attention. I think you might have left out some parts of this story, but one day you may be confident enough of my friendship to tell me the rest."

Chapter 30

Paul followed Sarah and Tamara back to the villa and into the cooking area. As Sarah began preparations for the evening meal, she told Paul about the children's lessons, including what they had already learned and how each child had progressed. While they talked, Dorcas, who had been away when they returned from the marketplace, entered the kitchen.

"Hello, mistress," Sarah said. "We went to see Jonas. He is sending word by way of his contacts to tell the master to come home."

"Thank you." Dorcas rubbed her forehead. "I have a few contacts too. I hope Hamath will receive the word to come home. I should never have told him he couldn't come home without Paulos." She turned and walked back into the house, her shoulders slumped.

Tamara clung to Paul the entire day. She hadn't let him out of her sight since he showed up that morning. She wanted to sleep with him on his pallet, but Paul shook his head and put her down on her own bed. Once Tamara was asleep, he turned to his wife.

"Sarah, there's something I promised the old woman, Mehida— the one who saved my life. Um, one of my lives? Anyway, I promised her I'd try to find her daughter, Emma, who's married to a fisherman named Ebenezer. She said they moved to somewhere on this coast, but Mehida didn't know if it was Ptolemais, Tyre, Sidon, or some other coastal village. Maybe Jonas can help us find her. I thought about her while we were talking today, but that memory didn't fully come back until later. I'll talk to him again tomorrow."

"He's almost always at his shop, except for the Sabbath. He's a rabbi."

"What's today?"

"Thursday."

"Then I'll go see him tomorrow. Meanwhile, it's so ... well, miraculous to be back with you again ... and to see Tammy alive!" His voice caught in his throat as he pulled Sarah to him.

"I know. I thought I was dreaming for a few days, but I kept waking up in the mornings with Tammy still here." Sarah paused. "She's been active today. I think the adrenalin might have boosted her, but, Paul, she's still sick. She still has the tumor. I'm afraid ... afraid we'll have to watch her die again, and there's no stopping this replay of her death that tore us apart before."

Paul frowned. "But why would Jesus pull us back here and force us to go through her death again? Somehow, he doesn't seem like that kind of guy. I wish we had a Bible. Maybe there's something in there that would tell us."

"I don't know. I remember some of the old Bible stories. There is one about this area—a Canaanite woman and a child with a demon, but my memory is pretty sketchy."

"A demon? Tammy didn't have a demon. She had brain cancer."

"I know. But people in this century don't know about cancer. They see someone writhing on the ground, and a demon sounds logical to them, I guess."

"Does anyone else know she has seizures?"

"Yes. Jonas and a physician named Nicolas. I've been afraid to tell anyone else."

Paul gathered her in his arms. "I've missed you so much, Sarah. Before you disappeared, I thought you didn't care for me all that much. I thought I didn't love you anymore either. But after you were gone, the hole in my life was too huge to bear. I don't want to ever be apart from you. Not ever again."

Sarah nodded. "I felt the same way when you disappeared from here. I existed from one day to the next, hoping against hope you'd return. I don't know if you remember, but we had a big fight that morning. I was afraid you'd left because you were angry or because you were unwilling to have your leg reset. I even worried that you might have killed yourself. I'm so grateful you're back. And that you came here from the future ... or whatever. Please don't ever leave me again, physically or emotionally."

"I'll never leave you. Never. That man in white has given us one more chance to get things right. Let's not mess it up again." He pulled her closer, tipped up her chin, and kissed her.

The next afternoon, Paul took over teaching the children. Sarah, between meals, sat with them. About halfway through the lesson, Dorcas entered the room.

Paul, who'd been sitting cross-legged on the floor, stood; Sarah followed suit.

"Dorcas—I mean, mistress—the children also need to learn mathematics and a few other subjects. If I taught them in the mornings, we could work on these other lessons. Would that be all right with you?"

Dorcas gave him an approving smile. "Yes. First though, I've been thinking about your status here. You and Sarah should begin calling me by my name. Let's just say you are now privileged servants, and I will increase what you earn. I realize this probably doesn't make up for the loss of status in your other life, but it's a small step."

Paul grasped his wife's hand. "That would be better than wonderful. Thank you."

"Second, yes, your idea to teach the children more sounds good. They will need to learn how to become good stewards of their inheritance. Even though she's a girl, I also want Orphah to learn these things. She might not be able to do as much as a man, but she will be responsible for a household when she is grown and married. And who knows, she might even need to be as I am—the one who manages the money because her husband can't or won't. And of course, Tamara may sit in with her.

"Third, I've decided to promote one of the slaves to the position Paulos once held. I've been watching a young man named Amad. He's faithful in his duties and works without being told to. He finds things to do or asks for work when he could be doing nothing. You, Paulos, can tutor the children. I think we can come up with a better place for your family to live than that shabby house by the stables too. Amad's first task will be to build something for you, maybe next to the street rather than by the stable."

"Oh, mistress—I mean Dorcas—that's beyond anything we hoped for!" Sarah dropped Paul's hand and grasped the mistress's. "We talked for hours last night, and I told Paulos how much you've done for us. Even living in a one-room house with dirt floors wouldn't make us want to go back to where we were before."

"True," Paul agreed. "We're in your debt. Any task you ask will never be too much."

"Nonsense! This is to our benefit much more than it is to yours," Dorcas said. "Now, I must be about my own work. I'm sorry for interrupting the lesson."

After the day's lessons, Paul walked to the marketplace to talk to Jonas again. Of course, Tamara had to go with him. She skipped ahead, stopping to show him the flowers and tell the other children her papa was home.

Jonas greeted Paul with a kiss to each cheek and Tamara with a wink and a pat on her head. "What brings you back to my shop so soon?"

"Mehida—the woman who took care of me—she had a daughter named Emma, married to a fisherman called Ebenezer. I don't suppose you'd know them?"

"I might. There's a fisherman in Tyre named Ebenezer, but I don't know his wife's name. You can probably find him in the afternoons at the port. In the mornings, I'm sure he's out fishing."

"Thank you, friend Jonas. I need to try to find him. Come along, Tammy."

Paul walked toward the north port. Before long he was carrying his tired daughter. After asking several people, he found a sunburned, scowling man mending his nets.

"Hello, Ebenezer. My name is Paulos. I'm a friend of Jonas, the cloth merchant, and a servant at the house of Hamath and Dorcas. Is your wife's name Emma?"

"Why do you want to know my wife's name?" Ebenezer demanded.

"If that's her name, I have a message from her mother, Mehida. Mehida saved my life when I was injured."

"Mehida." He spat out the name as though it were a swear word. "The woman tried to stop us from getting married. My Emma had to sneak out of their house and come to mine to be wed. We went to her parents after our marriage, but Mehida railed at us until we left. After that, we moved here and never went back."

"She's a lonely old woman. She was strong for her age when I saw her a few days ago, but it won't be long until she needs help."

"I'll tell Emma, but I don't want Mehida to live with us. I think my wife will agree."

"Mehida was kind to me. If you won't take care of her in her old age, I'll take her in, even though there isn't much room in my house." Paul started to leave, then turned back. "If you should wish to talk about your decision, my wife Sarah and I live next to the home of Hamath and Dorcas. If we're not there, check at our master's house."

"It's not likely you will be seeing me or my wife. Mehida might have been your life-saver, but she made Emma's life—and mine—thorny. Goodbye, Paulos." Ebenezer snorted as he turned his back and picked up his nets.

Chapter 31

Sarah was forming bread into loaves when Dorcas joined her in the outside kitchen.

"All I thought of all night long were the things in this future time. Could you explain more about these cars, trucks, and calling things?"

Sarah placed the bread dough in the oven, then scrubbed her hands clean. "I'll try, Dorcas. That's not where my education is, so I don't know how well I can explain any of those." She paused to find words.

"Hmm. You've seen lightning. That light you see is called electricity. A small version of electricity is the spark that flies between you and another person or object sometimes when the weather's dry. Cars produce small sparks that make little explosions of fire that force metal gears, cogs, and spindles to move."

She made a circle with her thumb and a finger, then a larger one with her arm to her shoulder. "These smaller cogs make the bigger wheels move. Some cars can go several times faster than the fastest horse you've ever seen. A truck doesn't go quite as fast, but it's still much faster than a horse. A car doesn't need to stop or slow down for a rest, and a trip from here to Ptolemais, for instance, might only take an hour."

"A winter hour or a summer hour?" Dorcas asked. "Although it doesn't matter. Either would be impossible. Ptolemais is at least a summer day's journey from here." She sat on a stool, gazing at Sarah with wide eyes.

"In that future time, the population of the world will have grown unbelievably. Most of the adults where we live each have a car. The small explosions in the cars and trucks produce noise and smoke. If you live in a large city, there are few places where you don't hear the constant noise of the traffic. Oh—when cars and trucks move along roads together, they're called 'traffic'. The smoke makes the air look like a dirty fog."

"I have a hard time fathoming so many people and so many cars." Dorcas frowned. "How would you ever be able to walk across a road?"

"It's difficult sometimes. There are signals in the cities—different colors of lights—green for go, red for stop, and amber for be careful because the green light is about to change to red. When the cars stop for the red lights, people hurry across the street. Sometimes there are bridges for people and cars to pass over other cars."

"How do the lights work? Does someone hold up the different colors of lamps?"

Sarah laughed. "Mistress, you're trying every limit of my knowledge! All I really know is that people learned to make and control electricity to light our homes, operate the traffic lights, and do lots of other things."

Dorcas shook her head. "My head is too full, Sarah! I think I've absorbed as much as I can for one day. Maybe we should talk another time about that 'calling' object, but for now I shall have to think about the things you've already explained. I'm assuming there is much, much more that's different about this other time."

"Yes, In fact, there isn't much that's the same. Maybe next time we can talk about clothes. I have a little more experience with that."

"Oh, wait! I must know about the clothes. Maybe just one more thing won't hurt."

Sarah laughed merrily. "I need to serve breakfast, Dorcas. You and I might love to discuss clothes rather than eat, but I doubt that the rest of your family would agree."

"Oh, all right. But right after the meal?"

At least the connection between women and pretty clothes hadn't changed. Sarah smiled as she carried the tray of food to the dining room.

After the meal, Dorcas followed Sarah back to the cooking area, even carrying one of the trays to speed the process.

"I've been thinking about how to explain clothing," Sarah said. "Maybe it would be easier to draw them on the children's wax tablets."

Dorcas brightened. "That would be perfect. Maybe you can draw some of the other things you talked about, too. I'll go get something to write on while you prepare the meal for the servants. Paulos could make a tablet for us, or we might even put these down on papyrus."

"Oh, no, mistress, that wouldn't be wise. Papyrus sometimes lasts thousands of years, and folks in the future might wonder how people in this age knew what cars, telephones, and clothing looked like."

"Hmm. All right, no parchment."

Dorcas left in search of Paulos to make a tablet for them. Sarah hoped for a large tablet, so they wouldn't have to melt the wax too often.

When Dorcas came back with the tablet, Sarah began to draw. "These are the dresses. Some are much shorter."

Dorcas sat back, her eyes wide. "Their limbs are showing."

Sarah laughed. "Wait till you see the swimsuits." She sketched a lady in a bikini.

"No! I can't believe a woman would expose herself so. Not even a prostitute would wear something like this. Are there no modest items of clothing?"

"Well, some dresses and coats are much like tunics, cloaks, and mantles. They can be full length to the ankles, or just cover part of their outfits."

"Out-fits?"

"That is what we call items of clothing worn together. Sometimes an outfit can be a one-piece dress, but often it's two or even three pieces: a skirt or pants, a blouse, and a jacket," Sarah explained, drawing each as fast as she could. *Thank goodness for the art class I took in college.*

"Fashions change for women every year or so, at least for wealthy women. Most of us can't afford to do that. I think the clothing designers and manufacturers scheme so that women will buy new clothes every year. And shoes too. Except, I think some shoes must have been designed by people who hate women. The shoes pinch the feet into painful triangles and make women walk on their toes." She drew a pair of stilettos, top and side views.

"Why do women buy them?"

"I'm not sure why. I guess because we think men like the way our ankles look with them."

Dorcas's mouth twisted into a wry smile. "I think women didn't get any smarter over time. We wear hair ornaments and embroidered tunics to attract male attention or to show other women how wealthy we are." She leaned forward. "So, what about men? Are their clothes so astounding too?"

"Not quite so much. They mostly wear slacks and shirts and sometimes a suit coat and a tie—sort of like this," she said, sketching again. "But some of the young men wear very baggy pants that hang off their hips and threaten to fall down. Nauseating."

Dorcas laughed again. "Hm. Young men don't get any smarter through the ages either."

"Good morning, Jonas. I saw some merchants arriving, and I wondered if any of them brought you word of Hamath."

"Shalom, Sarah. No. I wish I could give you better news for Dorcas, but no one has seen or heard anything about him."

"My poor mistress is losing sleep. She often goes to the rooftop and stares at the road to the south. I'm sure she wonders if he was killed by robbers on the way."

"I hope not." He paused. "I understand that your husband is now a tutor and no longer doing maintenance. Do you think he'd be willing to take on one more student? I don't have time or as much ability to teach Dathan sums. Of course, I'd pay Paulos for this."

"I'm sure he'd be willing and happy to teach Dathan, but I'm equally sure Paulos won't accept payment. We would need to ask Dorcas for permission. I can let you know tomorrow, if that's soon enough."

"Yes. Dathan's gone fourteen years knowing only the basics of numbers, so a few more days can't hurt. I'd be grateful to Paulos for his help, and I can afford to pay for his service."

Sarah grinned. "You may be grateful, and you may be able, but you may not pay for his work. You have done so much for us that this is a pittance we can give in return. Besides, this is what friends are for."

Sarah relayed Jonas's request to Paul and Dorcas. Both agreed, and Dathan began coming to the morning sessions. He already knew much more than the younger ones and often helped Paul with them when he wasn't busy with his own lessons.

The days passed, and life settled into a routine with few disruptions, except when Tamara was sick. Her sick times increased, and she often staggered or ran into things. And then there were tummy upsets, fevers, and seizures. Between bouts, she acted like her typical happy self, although not as perky. Sarah wondered where the pain Tammy experienced before had gone—now she never complained of pain. Sarah resolved to thank Jesus that night.

Tammy still clung to Paul whenever she could, and he was equally happy to be clinging to her. *And to me too.* Sarah's cheeks warmed at the thought.

Their new stone house, with two bedrooms and a separate living area, was finished. They talked Tamara into sleeping alone in one room only after a door was constructed between the two bedrooms. A sand-colored drape hung between the rooms, so if she needed them, she had only to move the curtain aside to make sure Papa and Mama were still there. The doorway also allowed Paul and Sarah to hear Tammy if she cried out in the night, or when they heard the thumps and bumps of another seizure.

A runner arrived with the news Dorcas's parents, Proteus and Thecla, would be returning for another visit. Sarah and Martha made their way to the marketplace with the donkey to stock up.

That evening after they retired, Sarah patted Paul's arm. "Are you awake?"

"Yeah. What's up?"

"I'm excited. I can't wait for Dorcas's parents to get here. They have a young slave called Benoni who has seen Jesus. He's the one who went with me the time you went missing. He raved on and on about him that night, and I tuned him out. Now that I believe in Jesus, I want to know more about him. I wish I could remember more of my childhood Sunday school lessons."

"At least you have something to try to remember—I'm wishing Mom had taken me to church when I was a youngster. The only things I know about Jesus is what Evie tried to convince me of. It's too bad I didn't talk to her more. Tammy has no doubts, and I have just the beginnings of belief. I still don't really know what to think about the man who brought me here."

"All the time we out were looking for you, Benoni kept going on and on about Jesus. I didn't really want to listen because I didn't believe in God, but so much has happened since then that I'm curious now. Maybe Benoni can tell us more about Jesus while he's here. And this time I won't close my ears."

Paul nodded. "It would be nice to talk to someone who has actually seen Jesus under normal circumstances, whatever normal is." He gave her a squeeze. "We'll give this kid a shot tomorrow, maybe?"

"Right. Now, we better get some sleep while we can. Tammy never gives us much warning about when her convulsions will hit.

But when Dorcas's parents arrived, the young man wasn't with them.

Sarah was hesitant about talking directly to them. "Dorcas, may I ask a favor of you? Would you be willing to ask your mother or father what became of their young litter bearer, Benoni?"

"I already know. We talked about him last night, although I didn't remember his name. I remembered what a help he had been, going with you that night you went looking for Paulos. My mother said someone bought the slave, and he's not with them anymore. The other servants might know more if you want to ask them."

Sarah nodded, her heart heavy. "All right. I'll go see them this evening." She waited until after the evening meal, then helped Amad carry the trays of food for the servants and slaves.

"Shalom," she said. "My name is Sarah. I'm one of Dorcas's servants. I was wondering if you would tell me about Benoni, the boy who was with you the last time you visited here. I understand he was sold to someone else."

Mary, Thecla's personal servant, nodded while she picked some cheese and grapes from the trays. "Yes, he was. All of us were sad to see him leave."

"Last time you were here, Benoni told me about seeing a man called Jesus. Do any of you know about him?"

Mary and four of the others glanced at each other. Mary spoke. "We were in Samaria when Jesus was there with his disciples. He spoke to the citizens of the town, and then he healed someone who couldn't hear or speak. He was awe-inspiring."

"May my husband, my daughter, and I come here and talk to you about him?"

"Of course. We love to talk about him," Mary said. Others nodded in agreement.

"Wonderful. I'll go get Paul and Tamara and be right back."

She ran to fetch her husband and daughter. Together they hurried back to the servants' dining area. The visiting servants and slaves vied with each other, telling tales they had heard of Jesus and the things they had seen. The expressions of those who listened, including Paul, ranged from disbelief to eager interest.

Every eye turned toward the child when Tamara told them Jesus was her friend.

"How do you know him?" Mary asked. "Has he been here?"

"He talks to me mostly in my dreams. And he held me one time when I was really sick and Mama and Papa were crying."

"Tamara sometimes has severe illnesses," Sarah said. "Once the fever was particularly hot, and she was near death. She tells us Jesus picked her up and held her, then laid her on her pallet. The next morning, she felt better. Neither Paul nor I saw him."

Amad nodded. "She's sick often."

The others exchanged looks that weren't exactly believing.

Another slave, Crispus, spoke up. "I saw Jesus in Samaria too. When he looks at you, you feel he knows you as well as a brother. His gaze is so piercing, yet caring—like he can see right through your skin, all the way to your heart."

Mary nodded. "That's it exactly."

Tamara wriggled on Paul's lap. "He loves bigger than anyone! His hugs are so warm they make me feel not freezy anymore."

"I've been talking to a man who is a rabbi here in Tyre," said Sarah. "Jonas also sells cloth in the marketplace. He told me that Jews expect a Messiah to come and deliver them from the Romans. Their scriptures talk about a great leader who will bring about peace, one who will be a counselor. Benoni thought Jesus was the Messiah, but this Jesus you talk about sounds more like the peaceful counselor than a warrior."

The stories went on for hours. By the time Paul and Sarah went back to their home, Tamara was asleep on Paul's shoulder. They smiled at each other in the moonlight, talking softly and holding hands—almost like newlyweds again.

Chapter 32

July AD 30

Paul sat explaining some Greek verbs to the children when Martha burst into the room. "A man called Ebenezer and his wife wish to talk to you, Paulos."

"Thank you, Martha. Would you take them into the dining room? I'll be there in just a moment."

After giving the children work to complete, he went to meet his visitors, catching them in a whispered argument.

"Shalom," Ebenezer said, turning to face Paul. "This is my wife, Emma."

Paul smiled at the diminutive woman and nodded. Emma looked a lot like Mehida.

"My husband says you met my *ima*."

"Yes, I did. A slaver who kidnapped me thought I was dead or dying, so he dumped me by the side of the road. She found me and, along with a physician and his apprentice, worked to save my life. She's a lonely old woman, and she misses you."

Emma sighed. "She didn't want me to leave. I haven't seen her since just after Ebenezer and I were married fifteen years ago. Why should I reopen old wounds?"

"She wondered if you have children." When Emma nodded, Paul asked, "Have you ever thought about taking them to see her?"

"No." Emma lifted her chin. "Ebenezer's mother lives with us. She's been a good grandmother to them and as good to me as any mother could be. Much better than my ima was to Ebenezer."

"I've found that sometimes parents soften their views toward their son-in-law—or daughter-in-law—once there are grandchildren. I wouldn't be surprised if, by now, Ebenezer has become the best son-in-law ever known. Of course, if you don't want her to know her grandchildren, that's your choice."

Emma scowled. "It's not that I don't want her to know our children. It's just that I don't want her to reject them, and that's what I'm afraid would happen, like she did me when I married my husband." Emma's eyes brimmed.

"I don't think she would. We talked a lot, and she spoke of you with love. She thinks you don't care about her or want to take care of her when she gets too old to care for herself. She doesn't want to leave her home. She wants to stay there where her husband and their other children are buried, but I think she also knows there could be a time when staying there won't be possible."

Emma glanced at Ebenezer and then back to Paul. "My husband doesn't want her living with us. It's his home, and his mother's there too. They might not get along. My mother can be tyrannical."

"Is there room to build a separate house or room for her on your property?"

"No." Ebenezer held up his hand. "I don't want her there. I don't wish to live in a house of strife."

"As I told you before, we will take her into our house if you won't."

"Wait, husband," Emma said, her eyes pleading. "Ima wouldn't live with us unless she couldn't take care of herself anymore."

Ebenezer scowled. "Mehida won't live with us at all. I told you coming here would be a mistake. If Paulos loves Mehida so much, he can care for her." Ebenezer stalked out of the house.

Emma cast an anxious look at Paul, then turned to follow Ebenezer. Paul stepped between her and the door. "Does Ebenezer know your mother is probably wealthy?"

"Wealthy? We always lived like paupers in that little house. Where did she get any money?"

"She said your father was a successful merchant, and she's hidden the money somewhere nearby. That's all I know." Paul moved aside to let Emma through the door. "You should go after your husband."

"Yes, thank you. I'll tell him. I know the expense is part of his objection, although he's too proud to say so. Goodbye, Paulos."

Emma bowed her head and left.

Word had reached Bildad of a man who wanted his neighbors to disappear. The monger could always supplement those potential new slaves with any careless wanderers in the area, and he had not been on a "hunting journey" for a while. Some people still hadn't learned they shouldn't go anywhere alone. He chortled to himself.

He rubbed his fat hands together in glee and kissed his ring. *As long as I have this ring, good fortune follows me like a new lamb follows its mother.* Bildad and a select crew departed the slave compound, leaving Chilead in charge. The whip master remained behind as well. Bildad knew how much the slaves dreaded and feared the two men. His slaves would still be there when he returned.

He and his men made a few stops on the way north, adding the lone traveler or wanderer here and there to his collection. Each time, a full day of training was required before the new "recruits" saw the wisdom of compliance, allowing Bildad and his band to travel on.

They stopped in their usual camping place just south of Tyre in the late morning. Bildad went a good distance into the brush to be out of sight while he relieved himself. When he returned, he ordered the new slaves to raise the tents, gather wood, prepare the meal and care for the horses.

Long after sundown, he noticed his precious ring was missing. Frantic, he ordered his men and slaves to get on their knees and search the campsite. They found nothing.

Distraught, Bildad sat on a log by the campfire, peering anxiously into the dying flames. He was sure the ring must be in the fire and feared it might melt. He would sift through the ashes in the morning, after the ground cooled. Lowering his face to his hands, he cursed long and fluently.

As Sarah approached the marketplace, Jonas stepped out and waved her to his shop. When she entered, he whispered, "Please stay until I finish with these customers. I have news." He negotiated quickly with the two men for some canvas and sent them on their way.

Jonas walked toward her with a bounce in his step. "The slave master who I suspect took your husband is camped on the mainland, just south of the causeway. Paulos said he might be able to convince the slaver to release his prisoners?"

"If anyone can, Paulos can." Sarah grinned. "Especially if he can convince the slave master that serious harm might come to him if he doesn't let them go. As soon as I finish up here, I'll go tell him." Waving good-bye, she left to purchase the nuts and spices she had come after.

When she got back to the house, Sarah found Paul teaching the children in their play room. "Paul," she whispered in his ear, "the slave master is back. He's camped south of the entrance from the mainland."

Paul nodded. "As soon as the children are finished, we'll do some planning."

"All right. I have to fix lunch anyway."

She left for the outside kitchen, thinking how wonderful a real hamburger would taste. She wished she could fix French fries too. The thought made her salivate. However, it would be a few centuries before potatoes would be introduced to this part of the world, so that dish was out. Still, there was no reason she couldn't make a hamburger.

Taking a chunk of beef, she began to chop it into tiny pieces. When she was satisfied, she mixed the meat with an egg and crumbled bread to help it stick together, then added chopped onions, garlic, and several spices. After forming patties, she cooked them on an iron plate. While the burgers were cooking, she sliced the flatbread lengthwise. She placed the meat in the middle, adding thin slices of raw onion and a leaf of lettuce. Finally, she presented the result to Dorcas and the children.

Tammy, who continued to take her lunch with the other three children, noticed the dish. "Hang-g'bers!" she chirped ecstatically.

"Hang-g'bers?" asked Dorcas.

"They're called hamburgers." Sarah laughed. "It's a treat well known in the fu ... ah, to us before we came here." She glanced at

Darius, Gideon, and Orphah; they didn't seem to notice her near gaffe.

Dorcas wiped the hamburger juice from her lips. "You did it again, Sarah. This is delicious."

Sarah wondered what her former friends would think of a hamburger as elegant cuisine. "Thank you, Dorcas. I'll be happy to make hamburgers again for you any time you like." *Hmm. I wonder how they'd like onion rings.*

Chapter 33

Hurrying to Jonas's shop, Paul whispered his plan to Sarah. "What we need is to make me shine," he said. "Too bad we don't have florescent paint, but a white robe drenched in olive oil, my skin and hair also smeared with it, might be enough to make me look ghostly by firelight."

"Slow down a little, would you? My legs are shorter than yours." She grinned. "I like your shiny idea. How about a red stain, wine or maybe pomegranate juice, on the robe where your leg was bleeding? That may be a convincing touch."

When they told Jonas the plan, he laughed. "I can provide a white robe dipped in olive oil. The greasier it is, the more convincing it may be to Bildad. And if the bottom of the robe were black, it would look as if you were floating. Ah, I just had another idea. How about if I hide in the bushes and play a drum softly before Paulos appears? I have a few other friends who could play trumpets too."

Sarah clapped her hands. "I can hardly wait to see that slaver's face!"

Paul turned to her and grasped her shoulders. "No, Sarah, you can't be there. If anything goes wrong and you and I were both captured, Tamara would be without any parent. One of us has to stay with her."

Sarah inhaled sharply. "Oh, Paul, I don't want you to get hurt or be put into slavery again. What if this fails and both of you are captured? Poor Dathan would be without a parent too."

Jonas turned to Sarah. "There is danger, my friend. Maybe we shouldn't do this. We can't deprive Tamara of her papa again. Nor Dathan of his abba, I suppose."

Paul shook his head. "We have to do this, Jonas. Somewhere, the woman you love is in slavery, enduring God only knows what. We have to try. Do you have friends who would go with us in case we get into trouble?"

Hesitating, Jonas frowned, then nodded. "There are several people in this town who have lost family members to slavers. I know they'd help."

"I have friends in Hamath's household too," Paul continued. "We'll take as many reinforcements as possible, leave them in hiding, and hope they won't be needed."

After they finalized their plans, Jonas began to close his shop while Paul and Sarah made their way back home. At sundown, Jonas and Paul would meet back at his shop with their friends.

Before they left, Paul held Sarah and Tamara close. "If we don't come back in the morning, you'll know the worst has happened. We won't be able to get back in the gate until it's opened in the morning, so don't start worrying too early. I don't expect anything to go wrong. Bildad is superstitious, and God knows he has a lifetime of guilt that should plague him. Pray for us, all right?"

Tamara hugged Paul tight. "My friend Jesus said it would be okay. I told him, and he said he'll help you."

Paul, Sarah, Amad, and several other male servants and slaves met at Jonas's shop that evening. The men carried knives, clubs, and whatever else they could use as weapons. A few carried swords or spears. Dorcas, Proteus, and Thecla had been told of the plan, and they gave their approval for the men to go with Paul.

Paul was surprised at how many men had joined the group, and Jonas had the robe literally dripping with olive oil. A gruesome red stain ran down the front. Paul's brows did a high dance above his eyes. "What's this?"

"I slaughtered a goat for tomorrow's meal. What do you think?"

Sarah shuddered. "Sickening."

After one more embrace, Paul sent Sarah back home.

Not wanting to move in a large mass and possibly put the slaver's caravan on alert, the group made their way, two or three at a time, past the city gate. Sometimes willing people sold themselves into slavery to pay off debts, or unwilling debtors were sold to pay their debts, but Paul felt certain most or all of Bildad's slaves had been obtained by dishonest and unwilling means. The men Paul brought with him were all in servanthood or slavery by choice or by inheritance. Jonas's friends were probably all free men. On this night, it made no difference. They were united in their purpose.

Paul waited until all the men were hidden in a cave not far from Bildad's camp. He donned his ghostly cloak. As they whitewashed Paul's face and hands and poured oil over his head, the men joked that it would take all the soap in Tyre to get him clean again. Paul was just glad he wouldn't have to walk far in the heavy robe.

The men made their way from the cave to the slaver's camp. Paul was amazed at how quiet thirty men could be. He worked his way forward, easing from one tree or bush to the next until he was close enough to begin his act.

When everyone was in place, Paul stepped out from behind a convenient bush, rising to his full height. A soft drumroll began behind him. Trumpets blasted from all around the campsite. He deepened his voice and called out, "BILLL-DAAAD."

Bildad and his men jumped to their feet and looked around, probably more than a little afraid. Their activities weren't exactly legal. At the least, they should be thinking Roman soldiers could be coming after them.

Loud trumpets continued to blare around the perimeter of the camp until Paul lifted his arms. The trumpets and drums were abruptly silent.

The twelve men by the campfire fell over each other trying to escape, running into the large tent behind them. Even Bildad moved quickly for one so heavy.

Paul raised his voice and bellowed, "BILDAD! BRING ME BILDAD! BRING ME BILDAD NOW!" A louder drumroll echoed between each of his dramatic demands.

Three men came forward, dragging and pushing Bildad to the forefront. The slaver kicked and scratched, trying desperately to break free of his companions. They pushed him to his knees.

"BILDAD, YOU HAVE SINNED!"

Bildad fell to his face, loudly cursing the loss of his lucky ring. With his broad behind raised, he pressed his forehead to the ground and extended his hands in front of him. His voice rang unnaturally high and loud as he cried out, "Wh-wh-who, m-m-me? H-h-how did I sin, sir?"

"BILDAD, YOU MADE SLAVES OF FREE PEOPLE. YOU PROFITED FROM THEIR MISERY."

"Y-Y-Y Yes, sir. Forgive me, sir. Who are you, sir?"

"I'M PAULOS, WHOM YOU LEFT ON THE SIDE OF THE ROAD TO DIE."

"P-P-P-P-Paulos??? B-b-b-but you were given to me by ... by a f-f-friend. Honestly. I had no idea you were a free man," Bildad protested, his voice squeaking.

"SILENCE, SCUM! YOU KNEW IT WASN'T HONEST."

"Well, he said he had the right to sell or give you away, the miserable liar, but I've had my revenge on him." Bildad started to rise from his prostrate position.

His revenge? Paul signaled behind his back for Jonas to increase the volume of the drums. Again, Bildad pressed his forehead to the ground.

"*YOU* AVENGED YOURSELF ON *HIM*?" Paul bellowed. (Loud drumroll) "YOU HAVE NO RIGHT TO REVENGE. THE GOD OF ISRAEL WILL WREAK VENGEANCE ON YOU FOR ALL THOSE WHOM YOU HAVE HARMED."

Bildad moaned. "Please, no! I'm just a humble ..."

"SILENCE! THERE IS ONLY ONE WAY YOU CAN ATONE FOR YOUR SINS, BILDAD. YOU MUST FREE ALL THOSE YOU PLACED INTO SLAVERY."

"I can't do that!" Bildad cried, raising his head a little.

This had better be over soon, Paul thought. His voice felt strained and could begin cracking at any moment. "HUSH YOUR FOOLISH BABBLING! IF YOU DON'T FREE ALL YOUR SLAVES, TRAGEDIES WILL COME TO YOU AND YOUR COMPANIONS, ONE FOR EACH PERSON HARMED, INCREASING IN INTENSITY UNTIL YOU ARE FINALLY LEFT TO DIE, FRIENDLESS AND FORGOTTEN, AS YOU DID TO ME."

A budding comedian behind Paul howled like a stricken banshee. Paul almost lost it.

"TOMORROW, A RABBI WILL COME TO YOU. HE WILL TAKE THE CAPTIVES YOU HAVE WITH YOU NOW. MISHAPS WILL PURSUE YOU UNTIL ALL OF YOUR MISGOTTEN SLAVES ARE FREE."

"I promise, sir. I'll obey. Oh, please don't bring my poor old head to Hades."

"HASTEN TO ATONE FOR YOUR SINS, BILDAD. YOUR LUCK HAS RUN OUT, AND YOUR TIME GROWS SHORT."

Slowly and smoothly, Paul backed up, guided by a man who made sure he didn't stumble. When he was no longer in the firelight, he swiftly discarded the robe and wiped his face with a wet towel. The drumroll stopped suddenly, and a single trumpet sounded one last loud, long fading note with a quaver at the end.

Silently, Paul and his company brushed out their trail. Ghosts shouldn't leave tracks. With as little noise as possible, they made their way back to the cave. After wrapping themselves in their cloaks, they caught a little sleep, leaving one man to guard the entrance. Just before sunrise, they proceeded, two or three at a time, to the city gate.

Once inside, Paul hurried home. Kneeling beside Sarah, he whispered, "He swallowed the bait."

Sarah hugged him so tightly he could scarcely breathe. "Thank God. I prayed all night for you."

Meanwhile, Jonas walked back to the slaver's camp with a tale of being awakened in the predawn morning by a ghost who said he was to get some captives from him and take them to Tyre. Bildad and his cohorts herded six young men and a lovely teenage girl from a tent.

"Here—take them. These are tokens of my word. I vow the rest will be freed as soon as I return to Jerusalem. Will your God return my ring to me when they are let go? Please, would you petition him for it?"

"The ghost said nothing about a ring. However, if that's all the punishment you get for your crimes, you should give the One True God your eternal gratitude."

The remaining men broke up camp as Jonas left with the slaves, not once glancing back at the man he hoped would remain a repentant sinner.

Chapter 34

When Jonas and the slaves were safely within the walls of Tyre, he turned to the young captives, who were still bound, and carefully began cutting their ropes. The men, bearing whip marks and dressed in bloody tunics, stood silent with their heads down.

Jonas gently touched their shoulders, one by one. "You're safe here, neighbors. No one will harm you. Where do you come from?"

At first no one spoke, although they exchanged glances. Finally, a girl answered, "I'm from Ptolemais. These others were taken from between Ptolemais and here."

"We have people who will return you safely to your homes. I'm sorry for the ordeal you've gone through."

"Will the ghost take us home?" She shivered and gazed wild-eyed around them.

Jonas chuckled. "No, not him, but there are several others who helped him and will help you too. Come with me." He led them to Dorcas's villa. The young men stumbled, probably weakened by lack of food and the beatings they'd endured.

Sarah opened the door to them. "Welcome, friends. We've prepared something for you to eat, and we'll dress your wounds. After that, Amad will take you to comfortable beds where you can rest."

Dorcas joined them. "You can stay here for a day, and then tomorrow my parents will take you back to your homes. They're traveling to Galilee, and they have a large enough caravan to keep you safe."

When the visitors were fed and cared for, Amad took them to the servants' quarters.

Dorcas sat down at the table and turned to Paul. "Do you really think this slaver will release the other people? What if no tragedies occur as promised? Will you follow him? How will you know if he's released all of them?"

"I don't think we have to worry, Dorcas," Paul said. "He'll count any bad thing that happens to him now as part of his punishment. He's so superstitious that some things will happen because he'll make mistakes. And we have Jesus on our side to help out."

"I think your Jesus must be much more powerful than our gods."

Jonas stared at his shaking hands. "After all this time, I'm afraid to hope. Bildad has probably sold Mariah to someone else by now. And if she is freed, would she come back to us, or would she feel too ashamed? Slavers aren't always kind to their captives, particularly women who can be used in ways I'd rather not think about."

"Jonas," Sarah said softly, "all these years you have hoped and prayed that your wife would return to you. You can't stop. Your prayer should be even more fervent now."

Jonas laid his head on his arms and began to sob.

Dorcas reached out and touched his elbow, her own eyes glistening with tears.

Tamara patted his back and leaned against him.

Paul slid his arm around Jonas's shoulders and prayed, "Dear God, you know I haven't been one to pray much, and I think this is only the second favor I've ever asked of you. Please, please, send Mariah and Hamath back to their waiting families."

When Jonas had wept himself dry, he raised his head, using his tunic sleeves to wipe his face. "Thank you, my friends. I think I should go back to the marketplace. People will be wondering if I died and left my business to Dathan." With a watery smile, he took one last swipe at his eyes, bowed his farewell, and left.

Sarah walked in silence toward the kitchen, thoughtful about the events of the past few days.

Tamara tugged at her tunic. "Mama, why was Jonas sad?"

Sarah knelt in front of her. "Sometimes people cry because they're sad, sometimes because they are happy, and sometimes because they're mad. I think Jonas was crying because his wife was taken a long, long time ago, and now there's a chance she might be able to come home, but he doesn't know if she will."

"My papa came home. I'm going to ask Jesus to bring Jonas's wife home too. Jonas and Dathan must be lonesome without her, just like we were lonesome without Papa."

"That would be just the right thing to do, Tammy. Maybe while you're talking to Jesus, you could also ask for Hamath to come home."

Tamara squeezed her eyes and lips tight. "There, I did," she said matter-of-factly.

Sarah smiled as she entered the cooking area. The next meal wouldn't take long to complete. That would leave her time to go to their house and pray one more time, hoping one more prayer wouldn't hurt.

Chapter 35

Hamath stood and stretched. His stripes from the whippings had healed. His paunch had disappeared, replaced by muscle. He'd even become accustomed to the sparse, tasteless meals. A ratty linen blanket was sufficient to keep him warm at night. He'd learned to sleep with the discomfort of one ankle manacled to the back of the shed.

Bildad rented the slaves to farmers or businessmen who needed laborers. Hamath had come to anticipate those days with pleasure. When they worked for someone else, he could carry on furtive conversations with other slaves, and usually they ate better.

Hamath had struck up a friendship with a young man named Zillai. He knew on this day the two of them would be rented to a nearby farmer to build sheds for his sheep.

When they were chained to the back of the farmer's wagon, far enough away from the slave holdings to speak safely, Hamath nudged Zillai. "How did you fare last night?" he whispered.

"Well enough." Zillai chuckled softly. "The whip master must have been in a kind-hearted mood ... not one lash." Zillai was a more recent "recruit." He hadn't yet learned to hold his tongue.

"Where is your home ... that is, other than the slave sheds?" Hamath asked.

"I'm from Bozrah. I came to Jerusalem searching for the man called Jesus. I hoped to ask him to heal my father."

"Let me guess—you traveled alone?"

"Yes. My mother has often warned me I'm too impulsive, and this time I received exactly what I should have been guarding against. I didn't do much thinking. My father had been thrown from his horse, hitting his head on a rock, and he wouldn't wake up. I didn't want to wait for a caravan. I jumped on my horse, told my mother where I was going, and left. Now Bildad has my beautiful stallion, Sultan, and I have a striped back. I know my mother wished me to learn a lesson, but I'm sure she didn't intend the lesson to be this severe. If I ever get free, I'll go home and never again leave so impetuously." He touched a scab on his shoulder. "I should also admit to her she was right."

"Did you find Jesus?"

Zillai heaved a heavy sigh, then glanced at their current boss. "No, Jesus left before I arrived in Jerusalem. I camped on the outskirts of the city, not too far from here. Some men asked to warm themselves at my fire. I should have known better. It wasn't cold. I invited them to share my meal. I had a leg of lamb roasting over a fire. The next thing I knew, I was bound, and they were eating my supper. You know the rest of the story."

He shook his head. "The worst is not knowing if my father is still alive. If he is, it's no thanks to my efforts. If he's not, I'll never have a chance to tell him good-bye or that I'm sorry for the times I disobeyed him."

Hamath nodded. "That's my problem too. I owe a lot of apologies because I hurt a lot of people. I'm even responsible for the deaths of two of my servants." He gulped and continued. "I desired one of my women servants, so I gave her husband to Bildad. He said the man died of injuries. Another servant died trying to rescue me. This life is what I deserve, and I doubt I'll ever be able to say 'I'm sorry' to the people I hurt."

"You never know. As long as we're still breathing, a chance remains. Maybe some of our loved ones will send rescuers."

"I hope not. I'm afraid they could wind up as we are. That's what happened to me. I came to rescue the man I gave to Bildad, and here I am."

"May the One God grant that we might have a chance to tell my mother, my father, and your people how much we regret our foolish acts."

"Amen," said Hamath.

The day ended far too soon. Before the sun went down, the sheds were finished. The farmer took them back to Bildad's slave compound without feeding them.

"Did the slaves speak among themselves?" Chilead demanded of the farmer.

"If they did, I didn't hear them," the farmer responded. "Your slaves are silent. Why don't you allow them to speak?"

"That's none of your affair," Chilead snapped. "It's enough for you to know they're not allowed to speak, other than to answer if you ask a question. Were they respectful to you?"

"Yes, they were respectful, and no, they didn't talk among themselves." The farmer sounded irritated. "Why do you grill me? I'm not your slave. I paid for a day's use of these men, and I don't consider these questions part of the bargain."

Chilead growled in response but allowed the farmer to leave.

Hamath glanced at the slaver. He probably wouldn't kidnap the insolent farmer this close to home. Too many people would know where to come looking.

Hamath and Zillai had been returned to their shackles in the shed when a commotion began outside.

Bildad had returned. He and the ones who went with him were arguing with the men who had remained at the compound. Hamath could hear only snatches of conversation. All of them were shouting at the same time, but an occasional word came through, like ghost and slaves. Hamath was curious, thinking offhand it might be nice if the whole lot of slavers killed each other off. After an hour or two, the arguing ceased. The next thing Hamath knew, Bildad himself was removing Hamath's shackles.

"You're free to go." Bildad said.

"I don't care to be the sport of your men again, sir."

"Go, or you will be whipped …" Bildad clapped a hand over his own mouth and looked around with wide eyes. "Just go. Go!" He stood and started toward the next slave.

"Wait. You stole my money and my horses and killed my servant. It seems you owe me."

"Your servant is dead. He … had an accident. Fell on his sword. Yes, that's what happened. He fell on his sword."

"That's a lie. I saw him killed," Hamath insisted.

"Here, thirty shekels, the price of a slave. Now go. Leave this place! Go home!" Bildad pushed Hamath toward the entrance of the shed, where several other slaves stood, looking confused.

"Where are my horses?"

"Horses? The ghost said nothing about horses. Now get out of here. Do you choose to remain a slave?" Bildad's voice rose an octave.

Maybe Hamath had pushed the monger as far as was wise. He left, walking south toward Jerusalem. For thirty shekels, he should be able to find a nag of some sort. Some of the other slaves were running now, outdistancing him, but Hamath picked his way with caution, not wanting to fall over a rock or a log in the dark. He hadn't gone far when weariness overtook him. He and Zillai had labored a long, hard day, and neither the farmer nor Chilead had fed them after their day of work. In the confusion and dark, he didn't see Zillai or any of the other slaves that he knew.

Hamath lay down to sleep, wishing he'd had the forethought to bring his blanket from the shed. Ah well, at least the night was warm.

When he woke the next morning, his stomach growled. Maybe he'd use some of the coins to buy a loaf of bread. He reached down for the bag of money Bildad had given him, but the bag was gone. Hamath searched the area where he had been sleeping. The bag wasn't there, but he found footprints close to where he slept. He began to swear but caught himself. "Sorry, Lord."

Hamath shrugged. No point in going into Jerusalem now. He turned, found the road north, and began walking. He stopped at a farmhouse and asked for a crust of bread. For a moment, the farmer's wife eyed him suspiciously, then handed him not only a loaf of bread but a piece of cheese and a skin of water, as well. Hamath thanked the woman profusely and again followed the road north.

The going was hard. Most days Hamath went without food, and his stomach was constantly growling. Whenever he met travelers or came to a house, he begged for food. Every crumb he received was better than gold.

"I'll never again refuse food to anyone who comes to my door, nor anyone who asks for help when I'm traveling," he vowed. "That is, if I get home."

Only two weeks had passed when Sarah began to notice the rejoicing in and around the town. So far, Hamath and Mariah were still among the missing, but at least two dozen people had returned to Tyre by the end of a month. Word came from Martha's sister in Sidon, saying missing people were reappearing there too.

Miraculous!

Chapter 36

As Paul and Tamara were about to leave their little house to begin morning lessons, they heard a knock at their door. Opening the door, Paul invited the couple in.

"Hello, Ebenezer, Emma. This is my wife, Sarah."

"Shalom, Paulos, Sarah," Ebenezer said.

"Papa," Tamara said, tugging on Paul's tunic, "Jesus told me 'bout Emma in my dream last night. He told me something to tell her."

Emma and Ebenezer looked startled.

"Who is Jesus?" Emma asked.

"He's my friend, and he knows everything. He told me last night you need to hurry to see your mama. She doesn't feel good, and she wants to see you before she dies." Tamara stared anxiously up at Emma.

Emma's eyes narrowed. "Before she dies? How do you know about this? Paulos, what did you tell this child?"

"I told her nothing. This Jesus talks to her often in her dreams, and thus far, all of what he has told her has happened. We believe Jesus is the promised one from God."

"The promised one?" asked Ebenezer. "You mean the Messiah? Has he actually come?"

"Well, that's our belief. And he's been seen by a lot of people, not just Tamara."

"Have you seen him?"

"I have, although Sarah hasn't."

Ebenezer lifted his hands toward heaven. "That is indeed good news! He has sent the Messiah to save his people."

One edge of Ebenezer's mouth tipped upward, the first hint of a smile Paul had seen from the man.

Emma took a small step toward Paul. "We came to tell you we're taking our children to see my mother."

Paul smiled at her. "I'm glad. I can't leave now. Tamara has been ill, or I'd ask Dorcas if I could go with you. Please give Mehida my greetings and tell her that her almost adopted son sends his love. May God go with you."

Mehida lay on her bed, staring at the ceiling. "Adonai," she murmured, "I know I'll soon join my children and my husband where they lie. I don't fear death, but I pray I can see my daughter one last time. I need to tell her I'm sorry. Yes, I know, I probably should tell that fisherman she married I'm sorry too and give them my blessing. I know I was wrong. If I don't see them, great Yahweh, please, would you tell them for me?"

Tears trickled from her eyes onto her bed.

"She won't live long now," Joel said. "She grows weaker."

Abidon nodded. "I'm glad we stopped to see her when we did. She'd have died there on the ground where she fell."

"To the goats' credit, they were warming her. Or was it that enjoyed the taste of her sleeves?" Joel grinned.

"Whichever, they did seem to help her. They lay down close to her and kept her warm during the night." Abidon stroked one of the friendly goats.

Joel glanced at the house. "She said she wants to see her daughter. Even though we sent word by the next person who passed on his way to the coast, I don't think anyone will find the woman in time. Mehida might live another week, but it could take more than a week to get to the Great Sea and back, even if the messenger hurried and knew exactly where to look for her family."

"A miracle will be needed to get the daughter here in time. Maybe she'll give us a message for her daughter."

"Perhaps. I'll talk to her again." Joel rose and walked into the house.

Mehida was still staring at the ceiling when Joel entered. She turned her head at the sound, squinting. "Is that you, physician?"

"Yes, Mehida. How do you feel?"

"I don't feel anything. It's as though I'm floating somewhere." She cackled softly, sounding a little like the old Mehida. "The view is dreadful. I remember myself as a young woman, yet here I am, old, crippled, wrinkled, and weakened by too long a life."

"Such happens to all of us, Mehida. You've had a good life, haven't you?"

"Some good, some bad. Some joy, some sorrow. Now I'm at the end of this life, and I don't know what lies ahead."

"A man called Jesus said if you believe in him, you would have everlasting life with him. Jesus is the Son of God."

"I believe in the One God. I didn't know he had a Son."

"He does, and the Son's name is Jesus."

"How do you know he's God's Son?

"Several reasons. He raises the dead to life; he heals the sick; he speaks with the wisdom of the ages. The biggest reason I believe in him, though, is because his words reach my heart."

Joel gazed out the high window above the fireplace. "Then too, I was on the banks of the Jordan River when a prophet named John baptized him, and God spoke in a voice like thunder, saying, 'This is my beloved Son in whom I am well pleased.'"

Mehida listened in silence, looking thoughtful. Finally, in a soft voice, she said, "If anyone but you had told me this, I'd think he was lying, joking, or out of his mind, but I believe you. Therefore, I will believe in him." She added wistfully, "I wish I could see him."

Mehida coughed and held her hands to her chest. Joel held some water to her lips.

"You need to rest, but I have to ask you one question," Joel said. "You don't have much time left here with us, Mehida. I sent someone to find your daughter, but I don't think she'll get the message and get back here before you step through the curtain between here and heaven. Do you want me to tell her anything?"

"I might fool you yet, physician. Remember when you thought Paulos would die? We fooled you then, and now I might fool you too." Mehida smiled a weak version of her old toothless grin. "I'm stronger than I look."

"Yes, Mehida, you're one amazing old woman. I agree. I just don't want her to miss your last words to her."

232

"I think I have another day or two left. Maybe more. If I think I'll die before Emma gets here, then I'll tell you what to say to her."

"All right, Mehida. Now I'll go outside and let you rest. Abidon and I are making some good chicken stew that should be ready in an hour or two."

Joel went back out where Abidon was stirring a steaming pot, cooking one of Mehida's old chickens with some fresh vegetables from her garden. The air filled with a mouth-watering aroma.

"Mehida doesn't think she will die today," Joel said.

"Do you agree?" Abidon blew on a spoonful of the stew.

"She feels well enough to argue, which might be a good sign. I hope she is. We can only try to keep her alive until her daughter arrives, but I can't believe the daughter will be here in time. I don't know how to work that miracle. The trip would take too long, if she comes at all. The traveler we gave the message to might not even find her. Mehida doesn't want to tell me until she's closer to death. I fear that if she waits that long, she won't be able to tell me. On the other hand, if I press her, it could worry her to the point where her heart fails. I pray she'll be able to say goodbye to her daughter."

"I'll pray too. We've seen miracles happen, remember. If only Jesus would pass by here, perhaps he would heal her."

"Perhaps, Abidon, but I think she is ready to go. The only reason she holds on is to see her daughter one more time. That's what I'm praying for."

"Then that will also be my request to the One God."

Mehida faded in and out of consciousness. Joel spent the night sitting by her bedside, hoping and praying. At daylight, when

Mehida stirred slightly, Joel took her hand. "Mehida, can you hear me?"

"I hear you."

"Do you have any words to pass on to your daughter?"

She rolled her head from one side to the other. "I'll tell her."

"She's not here, Mehida."

"Soon. She's coming," Mehida murmured as she drifted off again.

Joel shook his head and went outside.

Abidon lay on the ground next to the house, a young nanny goat nestled next to him. Awakened by the closing door, he sat up and scratched his head.

"Any change?"

"I don't believe she'll live through the day, Abidon. We can do nothing more than sit with her. It may be a comfort to know she has friends here. And if we can find it, we can place her in the tomb with her husband and children. I don't know anything else we can do."

"You should get some sleep, Joel," Abidon said. "I'll sit with her."

"No, my friend. There will be time for sleep after she is gone. I'll stay awake for that long. Would you search for the tomb?"

"Of course." Abidon reached for the cheese and grapes left from the previous night. "Here ... at least have something to eat."

"Thank you, Abidon. You should eat too."

"Should we prepare some crushed fruit or broth for Mehida?"

"I don't think she will want it, but we can try."

Abidon glanced toward the road. "Did you hear voices?"

"No. Wait ... yes, I do."

A woman, a man, and three children led a sweaty donkey pulling a cart. They walked wearily toward the house.

"Shalom, friends. May we offer you some cheese and grapes?" Joel asked.

Chapter 37

Ebenezer scowled at the two strangers. He reached for the prod from the wagon in case he needed to fight. "What are you doing here at the house of my wife's mother?

"I'm Joel, a physician and Mehida's friend. This is my assistant and apprentice, Abidon." He turned to Emma. "Are you her daughter?"

Emma's eyes were red, her voice tired. "Yes. Where's my mother?"

"She's in the house. I fear she doesn't have long. She fell and broke a hip, and we don't know how long she lay there on the ground before we found her. She's very weak. How did you get here so quickly? We only sent the message three days ago."

Ebenezer unhitched the donkey, tying the rope from his halter to a tree limb.

Emma's eyebrows rose. "Three days ago? We received a message two days ago, but not from any messenger. A small child named Tamara told us my mother was dying. Someone called Jesus told her in a dream. Tamara said my mother wanted to see me before she died. We've been walking without stopping since then. Our children slept in the cart, and once my husband or I also slept, but our poor donkey has had little rest."

The beast had stood with his head down and his legs splayed while they talked. As they spoke, he lay down on the grass and with a contented groan stretched his head forward and shut his eyes.

Ebenezer placed his arm around Emma's shoulders. "The girl who told us about Mehida is the child of a man named Paulos. Paulos was rescued by my wife's mother a few months ago."

Joel smiled. "And so, the circle continues. We know Paulos and how Mehida helped him. Come. If Mehida is awake, I know she'll want to see you. The hope of seeing you again is the only thing that's kept her alive. Her heart is worn out."

Joel opened the door. Ebenezer and Emma entered, followed by the three children. Though the sun was up, the interior of the house was dim, so Joel pushed the wick higher on one lamp and lit another, placing the lamps on a stand beside the bed.

"Mehida, are you awake?" he asked.

"Is Emma here?" A touch of excitement strengthened Mehida's whisper.

"Yes, Ima, I'm here. Are you in pain?" Emma's voice faltered. She stood by the old wooden stool and lay her head on her mother's shoulder.

"No pain unless I move. I told him you'd come. I had to see you one more time."

"I'm so sorry I left in anger. I love you, Ima. I've missed you. I was young and foolish. I know I hurt you. Will you forgive me?"

"You are forgiven, but I'm the one who was foolish. I drove you away." Mehida paused to cough. "If I hadn't driven you off, I could have come to see you." She paused again. "Beloved daughter, I give my blessing on your marriage." She paused again, her breathing labored. "May you live long and have many strong and happy children. Learn from the mistakes of your mother, and tell your loved ones often how precious they are." Mehida's voice cracked and fell still.

"Ima?" Emma cried.

Joel touched Emma's shoulder. "She's only resting. See? She still breathes."

Ebenezer stepped up beside his wife. She turned, sobbing against his chest.

"Stop that." Mehida opened her eyes a bit. "Save your tears. I'm not gone yet." Her voice wavered. "I have a gift for you, my daughter. Is your husband here?"

"I'm here, Mehida," Ebenezer said.

"Good. Have you been kind to my little one?"

"We share a deep love for each other and for our children," Ebenezer said. "The One God has blessed us."

"You have children? Are they here?"

"Children, come and greet your grandmother," Emma said. The three children hesitantly came closer. The oldest, a boy, climbed onto the stool and reached for his grandmother's hand.

"I'm Abner, *Savta*. I'm ten years old. I'm the oldest."

"You are named Abner?" Mehida's eyes widened a little and her lips tilted up. "A good name."

The girl clambered onto the stool. Holding onto her brother with one hand and reaching with her other hand, she patted Mehida.

"I'm Tabitha, Savta. I'm five." She held up five fingers, sticky with grape juice.

Mehida smiled again. "A girl. Good."

Ebenezer lifted the youngest, who buried his head in his father's shoulder. Ebenezer took Mehida's hand and placed it on the boy's head.

"This is Aaron. He's two years old and shy."

Mehida's tears flowed again. "I cheated myself out of getting to know them, and now there's no time."

"No, Ima, don't say that," Emma cried. "It's not too late. We've come to take you back with us. We brought our donkey with a cart. We made a soft bed in the back."

"Ah, if only I could," Mehida said. "My heart is too old. But I give you a parting gift. In the goat shed, under the straw. In the wooden floor, a trap door. Your abba's savings. Yours now. I won't need it. I go to be ... with my God, my husband, and my other children."

"No, Ima, no. Not yet, don't go. Please, don't go." Emma put her cheek next to Mehida's, and their tears flowed together.

"I'm old and tired, child. Need to rest."

"Come away." Joel whispered softly to Emma. "Let her rest awhile, and you may yet talk to her again."

Emma nodded. "Rest then, Ima. I'll be here when you wake."

Ebenezer wasn't sure whether Mehida heard her or not; the old woman's eyes were closed. However, her chest still rose and fell under the blanket covering her thin body. Emma gently placed her mother's hand on the blanket and came away from the bed. They walked outside the house, leaving the door open so they could hear Mehida if she called.

The group sat on logs they had dragged from the nearby woods, silent in the warming day.

Quietly, Joel said, "Mehida will want to know you found her treasure. Perhaps you should look for it."

"I'll do it." Ebenezer stood.

"Shall I help, Abba?" Abner asked.

Ebenezer smiled at his son. "Come," he said.

"Me too, Abba?" asked Tabitha.

"Yes, you may help too."

Aaron nestled on his mother's shoulder and closed his eyes as Joel guided the father and young siblings behind the house to the goat shed. The shed was little more than a lean-to with three sides and a floor, the wooden base covered with straw.

"Let's clear the floor, son. Be careful of splinters."

When they had moved the straw outside the shed, Ebenezer stood and scratched his head. "I don't see a trap door, but this is the only shed. Let's try pulling on those iron rings." He pointed at the rings set along the floor to tie the goats for milking.

If Mehida hadn't told them it was there, he would have suggested they look somewhere else. When he pulled on the last ring, a panel came up from the floor. The leather hinge was barely visible.

"All I can feel are goat skins, Abba. See?" Abner lifted the hides out one at a time.

Ebenezer felt around the edge of the rock-lined cavity. One side had a piece of shale that seemed loose. "Hah! There's another opening." He lifted the thin, heavy rock.

Ebenezer reached his hand into the dark cavity. "There's a leather bag in here." He pulled it out of the hole and handed it to Abner. Reaching farther into the hole, he found two more. He handed the lightest bag to Tabitha.

She tried, but she couldn't lift it. "It's too big to lift, Abba. But I can pull it on the ground. See?"

Ebenezer ruffled her hair. "May I help you carry it?" He lifted it and let her bear part of the burden. Together they hauled the bags to where Emma sat and dropped them in front of her.

She lifted one of them with a little difficulty. "They're so heavy." She untied the leather thong and peered inside. She gasped, and her eyes widened. There were hundreds of silver shekels in the bag. Another held a small handmade bronze cup, a child's tunic, and a toy made of goatskin—and more coins. Emma covered her eyes and cried again.

"These were mine … my cup, my tunic, and my toy dog, Yappy. So, these were parts of her treasure. All those years we wasted when we could have been together."

"The fault was mine, Emma," Ebenezer said softly. "I kept you apart. And it was I who delayed our coming to see her. Will you forgive me?"

"It was no more your fault than mine. I was stubborn and proud, thinking she should come to me. I couldn't see my own fault in this; I only blamed her."

"You can't undo the past," Joel said gently. "You're here with her now when she needs you. Make her last hours pleasant, and she will ease into the arms of her Lord with peace in her heart."

"Is she really going to die, physician? Can't we take her home with us?" Emma's eyes pled with him, but he shook his head.

"I'm afraid not, my friends. She may not die until tonight or tomorrow morning, but she is too weak to last more than a few precious hours. Even if she were stronger, she would suffer too much pain in the wagon before you reached your home."

Emma rocked back and forth, kneeling next to Mehida's treasure, weeping silently until Aaron tugged on the sleeve of her tunic. Emma raised her gaze to the baby.

"Sava," he said, pointing into the house. "Sava wake."

Everyone followed Aaron as he trotted back into the house.

"Shalom, Ima, did you rest all right?"

"Rested," Mehida breathed. "Grandchildren, please?"

Emma and Ebenezer lifted the younger children onto the edge of the bed, while Abner climbed up over the end of the bed. When all three were seated by her, Mehida smiled. "My eyes are dim, and I can't see you," she said, pausing often for breaths of air, "but I know you're here. Children, I have ... something for you. Small ... piece ... wisdom. Remember, even when ... you ... argue, your ima ... still loves ... you. Even ... if she ... yells ... at you." She shut her eyes for a moment, then opened them. "Pots ... honey ... shelf. Remember ... I love you."

"I love honey, Savta. I love you too," Tabitha said. After she laid her head briefly on Mehida's shoulder, she held her arms out to her father to help her to the floor.

"Me too, Savta. I love you too," Abner said. "Thank you for the honey and for the wisdom. Ima never yells at me, though."

Mehida's old cackle was faint but there. "She will." With her eyes shut, she breathed in shallow gasps.

"Me too," Aaron said, not to be outdone by big brother or sister. Patting her face, he repeated, "Me too." He leaned forward until his nose nearly touched hers.

"You too." Mehida opened her eyes a crack.

Emma leaned in close to her mother. "Ima, thank you for the bags of sheckles. We found them. You kept my cup, and my tunic, and my Yappy."

"Yes. Good. You found ... them."

"You hid them well, but yes, my Ebenezer found them."

"Yours ... with ... blessing.

"Ima, I love you so much. I wish I could make all the years up to you."

"You have. Tired. Time ... to go. They ... wait."

"Who, Ima?" Emma had tears rolling down her face again, but she kept her voice under control. "Who is waiting?"

"Abba ... children ... *Adonai*." Mehida's voice was so soft Emma could scarcely hear her.

"Say shalom to Abba for me, Ima, and tell him I miss him. I'll miss you too, Ima."

"I'll ... wait ... for ... you ... there." One more tear rolled down her cheek. She sighed as she left them.

Joel and Abidon, who had entered the room by then, stepped forward. Joel held a feather in front of Mehida's mouth and nose, listened to her chest, and turned to look at Emma, sympathy in his eyes.

"She has gone," he murmured.

Emma bent to kiss her mother's cheek. Slowly, she turned away, keening softly. One after another, each of the children kissed their grandmother.

Ebenezer gazed down at Mehida's still form and whispered, "You were a fine old woman, Mehida. I misjudged you." Then he and the family left the house and waited outside for Joel. Abidon followed them.

"I'll go into Nain and buy the spices," Ebenezer said. "I should return by nightfall." He reached into the bag of money and brought out a half-dozen coins. "Is there anything else we need?" He pulled the protesting donkey away from a patch of grass.

"Thank you, no, Ebenezer. We will be here, and a meal will await your return," Abidon said.

Emma had cried so much her eyes burned. The children hadn't seen death up close before, and this grandmother they barely knew wouldn't evoke the emotion as the one they had known all their lives. Even so, Abner and Tabitha glanced wordlessly toward the house. Little Aaron, however, wasn't so reserved. He tugged at his mother's sleeve.

"Sava sleep?"

"No, Aaron, your savta won't wake up any more. She went ... she went away from her body."

"Where?"

"She died and went to see my abba."

Aaron looked off in the direction his abba had gone.

"No, Aaron. Not your abba, my abba."

Aaron looked confused. "Ima's abba?"

"Yes, Aaron. I used to be a little girl, and I had an ima and an abba like you do. Your savta was my ima. My abba died a long time ago." Emma released a small sob.

Aaron regarded her with a slight frown. She hadn't cried in front of him before, and all of her tears must seem strange to him.

When Ebenezer returned in the afternoon, several people came with him. Some were vendors and townspeople who knew Mehida; others who would play the flutes, and the wailers who began crying as soon as they arrived. The physicians had killed and dressed one of the goats, Emma had roasted it and boiled some leeks, expecting a small crowd, This had been her family's home for generations.

After they ate, the women helped Emma anoint and wrap Mehida's body in a shroud. Emma showed them where the burial tomb was located, about five hundred cubits from the house in a hillside. The men rolled the boulder away from the entrance, then solemnly carried her in procession to the hillside cave and laid her on an empty shelf. With the wailers in full volume, the men rolled the large stone back across the entrance to the cave.

After the villagers left, the rest rolled up in their cloaks to lie down wherever there was an empty spot.

Despite her exhaustion, Emma couldn't sleep. Memories flooded her mind. She remembered when her parents had taken her to Jerusalem for her first Passover. Even though she wasn't a boy, her parents had sacrificed two doves in gratitude that one child had finally lived. She didn't recall what age she had been then, but she couldn't have been more than three or four years old.

She remembered the first time her father scolded her fiercely when she had answered her mother with anger. She had cried because he had never scolded her before.

Emma remembered the birth of yet one more child, a boy, who died the day after his birth.

So many memories that finally faded, one into the other, as she fell asleep.

The next morning, Joel and Abidon bade their farewells and took their leave. Emma had offered to pay them for their time and trouble, but they insisted Mehida's friendship was payment enough.

Ebenezer and Emma loaded as many of the household items as they could on the donkey cart, along with the chickens in straw baskets, then tethered the goats to the back of the cart. Emma turned and looked once more inside the house. She sighed, then turned back to her family. "Let's go," she said. "It's a long way back to Tyre."

Chapter 38

Hamath's worn sandals fell apart about half way to Tyre. He continued barefoot, making poor progress on the hot road until the blisters on his feet became calluses.

Discouraged, Hamath sat down on a short section of a rotting log by the side of the road. Two days had passed since he last ate, and he felt incredibly weak. Maybe a nap would be all right, just for a while. He curled up and slept as the sun sank low on the horizon. When he woke the next morning, he saw something moving at the base of the old tree. He pushed the log, rolling it halfway over.

Grubs. Dozens of fat, wriggling grubs. Hamath stared at them, at first in revulsion. On further thought, he decided this could be better than the angry growling in his stomach. Slowly, he picked up one squirming grub, brushed off the dirt, and placed it in his mouth, crunching and swallowing quickly. He ate as many as his stomach could stand, then drank some water, rolled the log back over, and stood.

He wasn't far from home. He had passed through Araba some days before, and now he could finally see, at a great distance, the buildings of Ptolemais and the sea. He would be home in just a few more days.

What if Dorcas won't let me stay? The house had been hers before they married. He felt so unworthy of a home now. Jesus had no home, either. *Not that Jesus was unworthy; he apparently chose to live that way.*

If Dorcas won't accept me back, then I'll try to find Jesus and follow him. But I want so much to see Dorcas and explain. Yet, how can I hope for her forgiveness when I can't justify, even to myself, the things I've done? It's too much to ask of her ... but I'm going to ask anyway.

"Dear God," he prayed aloud, "if I could just see Dorcas and my children again, I would try to make it up to them. And to Sarah."

Two more days passed with no food, and Hamath's steps became slower. He had to stop and rest frequently. Travelers passed him, staying as far away from him as possible. If he approached to ask for food, they turned their backs and held their cloaks over their noses. Hamath hung his head.

One more step. And another. And ... He fell and crawled to the side of the road. He pushed a log over, but found no more grubs. He took the last swallow of water from the skin he carried.

Hamath struggled to his feet and walked on, staggering to the top of a rise on the road. The world spun, and he fell, tumbling over and over until he came to rest against a large rock. Defeated, he closed his eyes and lay motionless in a dirty heap.

A traveler approached and stopped, looking down at Hamath. He lifted his eyes heavenward, then tenderly turned his gaze to the unconscious man. Crouching down, he lifted Hamath onto the back of his donkey and continued on his way.

The next morning, Hamath opened his eyes. He lay beside a small stream with a cloak spread over him. As he pushed himself up, his left arm hung useless and in agony at his side. Raising his head, he blinked and rubbed his eyes. Odd. Where did this cloak come from? And when did I pass Ptolemais? There's Tyre. Or am I dreaming? The morning sun lit the walls of the city as though in welcome. A dried fish and some grapes lay on a cloth beside him.

Thus far, the day had not been a good one. Sarah brushed limp hair away from her sweating cheek and wondered if Paul felt as weary as she did. Tamara's face next to her pillow looked ghostly pale. They had been through a long night, with Tamara's convulsions coming one after another. They'd just finished the midday meal, and Paul was teaching the other children while she took Tamara back to their house to nap.

Sarah had just dropped her own head on the pillow when she heard a knock at the door. Opening the door, she gave a glad cry as she pulled the young man standing there into a hug. "What a glad surprise, Benoni! It's so wonderful to see you! Come in!" The young man looked thinner, a little ... well ... scruffy ... and tired.

"Are you well, Sarah?"

She knew Benoni's gaze was taking in the deep, dark rings under her eyes. "I'm tired, but I'm well. Oh, you must meet Paulos. He's come home."

Tamara walked into the room, rubbing her eyes with one hand and holding her doll with the other. "Benoni, do you remember my daughter, Tamara? Tammy, this is the man who helped me search for Papa when he disappeared."

"Are you the one who has fevers, Tamara?" Benoni asked.

"Yes," Tamara said, yawning. "You couldn't find my papa because he was stolded, but he's back now. Jesus bringed him back to us."

"Jesus did?" Benoni's eyebrows bounced up. "How did he do that? I thought Jesus was in Galilee. Was your papa in Galilee?"

"I don't know," Tamara said. "But he's home, and his leg is all better."

"His leg has healed too? Amazing!"

Sarah laughed. "You would have to talk to Paulos. I'm not sure even he knows exactly where he was, but yes, his leg is mended."

They began the walk through the courtyard. "There is something else new. We've become Jesus's disciples, even as you are."

Benoni hung his head and didn't meet her gaze. "Oh, Sarah, I haven't been following him. I earned my way to freedom by saving my new master's son from a lion stalking the boy. But when I was set free, I didn't go to find Jesus. I followed myself instead."

"But Benoni, you were so enthusiastic for Jesus. What happened? You were a big part of the reason I began believing in him."

"My master was so grateful his son wasn't eaten by the lion that he also gave me fifty pieces of silver. People had been telling me

what to do for so long that I didn't know what to do with myself."
He blushed crimson and glanced at Tammy. "A pretty ... umm ...
woman approached me as I was walking on a road in Damascus. I
spent all the money my master gave me within the next week. When
I had no more coins, she threw me out. I was so ashamed. I didn't
think Jesus would be interested in having me for a disciple after that.

"Now I have nothing. I have to depend on the generosity of
strangers. I went first to the house of Proteus, but no one was there.
I decided to come here in hopes that perhaps you might recommend
me to Hamath. I could be his servant or slave. I didn't do well with
freedom. I guess I'm not wise enough to be on my own in this world."

Sarah put her arm around his shoulders and squeezed. "You're
not the first person to make stupid mistakes, Benoni. Everybody in
this world has done shameful things. The past can't be undone, but
I think it can be forgiven. There's a psalm of King David that Jonas,
a rabbi here, told me about. David had done something far worse
than what you did. He committed adultery with the wife of one
of his soldiers, then gave orders that caused the soldier to be killed
in battle. David wrote down his shame and his repentance in the
psalm. The poem says the sacrifice the Lord really wants is a broken
and contrite heart."

"That fits me. My heart feels like it's broken and bleeding, like it
will never mend. I'd do anything to make my sins up to him."

"Then tell him that. Find yourself a quiet place and tell him
what you did and how you feel."

"But he isn't here. How can I tell him?"

"I don't know how, but Tamara says he can hear you anyway.
Just ask her."

Tamara, who had been petting Keddy, looked up at the sound of
her name. "What, Mama?" she asked.

"Does Jesus hear you when you talk to him, even if he's not here?" Benoni asked her.

"Yes, he hears me, and he talks to me too."

Benoni looked hopeful, or at least a little more so than the woebegone youth who arrived moments earlier.

"Now," said Sarah, "Let's go find Paulos, and then Dorcas. Hamath isn't here, but Dorcas is. Maybe she will hire you or knows of someone else who needs a servant."

She picked up Tamara, and they walked into the villa. Paul was in the great room, preparing lessons for the children. "Paulos, do you remember when I told you about the young man who helped me look for you?"

Paul stood. "The one Proteus sold?"

"Yes. This is Benoni. His new master set him free when he saved the life of the man's son. He's looking for work and wondered if Dorcas might be willing to hire him."

Paul grabbed Benoni's right hand and pumped it. Benoni was obviously bewildered. Paul gave Sarah an "oops!" look.

"A Greek and Roman custom," Sarah said, covering for Paul's modern-age blunder. "It's called a handshake. Some people greet each other this way, especially men when they first meet. You might have seen the image of a handshake on a Roman coin."

"Oh," Benoni replied, "I'll remember that."

The three of them went in search of Dorcas and found Martha instead.

"She isn't here," Martha said. "The mistress went out to look at a piece of jewelry a vendor told her about. The piece is beautiful, so she said—obsidian and gold in the shape of a fish. The vendor said the piece was owned by an Egyptian princess or someone else of royal blood somewhere. Maybe the jewelry belonged to a Babylonian princess or an Egyptian prince. I don't remember. She should be back soon—the mistress, not the Egyptian princess—and I can tell her you wish to speak with her."

Sarah nodded. "Martha, maybe you can help us. Do you remember Benoni, Proteus's slave?"

Martha's face spread in a wide smile. "Oh, yes, of course I remember you, Benoni. Welcome back. Did you come to tell us that Proteus and Thecla are coming back to visit already? Oh dear, I'll need to air out the guest quarters again. Oh, wait. Didn't Proteus sell you to someone else? So, did you bring us other guests? Are you come to give us some other news? Oh, yes … hmm … and you wanted to know if I could help with something?" Martha scarcely took a breath between questions, and her face danced between welcome, consternation, curiosity, and concern.

Benoni's eyes twinkled. "I don't know if they are coming back to visit. Yes, Proteus did sell me to another master. No, I didn't bring any other guests. No, I don't know any other news. And yes, I hope you can help me with something. Do you know if Dorcas wishes to hire any more servants? Or maybe you know another household that needs a servant or slave? I'm in need of a place to eat and sleep."

Martha blushed and chuckled. "Oh, I do chatter on sometimes, don't I? I don't know if the mistress needs more help, but you should ask her. There is another family I heard was looking for a stable boy, but I think they wanted to buy a slave rather than hire a servant. You should ask Dorcas first. And you look like you could use a meal. Come with me." She turned toward the doorway. "There was a bit of food left in the servants' quarters after the midday meal that might sustain you until the evening meal is ready."

Benoni followed the still chatting Martha to the servants' quarters. Paul hugged Sarah, then they went their separate ways, Sarah to prepare the evening meal and Paul to prepare the next morning's lessons.

Chapter 39

By the time Sarah had prepared the evening meal, Dorcas had returned, her new treasure in hand. Sarah admired the piece, turning it over and looking at it from every angle. "This necklace is beautiful, Dorcas. I'm curious: Was it the property of an Egyptian princess or a Babylonian prince? Martha was a little vague on that point."

"Martha told you I went after the necklace?" Dorcas frowned slightly.

"Oh, dear. I'm sure she didn't mean to gossip, and she would know I wouldn't be telling anyone who shouldn't know. You know how talkative she is. When I asked her where you were, she said you'd gone to see a vendor about a piece of jewelry, and so the story continued. Do you remember Benoni, the young slave of your parents?"

"The one who helped you look for Paulos?"

"Yes. Benoni was here the day Paulos disappeared, and the young man went with me the night I searched for my husband. After your father sold Benoni, his new master freed him as a reward for saving his son's life. Benoni found he didn't do well as a free man. He'd rather be a servant or a slave, following orders, so he came here looking for work."

"Do you recommend this young man, Sarah?"

"Yes, I do, even though he acted without thinking after being freed. He's young, and the young don't always act with wisdom, especially when they haven't made many decisions before. When his master gave him fifty shekels, he spent it all foolishly, but it was a lesson well learned. He found he was better at serving than living on his own."

"Not everyone is good at independence, which is perhaps a very good thing, considering nothing would ever get done unless there are also those who serve. So, what can this young man do?"

"He was a litter bearer for your parents, and they trusted him, but other than that I don't know. Would you like to talk to him, Dorcas? Martha took him to find something to eat. He looks like he hasn't eaten well since he was last here."

Moments later, the young man came to her, bowing deeply. "Sarah tells me you wish to talk to me, mistress," he said, eyes lowered.

"And Sarah tells me you're looking for employment. What have you done in the past other than being a litter bearer?"

"I was also a stable boy for your parents, mistress. For my new master, I was to replace his son as a shepherd. His son showed me how to take care of the sheep and where they were to feed, but that ended when the boy's father freed me. When I was ten, my parents sold me into slavery rather than starve, but before that, my father taught me sums. He hoped that would serve me well in the future. So far, I haven't used that skill."

"You are well spoken, Benoni. Have you been taught languages?"

"No, mistress, other than what I've learned from my masters and family. I know Aramaic and Greek and a little of Egyptian and Latin. I learn fast, though. I pick up new words in different languages easily."

"I don't need any more workers now, Benoni, but you may stay here for a time. I'm sure there's room in the servant compound. I'll talk to Martha about that. I may know someone who could use you, but I'll have to talk to him first. If he wants to talk with you, I'll have him come here. Meanwhile, I think you will find your evening meal in the servants' dining area." She smiled at the young man as she dismissed him. He bowed again and left the room.

It's too bad I can't use him here. He tried to help Sarah, and he earned his freedom from his last master. Ah, well, maybe another family can use him. She picked up a candlestick to take to her room. As she turned to leave the dining area, she ran into a man who had come through the door, knocking him to the floor.

Dropping the candlestick, she gasped. "Hamath!"

Chapter 40

Dorcas couldn't stop smiling as she helped Hamath to his feet. He threw his right arm around her and pulled her tight. His left arm hung useless by his side, and he wore a dark bruise that covered one side of his face. He smelled of too many days without bathing, and his tunic was little more than dirty scraps on his emaciated body. She didn't care about the dirt or the smell. He was home.

"Oh, Hamath, where have you been? What happened to you? I've been so worried."

"Please let me sit down, Dorcas, and may I have some food? I'm hungry enough to eat our old rooster, feathers and all."

Dorcas ran to the kitchen. Sarah wasn't in sight, but bread and cheese, covered by a cloth, lay on the work shelf. She placed a knife and the bread and cheese on a platter and hurried back to the table. After slicing the cheese and bread, she returned for a skin of watered wine and a goblet. She placed the food and cup before her husband, resisting the urge to touch him again, to hold on to him. She waited, patient and silent, until he finished eating.

"Would you like for me to have Martha draw a bath for you?"

"I would," he said. "I don't think I've bathed since I left here. You wouldn't believe what's happened, Dorcas."

"Wait here, my love, while I set Martha to heating water." She hurried off to find Martha, locating her in the guest quarters. "Martha, Hamath has returned," she announced joyfully. "He wishes to bathe. Please have a bath drawn for him and lay out a clean set of clothes."

"Oh, mistress! How, um ... how nice. You must be so pleased to have him back." Martha smiled. "I'll have the slaves begin heating and hauling the water now."

Dorcas nodded and turned to go back to Hamath. "Yes, do," she said over her shoulder.

When Dorcas returned, he was nearly asleep at the table, his head resting on his good arm. His other arm hung straight down.

"Hamath, please wake up and talk to me. Your arm—do you need a physician?"

Hamath nodded. "My arm hurts, and I can't move it. I don't know what's wrong. I fell ... I think."

"Do you feel like talking?"

"I'm tired, but I want to tell you what happened, and then you can decide whether you will allow me to stay." He dropped his eyes to the table.

"What do you mean? What happened after you left here?"

"The story is terrible, but with some good too. When I left to look for Paulos, you remember I took Enoch? Well, we no longer have Enoch." Hamath's moist eyes focused on the table. "He was killed in Jerusalem. We traveled without incident to that city, arriving in less than a week. We went to an inn for lodging and food, then began searching for Bildad, the slave monger.

"A man called Jesus was there in Jerusalem. He's amazing. I listened to him, and I felt like he spoke just to me, though I was part of a crowd. I had the strangest feeling, as though he could see inside of me. He could have condemned me with what he was seeing, but instead he just looked at me with sad eyes. He spoke of blessings to peacemakers, and I thought of the times I created turmoil here in my own home. He talked about blessings to the poor in spirit, and I thought of my arrogance. Jesus gave blessings to the merciful, and I thought of my cruelties, especially to Paulos. He mentioned blessings to those who mourn, and I thought about how I treated Sarah when she was mourning Paulos's disappearance. He spoke of blessings for the meek, and I thought of how I looked down on everyone. And he said there would be blessings for those who hunger for righteousness, and I thought of how unconcerned I was of whether I acted rightly or not. I couldn't help myself. I told him I was sorry. I was way back in the crowd, whispering, but he heard, and he forgave me. I know this isn't making much sense; maybe I can talk more sensibly later." He shook his head and choked on a sob.

Dorcas sat back on her chair in astonishment. Her Hamath, weeping!

His shoulders shook for a time and then remained slumped. Dorcas waited, silent. At last he lifted his head.

"We stayed at the inn in Jerusalem while we searched for Bildad. Two days later, we found him. I told him who I was and that I wanted to buy Paulos back from him. He became angry. He ordered his men to grab me, saying Paulos had died and I must take his place. Enoch tried to defend me and was killed. They took me captive. Dorcas, I did try to find Paulos. I'm so sorry that he died, and Enoch too. That really wasn't in my shortsighted plan ... Why are you smiling?"

Hamath didn't wait for her to respond before continuing, his words nearly tripping over themselves. "Bildad made me a slave.

They put me in shackles, fed me weak broth and gruel, and beat me when I didn't do things exactly to their pleasure. Several days ago, Bildad set me free. He paid me thirty pieces of silver for Enoch and almost shoved me out the door. He kept my beautiful horses, though, and didn't pay for them."

"We have other horses. Although I wish Enoch hadn't died, it gratifies me to know how courageous he was." She motioned for him to continue.

"Bildad said something about the horses not being part of the bargain with a ghost, whatever that meant. But I was free. I didn't want to protest too much, because he might change his mind. After thieves stole the coins he gave me, I began to walk home, depending on the charity of others for food. I was so hungry; I even ate locusts and grubs."

He ran his hands through his hair. "Yesterday I passed out. I don't know if I fainted from hunger or if I fell. At least, I think it was yesterday, except that I don't remember passing Ptolemais. I woke up at dawn. Somebody had covered me with this cloak, and I was just across the causeway from here."

Hamath dropped to his knees in front of her. "I have failed you, Dorcas. Not just this time, but so many other times over the years. Please, will you forgive me? And may I stay?"

Dorcas wept. "Oh Hamath, I've wished so often I could take those words back about Paulos. Yes, you are home, and I hope you are home to stay. But before you take your bath, come with me."

She helped him to his feet and led him to the children's play room, where Paulos sat cross-legged on the floor with his back to them, telling a story to the children. Darius, Gideon, and Orphah jumped up. "Papa?" Orphah ran to him. The boys, not quite so demonstrative, were smiling and coming toward him..

Paulos turned his head toward Dorcas and Hamath.

Hamath gasped. "Paulos?"

"Who ... Oh, uh, hello, Hamath," Paul said, as he stood up. "Bildad said something about having his revenge on you, and I feared he might have killed you. But I guess he must have captured and then freed you. Good."

"You're not dead! And you're here. And your leg ..."

"Yes, sir. I'm alive and well."

"Bildad said you were dead! How is it that you live? I'm so glad you're alive!" He grasped Paul's shoulder with his good hand.

"So am I, but it's just as well Bildad keeps thinking I'm dead. I appeared to him as a 'ghost' a little over a month ago and ordered him to free all the people he kidnapped and enslaved. We hoped you'd be home much sooner. Dorcas has been anxious for you to get here. I'm thankful you were freed and are home."

Dorcas nodded, her happiness bubbling like a fresh-water spring.

"So that's what happened. Mine is a long story, Paulos, and yours must be as well. Perhaps tomorrow we should talk. Meanwhile, a bath has been drawn for me, and then I think I'll sleep for a long time."

"As you wish, sir," Paulos replied.

Hamath waited in their chambers for his bath. Dorcas returned to the dining area and sent Martha for Benoni. When he arrived, she asked, "Would you like to be Hamath's personal servant? That means you'd be responsible for helping him bathe, seeing that his clothes are clean and ready for him, and following any orders he may give you. If necessary, you must be willing to lay your life down for him if he should be in danger."

"Oh, yes, mistress, I'd be happy to be his servant, and I promise to protect him with my last breath, should that ever be needed. Thank you." He knelt and bowed his head to her feet.

"Good. Your first job is to get one of our servants or slaves—any of them, they all know the way—to go for Nicolas the physician. Anyone but Sarah, that is. Then, you will go to Hamath's quarters to help him bathe."

"Yes, mistress, as you wish," he said. He stood, turned on his heels, and ran toward the servants' quarters.

She smiled. *Well, that's a good start. There doesn't appear to be anything lazy about this young man.*

Dorcas made her way to their room, where Hamath had submerged himself in the hot water.

Chapter 41

Sarah had been searching through the dugout for a piece of cod to prepare for the evening meal with Tammy close by. When they returned to the kitchen, some of the food was missing. *That's odd. I know I left more cheese and bread out. Ah, well, no matter. Maybe someone got hungry and wanted a snack. There's more cheese in the dugout, and what bread is left should stretch through the evening meal.*

Paul joined her. "Hello, wife." He pulled her close and nibbled on her ear.

"Paul, the other servants! Whatever will they think?" She giggled and glanced around. No one was within sight, except for Tamara playing with Keddy.

"They will think I have the most beautiful wife in the world and that I'm the luckiest man in Tyre. By the by, my dear, Hamath has returned."

She made a face. "Oh. Well, at least Dorcas will be happy."

"The children seem happy too." Paul sobered. "You know, I could be wrong, but I think there might be a change in Hamath. Other than the fact that he is in sorry shape—one arm is hurt, he's badly bruised, he's thin, and he and his clothes are filthy and smelly—he behaved differently, taking into consideration, of course, that my recollections of him are not all that clear. Sort of like remembering a dream … not that he's much of a dreamboat. Unlike the dreamboat standing here next to me."

"That would be a nice change … in Hamath, I mean. I hope you're right."

The evening meal went well. Hamath wasn't there.

"My husband is in our bed chamber. I'll carry a platter to him when we're finished eating," Dorcas said. "His arm was dislocated, and by the time Nicolas was able to put the shoulder back in place, Hamath was nauseated and exhausted. He didn't feel like eating."

"I'm happy for you that he's back, Dorcas." Sarah didn't miss seeing Hamath. Tomorrow might even be too soon.

That night, Tamara convulsed again. The seizures went on for a longer time and occurred on and off throughout the night. Paul and Sarah took turns keeping cool, wet cloths on the child's head and stomach. She was convulsing too often to let her chew the bark, so Sarah boiled some tea for her. By morning, Paul and Sarah were both exhausted, but Tamara had at last dropped into a natural sleep.

"You stay here with Tammy. Okay, honey?" Sarah whispered. "Catch a few more winks while I make breakfast. I'll bring a tray back here, but I won't wake you. Then I'll take the children for a hike in the hills. They can afford to miss one lesson."

Paul nodded. "That sounds like heaven for me, but when will *you* rest?"

"I'll lie down for a while after lunch. You'll have your turn with the kids then. I just felt Tammy's head, and she's cooler this morning. Still, I think we should keep her in here today. What do you think?"

"Let's wait and see," he said, rising on his elbow. "Sometimes she's better for a few hours during the day. We should be able to tell by lunchtime."

"True. I'll bring lunch over later, and we'll see how she is then." She bent over and kissed him. "Sleep tight, lovey."

Sarah entered the cooking area just as Hamath came out of the house. She turned and braced herself, but he stopped about six feet—um, four cubits—from her.

He bowed his head and said, "I have an apology for you, Sarah." He almost sounded humble.

Her face must have echoed her astonishment. Hamath smiled a small, inoffensive smile. "I should not have treated you as I did. I'm sorry, and it won't happen again. Paulos's disappearance was my fault, and I'm sorry for that too. I'm happy he's back and well. I hope you will forgive me."

Sarah's mouth gaped even further. Closing her mouth with a snap but unable to speak for a moment, she finally cleared her throat. "I will forgive you, Hamath." Maybe not at this precise moment, though. "Dorcas is very happy you've returned, sir."

Hamath nodded. "Yes, she is, which is amazing all by itself. And I'm happy to be here. For a time, I didn't think I'd ever see home again, or that I'd be welcome if I did. I give thanks that Paulos is alive despite my terrible decisions. I had a lot of time to think over the past months. Obviously, I didn't do much of that before. Now I know what a wonderful, loyal wife I have and what beautiful children. I wasn't as good to them as I should have been. I want to change that."

Sure. I'll believe that when pigs fly.

"Dorcas told me how helpful you and Paulos have been to her and the children. You even started a search for me. I'm humbled and grateful, even though the search was unsuccessful." Hamath turned to leave.

Humbled? Grateful? Should she give him another chance, as Dorcas was apparently doing?

"Sir?" Sarah said. He turned back toward her. "Let's start out with a clean slate—that is, let's start all over again. As though the past never happened."

"I'd like that. Now please excuse me. Is Paulos around?"

"He and Tamara are resting. She had a fever most of the night, and we were both up all night trying to cool her off. This morning after breakfast, I'll take the other children for a hike. Paulos will be here after the midday meal. He'll continue their lessons then."

"I want to talk to him about what he did to Bildad to make that evil man give up his slaves."

"The story is a good one, sir. He'll enjoy telling you."

"Would you mind if I kept the children with me today, instead of you taking them on a hike? I'm not quite ready to go walking yet, but I'd like very much to have them around me. I've missed them."

"No, not at all." She shook her head. Wow.

Hamath went back into the house, whistling for Keddy. Sarah stared after him.

Once breakfast was out of the way, Sarah walked to the marketplace. She needed some spices, and with Hamath back plus Benoni and his teenage appetite now with them, they would need more supplies. Besides, she should let Jonas know that Hamath had returned and ask if he had word yet of Mariah.

A light breeze blew from the sea, heavy with moisture and the smell of fish. By the gathering clouds, rain seemed likely.

When she arrived at the marketplace, she noticed Jonas's drawn face. His eyes, usually sparkling with humor and goodwill, instead looked haunted and unhappy with new lines around his eyes and mouth. So many people had returned, but apparently not Mariah.

"Good morning, Jonas." She glanced around for Dathan. "Has your son already left?"

"Shalom, Sarah. No, Dathan stayed home today. My sister, Miriam, is fevered this morning, and Dathan stayed to help her. If Paulos will bring the day's lessons to me, I'll make sure my son completes them."

"Actually, I'm glad he didn't go. Paulos is getting some rest this morning. Tamara, too. She had a bad night, and none of us got much sleep."

"Ah, that explains the dark circles under your eyes, my friend."

"*My* eyes have dark circles?" she said. "You should see your own, Jonas."

"Is it so obvious, then?"

"I'm afraid so."

"I fear for Mariah's life. Sometimes slave masters can be cruel, and slave lives are cheap. Especially if that slave master got her for nothing." His mouth twisted down.

"I know you're worried, Jonas, but we won't give up hope. Are there others still waiting?"

"Yes, but very few. Most of the missing have returned. There may be a few who perhaps wouldn't wish to come back, and some have spouses who don't want them back. A few husbands have since remarried. Then again, if slaves are well-treated, they might choose not to leave their masters, even if a chance comes to be free. Some women even become wives of their masters. Maybe that's what happened with Mariah. Did she choose to stay with a new master? I might never know." He scrubbed at his eyes with a sleeve.

Sarah said nothing, letting him regain control of himself.

He took a deep breath. "If that's what's happened, I want her to be happy. I don't want her to be sorrowful."

"I know how hard this is for you, Jonas. I wish I could help. If it provides any comfort to know that someone grieves with you, please remember that Paulos and I do. Also, I wanted to let you know Hamath has returned. He's acting different. He even apologized for the way he treated me and for selling Paulos into slavery."

Jonas raised a skeptical eyebrow. "Hamath apologized? Somehow, this doesn't seem like something Hamath would do, no matter how offensively he behaved. Are you sure he was serious, or are you even positive it is him?"

"He looks like a thin version of Hamath, and his voice is the same. Whether words will be matched by actions is yet to be seen." She lifted her hand to push hair back under her scarf. "I need to get back. Dorcas will be trying to feed Hamath back to his old corpulent self. He must have been starved during his absence."

"Hamath, thin? That's hard to visualize, especially in view of the relatively short time he was gone. Be well, Sarah. And be wary of your master. I have trouble believing he's changed so completely."

Chapter 42

Sarah hadn't much more than put away the day's purchases and begun the midday meal when Dorcas walked into the cooking area. "Thank you for recommending Benoni. Hamath likes him, and so do I. The boy hastens to help whenever asked, he looks for work when he might otherwise remain idle, and he's conscientious and honest. He even found a silver coin behind a chest of clothing and handed it to Hamath. Some would have secreted the coin away."

Sarah smiled. "That sounds like him. Martha told me that yesterday when he finished eating the scraps left from lunch—and yes, he ate all of them—he cleaned up the room, then asked one of the stable boys if he wanted some help."

With Tamara nestled on his shoulder, Paul approached the two women. "Good morning, ladies."

"Shalom, Paulos and Tamara. My goodness, little one, you look so pale. Did you have a fever last night?" Dorcas raised her hand and brushed back the little girl's hair, feeling her forehead.

The usually perky Tamara just nodded, one thumb in her mouth. Sarah glanced at Paul, and reached up to stroke Tamara's cheek. "Would you like a bit of cheese, Tammy?" she asked.

Tamara shook her head and closed her eyes.

Dorcas spoke up. "I'm sending for Nicolas."

Sarah opened her mouth to protest, but Dorcas was already leaving the room.

Paul's gaze met Sarah's, and he shrugged. "What can we do? There's no hospital. Even if there were, I don't think they could help."

Not trusting herself to speak, Sarah could only nod. She cleared her throat and asked, "Tammy, would you drink some juice if I made some for you?"

Tamara opened her eyes slightly. "'kay," she said, her voice barely above a whisper.

Sarah picked up a cluster of grapes from the table. Wrapping them in a thin cloth, she mashed them in a bowl with a pestle, then poured the juice into a cup. With trembling fingers, she held the cup to Tamara's mouth.

Tammy drank all the juice and licked her lips. She laid her head back on Paul's shoulder, her eyes closing.

"I'll bring you some lunch as soon as I've fed the family," she said. "I'll make Tammy some more juice. How does that sound?"

"No more juice, Mama. I want to sleep some more."

"Stay awake for a little while, Tammy," Paul said. "Nicolas is coming to see you today. Then you may go back to sleep."

Sarah watched as her husband carried their child back through the gate. *God, please ...*

Dorcas returned to the kitchen. "I sent Benoni because I knew he'd run, and they're already back. Did Paul take Tamara to your house?"

Sarah nodded. "They just left." She finished serving and cleaning up, and then hurried home, carrying food and drink for Nicolas, Paul, Tammy, and herself.

Nicolas sat on the floor next to Paul, who held Tamara on his lap. The physician glanced up at her. "This looks good, Sarah, thank you."

The adults ate in silence. Tamara ate a miniscule bite of lamb and drank a sip of the broth.

Nicolas finished first. He stroked Tammy's hair. "Perhaps you'd like to take a nap now?" he asked.

"Yes."

Paul pushed the curtain aside, took her into the next room, and laid her on her pallet, pulling the lamb's wool blanket over her shoulders. The child lay limp, her eyes already closed.

As Paul returned, Nicolas looked down at his hands before raising moist eyes to gaze at them. "Tamara is seriously ill. You know that. I wish I could give you good news, but I don't want to tell you pleasant lies. I'm afraid Tamara won't live much longer, maybe a day or a week, perhaps as much as two weeks. You must prepare yourselves. I don't know how to help her. She's too weak."

Her heart aching, Sarah searched his face for any hope. "Isn't there anything more we can do?"

He lowered his gaze back to his hands. "All I can tell you is to keep her warm when she is not fevered, and place cool, wet cloths on her body when she is. Give her willow bark or tea. Try to get her to eat meats and fruit. Meat broth would be good. Even so, though you might prolong the inevitable, I fear the end will be the same."

Paul nodded. "We've thought so too. Thank you for your efforts, Nicolas, even though you haven't been able to find a cure."

Nicolas opened his mouth as though to speak, but instead he lifted his hand in farewell and left.

Paul looked at Sarah. "There is one more thing we can do that we, or at least I, haven't done yet. We can pray."

"I *have* prayed," Sarah said. "Still, Jonas says God is not offended by more than one prayer for the same thing." Together they knelt on the rock floor, and with hearts filled with pain, they poured out their hopes to God.

Chapter 43

The next morning, Sarah let Tamara sit with the other children while they had their lessons. She'd eaten a little breakfast. Even though she had suffered only one short convulsion during the night, she was far from her former bouncy self.

Soon after Sarah had cleaned up the morning meal, she heard a knock at the front door. Martha answered and brought the guests to the children's room, where Sarah sat holding Tamara while Paul taught the lesson.

"Jonas, Dathan, please join us." Paul rose to his feet and held out his hands.

Sarah's grinned. Jonas had more than just Dathan with him.

"Not today, dear friends, not today." Jonas beamed. "I just came to share our good news. Mariah has returned. He reached behind him and gently pulled a petite, blushing woman forward. "And she has some new additions to our family, Ezra and Zillah. I'm going to adopt them so there will be no doubt about them also being mine."

Two small children clung to Mariah's tunic, both staring, their thumbs in their mouths. "Ezra is two years old, and Zillah is three. Are they not as beautiful as their mother?" Jonas's smile couldn't have been much broader.

Dathan stood silent, his eyes darting from his mother to the two new siblings.

Mariah spoke with a soft voice. "Jonas told me a man named Paulos was responsible for our freedom. Are you that man?"

Paul nodded, smiling at the whole family. "I am Paulos. Jonas has been anxious for you to return. And he bears as much credit as I do for your freedom."

"I thank you, sir. You are our savior."

Paul shook his head. "I won't claim that title, Mariah, but I'm happy to be your friend. Jonas has been a good friend, and he's talked of you so often I feel as though I know you."

Paul bent to pick up a fallen quill, and the two younger children tore behind their mother. "Shh, it's all right," she whispered, "He won't hurt you."

Sarah's heart ached for the poor little ones.

Paul dropped to his knees and held his hand out to them. "I'm sorry, Zillah and Ezra. I didn't mean to scare you."

"It will take them a while to trust you. Or any man. They only have experience with men who are evil." She knelt and pulled the trembling little ones close to her.

Paul nodded and turned back to Jonas. "I've been doing some thinking, my friend. You have more contacts than I do. What if we formed a group of those who have returned, along with their families? Maybe even include the ones whose family members haven't returned, if they would like. It might help for people to talk about their experiences, to know they aren't alone in their troubles in readjusting."

Mariah stood. Ezra pressed his face against her neck, while Zillah clung to Mariah's leg. "While I was a slave, I saw some that I knew. We weren't allowed to speak, but sometimes we communicated by other means when the guards weren't watching. At night, I'd often hear weeping. Bildad rented us out to people wanting almost anything, from nursemaids to cooks. We weren't always treated with kindness. Although some of the renters treated us well, most didn't." She set Ezra back on his feet, patting his head.

Jonas pinched his lips, glancing down and then back up at Paul. "I'll make some contacts. Many of the people are Jews. Those who are could meet at my home on the Sabbath after the midday meal. Most of my rabbinical duties are finished by then. My house is central to Tyre, and people wouldn't have to walk far, no matter where they live in the village."

Paul stood. "Jonas, what about those who aren't Jews?"

He glanced down and a small scowl flitted across his face. "I'm sorry. We aren't allowed to invite gentiles into our homes. I would like to include all, of course, but as a rabbi, I must obey our laws."

"We're not Jews either, Jonas." Sarah said softly. "I think we believe a lot of the same things, but Paulos, Tamara, and I are not of your religion. Neither are Hamath and Dorcas."

Jonas shifted from one foot to the other, frowning at the floor. "Let me think and pray about this."

Dorcas came into the room, Hamath right behind her. "Did I hear our names? Oh, Jonas, this must be your wife!"

Jonas cleared his throat. "Yes. Dorcas and Hamath, this is my wife, Mariah. She brought two new members for our family, Ezra and Zillah."

Dorcas knelt in front of the two toddlers. "Hello, Ezra and Zillah. Are you happy to be home?"

They both hid their faces in their mother's tunic.

"Forgive them, please, madam. They're very shy," Jonas said. "They haven't even come to either Dathan or me yet."

Tamara rose from Sarah's lap and walked over to the two. "It's all right," she said to Zillah, who peeked at her with one eye. "Everybody is nice here. Nobody's mean. Do you want to play?"

Ezra shook his head, retreating behind Mariah. Zillah just looked at Tammy, wide-eyed and watchful.

Orphah ran up beside Tammy, and Zillah stepped back, ready to flee.

"We have a puppy. Do you like puppies?" Orphah asked.

Zillah shook her head hard. She held her hands up, silently pleading with her mother to save her from all these people.

Mariah knelt and put her arms around her children. Looking up at Jonah, she murmured, "May we go now?"

Jonas shifted his weight. "Um, Paulos, maybe we could talk tomorrow?"

Paul nodded. "I'll come to the marketplace after the lessons are finished."

"Yes. Well, it was good seeing you all." Jonas hurried his family out the door.

When the door shut behind Jonas's family, Hamath commented, "Hm. That was awkward. Did we offend them? What happened?"

"You didn't do anything, sir," Paul said. "I might have, though."

Dorcas gave Paul a quizzical look.

"I suggested that the families whose loved ones were missing and now are returned might like to get together and share their experiences. Jonas liked the idea and offered his house, but when we reminded him your family and ours aren't Jewish, the conversation became suddenly strained."

"Why?"

Sarah stood. "Jonas is a Jewish rabbi. The Jewish law says that if a gentile—that is, someone not of their faith—enters a Jewish home, that home becomes unclean until the next day. As a rabbi, he has to be especially careful to follow the law."

"Really? Hmm," Dorcas said, a thoughtful light coming into her eyes. "Hamath, what do you think? Could we host this gathering of families?"

Hamath rocked back on his heels and shook his head. "Absolutely not. Would you want a band of dirty stragglers ... ah, well, maybe we should. I was one of those dirty stragglers, wasn't I?" A sheepish grin brushed across his reddening face, and chuckles rippled among the adults in the room.

Chapter 44

The following day, Paul walked to the marketplace after completing the lessons. Maybe Tyre wasn't as hot as Phoenix, but the heat, combined with the humidity, left his tunic soaked with sweat, maybe like Phoenix nights during the monsoon season. He could use a cool swimming pool. Or air conditioning.

"Ah! Paulos, my friend. Come into the shade."

"Happily," Paul said, stepping under the wide awning covering Jonas's materials.

Jonas set down the roll of fabric in his hands. "About yesterday. I'm distressed. I slept little last night, I'm afraid. I feel like a hypocrite! We have a servant who is not Jewish, Arbah, yet she lives with us. Several others in the synagogue also have gentile servants. Our law also says we should welcome the stranger and treat him like family. So, why is it all right to have a gentile servant, but not non-Jewish guests, whether strangers or not? I will raise this question at our synagogue on the Sabbath."

"Would you and Mariah come Saturday afternoon to Dorcas and Hamath's for the gathering?" Paul asked.

Jonas ran a hand through his hair. "I've invited all the ones I know of who are Jews to my home. If it weren't on the Sabbath, my Jewish friends would probably quickly ignore the ban on gentiles coming into a kosher home. I'm in a thorny position as their rabbi. However, if things go as I hope, we should be able to combine the two groups next time."

"I understand your dilemma. Sarah does too, but Hamath and Dorcas might feel like they've been slighted."

Jonas winced. "What can I do to make it up to them? I'm not being the person I want to be. I'm ashamed, but I have to obey the law."

"Maybe you could send the ones you know who aren't Jewish to Dorcas and Hamath's?"

"I can do that. I know plenty. Several gentiles were there to help with your ghostly presentation."

Paul nodded. "That sounds good. I hope your conversations with your Jewish friends go well. Now, I need to return to my home. May peace attend you, Jonas." He held out his hand, and Jonas grasped it for a moment.

"Shalom to you too, Paulos."

A few people began arriving around dusk. Paul didn't know many of them, but Dorcas seemed to. Some apparently worked at their dye production plant; others must have been acquainted some other way. When all had settled, most sitting on the ground, Hamath welcomed them and introduced Paulos as one who had been kidnapped and had returned.

Paul stood and thanked Hamath, and then turned to those who stared at him—some with apprehension, others with hostility.

One man spat on the ground, eyeing Paul with suspicion. "You're the one who magically appeared inside the gate, aren't you? Are you a sorcerer?"

"No. I'm just an ordinary man. What's your name?"

"I'm Abram. My wife is one who was taken." He tipped his head toward the woman, obviously pregnant, who sat beside him."

"All of us are either people who were abducted by Bildad or part of the families of those enslaved. Some of you—or maybe all of you—are having nightmares, sometimes waking nightmares. You might wake up screaming, or you might be pushing your spouse away from you. You might even be fighting with or running away from your spouse. I just wanted to tell you what you're experiencing is common to almost all of us."

The crowd murmured in agreement.

Paul nodded. "Those of you who want to say something about your experience may do so. If you don't want to, don't worry. No one will be forced to talk. I'll begin because I'm one of you, and I've found that talking about the experience helps me get over some of my anxious feelings. My wife has been understanding, but since I've been back—just a few weeks now—she's gotten a few bruises because I'm often swinging my arms at night."

Sarah nodded, and she lifted the sleeve of her cloak to show them a bruise on one wrist. A few smiled and chuckled.

The next person to stand was a woman of perhaps thirty. One side of her face was scarred, her eye on that side looked milky, and her hair was more gray than brown.

"My name is Shalisha. I came home to find my husband has died. We had no children, and my parents died many years ago. I have no one. I don't know what to do. Is there a possibility any of you might have work for me? I know how to do most things needed in a home."

Hamath whispered something to Dorcas, then turned to the woman. "We have need of someone who can wash clothes and sew. Our housemaid is getting older and her hands are stiff. If you're able to do these things, we can use your help."

Martha, carrying a tray of cheese and wine to a table in the courtyard, opened her mouth. "But I ..."

Dorcas cut her off. "Now, Martha, you know you could use some help."

Several surprised gazes had turned in Hamath's direction. Paul suspected Hamath wasn't known for his kindness toward unattractive women.

Shalisha smiled gratefully. "I can do these things."

Another man stood. "I'm Ethan. I was betrothed when I was taken six years ago, but now my intended bride has wed someone else. I built a room for us on my father's home, but instead the room is now occupied by my grandmother. My parents say I have gone mad, and maybe they're right. They don't want me to stay, and I have no place to live." He flushed. "I've been sleeping behind your stables, Hamath."

Dorcas cleared her throat. "I'm sure they have a hard time understanding. Hamath, we have need of another man for dye production, don't we? Can you work in a place that smells like dead clams?"

"I can, lady."

"Then meet my husband tomorrow morning at the dye plant." She glanced at Hamath, who nodded.

Abram stood again, his chin jutted forward. "My wife is with child by another man. I would divorce her, but we have other children who need someone to watch over them and feed them. I suppose you think I should keep her."

Paul shrugged. "What did you do while she was missing?"

Abram flushed. "I married another woman. I assumed Norah was dead. When Norah came back, Hagar was furious and went back to her parent's home."

"Do you hate Norah?"

"She slept with another man. I would be justified in putting her aside."

Paul persisted. "Do you hate Norah and love Hagar?"

"What does that matter? My children need a mother."

"Who do your children want?"

"I am their father, and they will have who I say."

Paul blew out a breath. "So, who do you say? Who would God say you should have?"

"God? What has a god to do with my judgment? I could have her stoned, and no god would object."

With each of her husband's pronouncements, Norah shrank farther away from him, tears squeezing out of frightened eyes.

Sarah rose from where she'd been sitting, Tammy nestled on one shoulder. Fury laced Sarah's voice. "Norah, come with me. You deserve better than this beast."

Abram whirled and grabbed the front of Sarah's tunic. "Shut up, woman!" He shoved her, and she fell, twisting her body so Tamara wouldn't be crushed.

Paul grabbed the man's shoulder, turned him around, and landed a blow on his chin.

Abram dropped to the ground.

Paul stepped to Sarah's side, shaking the hand that had connected with Abram's chin. He helped her to her feet and took Tammy, who had started crying. "Are you hurt?

"I'm not. Tammy, are you all right?"

"Yes. Why did that bad man push us?" She sniffled, reaching for her mother.

Paul handed her back to Sarah.

Abram had gotten back to his feet. "Why did you hit me?" He lifted his hands, apparently ready to continue the battle.

Dorcas and Hamath had both rushed to Sarah's side. Dorcas turned to Abram, the icicles in her voice enough to freeze a forest fire. "Leave our villa. You are no longer welcome here."

Abram harrumphed. "Wife, we're leaving." He reached for Norah, but Dorcas was quicker, stepping between them.

"She may stay. You are the one who must leave. And I do mean now." She pointed toward the gate, and when Hamath and Paulos stepped to her side, Abram closed his mouth and stomped away.

Norah began sobbing, and Sarah wrapped her free arm around the woman's shoulders.

Dorcas turned to face them. "Norah, you're welcome to stay here. We have a place for you."

"B-but my children. What can I do? Barak and Shelah are without a mother. What if he brings that other woman back? She doesn't love them. She beats them if they don't eat, if they talk when she doesn't think they should, even if they cry. Sometimes *he* beats them too. I must go to them. Better that he vents his anger on me than on them, and better than if he brings Hagar back."

Hamath scoffed. "He doesn't deserve to be a father or a husband. What if we take the children from him?"

Dorcas shook her head. "The law won't let us do that, Hamath."

Norah brushed away her tears. "Then I must go. Thank you for your kindness, but my children need me." She bowed her head to them, turned, and walked out the open gate.

Silence followed her departure. Several of the guests exchanged glances.

Paul made a wry face. "Are any of you neighbors of Abram?"

"We are," a man said from the back of the group. The brawny man and his sweet-looking wife stood up.

"Would you be willing to watch over Norah and the children and give them protection if Abram goes on a rampage?"

"Gladly. He's as cruel as his father was before him. I don't want any harm to come to his wife and children."

Hamath turned to face the man. "If they need a place of safety, you may bring them here."

Paul sighed. "I'm sure not many of the returned were greeted so sadly. Has anyone else a story of their homecoming?"

Lots of murmuring, but apparently no one else wanted to offer anything.

"Would you like to meet again? Dorcas and Hamath told me they will gladly host you for as often as you want to meet."

Ethan cleared his throat. "There was also a meeting today at the home of that Jew, Jonas. Why didn't they come here?"

Paul rubbed his forehead. "The reason has to do with their religious laws. We wanted to meet all together, but because he is one of the religious leaders, he couldn't. He knew that many people of his synagogue would also not feel free to meet here, especially on their Sabbath, so he offered another choice to them. We—Jonas and I—hope to overcome the prohibitions so everyone can meet at one place."

"Huh. I got the feeling they thought they were better than we are and so wouldn't meet with us."

Paul lifted one shoulder. "I don't know. There may be some that think that way, but over the past months my wife and I have become good friends with Jonas. You know he was one who helped get the slaves freed, right?"

Ethan's eyebrows lifted. "No, I didn't know that."

"Many people participated in convincing Bildad to release the slaves. Some of them were Jews, and some were not. We worked together. Jonas, Dorcas, and Sarah, and many of you." He swept his arm to indicate everyone. "We had a part, remember?"

Those who had helped nodded, some grinning and elbowing each other.

"What do you think? Shall we meet and talk again?"

Again, nods from most there.

"All right. On Sunday evening, then?"

Chapter 45

The next day Paul hurried to the marketplace early, hoping Jonas would be there with good news.

Jonas greeted Paul with a broad smile. "Shalom, friend!"

"Good morning. Shalom to you too. How did your meeting go yesterday?"

"It went even better than expected. People were happy to talk about their return. Not so willing to talk about the troubles, though. I tried to get Mariah to begin that part of it, but she was too shy. How was yours?"

"Ah. Well, I knocked a guy on his keister and nearly started a brawl, but otherwise fine."

"Keister?"

"Onto his buttocks. The idiot shoved Sarah down. That would have been bad enough, but it was while she was holding Tammy."

"Hm. Your meeting might have been more interesting than mine. Are Sarah and Tamara all right?"

"Yes, they're fine. This guy, Abram by name, couldn't seem to make up his mind which wife he wanted. He remarried after his first wife was kidnapped, but it sounded like all he really wanted was someone to take care of his children."

"Oh ... Abram. I know him. I tried to warn both Norah and Hagar's parents of his quick temper and tendency for viciousness, but neither listened. He must have offered a good bride price."

"Someone mentioned you were also having a meeting and wondered if we gentiles weren't good enough, but I think I set them straight. Did your friends agree you could meet with us?"

"Some yes, some not enthused. The ones against had no one who had been kidnapped and returned, if that means anything. Nor did they come to the gathering at my home. I'm going to say we should all meet together, just not on the Sabbath. In addition, we can stay in the courtyard. A lot of the Pharisees sometimes stretch the limit of the law, and if we're in the courtyard, we're not technically in the home."

"I invited ours back on Sunday evening. How does that sound?"

"Fully acceptable to me. I'll spread the word. If this works without raising the hackles of our elders, the one after that can be at my villa."

"Perfect. I need to get back home now, Jonas. I'm glad you had a positive meeting and that we'll all meet together before long."

"That will indeed be a blessing. Go with God, friend." Jonas waved and resumed his work.

Sunday dawned cloudy and threatening rain. The weather suited their moods. Paul and Sarah were exhausted; Tamara, weaker. She had again spent the night with a high fever and seizures.

"Maybe we should stay here and not join the others for the meeting." Paul cast a worried glance at their child.

"No, you started the idea for the meeting, and you're the only one with training in counseling. You have to go," Sarah said. "I'll stay here with her."

"Some counselor, slugging the first guy who expressed the wrong opinion."

She laughed. "You came to my rescue. How could I fault my knight in shining armor? So, you go. Tammy and I will stay home."

Tamara shook her head, her gaze passing back and forth between them. "I have to go too. There will be kids there like Ezra and Zillah, and they need me. They're scared of grownups."

Paul hesitated, wanting to say no but knowing she was right. "All right, but I don't want you out of my sight. And if you start feeling bad, tell me or tell Mama."

"Okay, Papa," she said, her eyes brightening a little. She walked into her room and came back with her doll.

Tamara rested at home until time to go. Paul carried her into the courtyard. The morning had produced some rain showers, but now the skies were clear. Paul guessed the temperature must be close to sixty-five degrees. When the three arrived, only Hamath, Dorcas, their children, and their servants were there, but it was still early. Dorcas had set out fruit and bread in case their guests wanted to eat.

The crowd arrived soon after. Several children played, but most of them clung to their mothers. Although Mariah's two were among those clinging, Paul noticed them watching others who were laughing and playing with Keddy. The pup was ecstatic to have so many playmates.

He put Tamara down. "You may sit by Jonas's children," he whispered. Tamara nodded and sat on the log beside the two smaller children, apparently satisfied with her small mission field.

Tamara showed Zillah her doll. "This is my baby," she said. "Her name is Abigail, and I call her Abby. Do you want to hold her?"

Zillah held out her hand—the one that wasn't attached to her mouth—and took the doll. She looked puzzled about how she should hold the doll. Then she took her thumb out of her mouth and cradled the doll with both arms.

Ezra leaned toward them. "Bebee?" he asked Tamara, whispering around his own firmly entrenched thumb, pointing with his other hand.

Tamara grinned at him. "Yes. That's my baby."

"Bebee ... me?" This time the question was directed to his sister.

"Maybe," Zillah whispered back. "Be nice?"

"Nithe," Ezra agreed, taking the doll and cradling it like he had seen his sister do, except holding the doll bottom side up.

Tamara giggled. "Hold her head up," she said, turning the doll around.

"Uf." Ezra nodded. He patted the doll and rocked.

Paul grinned at Mariah, who smiled back.

"He will be a loving father one day," Sarah murmured.

Mariah, who had been studying Hamath, spoke softly. "Sir, did I also see you in Jerusalem?"

"Yes. I returned just over a week ago," Hamath said. He grimaced. "Bildad wasn't the gentlest master."

"That's true. It was hard to believe such a dramatic change. He set nearly all his slaves free."

"He was in an amazing hurry to get rid of us."

She lowered her eyes. "At first, he wanted to keep all the children, but he gave permission to take them when he realized he'd have to care for them himself. He had no one left who could tend the little ones. He turned us loose a while back, but we had no means to come home. There were ten of us women who left together as a group. We couldn't walk fast because of the children. As we traveled toward our homes, we worked for food for a few days, trying to gain a coin or two to last until we had to stop again."

Hamath cleared his throat. "Uh ... do you have dreams? I mean, ones where you wake up your spouse?"

"Yes, I have nightmares," Mariah said. "Several times I've awakened myself and Jonas when I've thrown myself off the bed."

Several people began to talk at once. Paul stood up and cleared his throat. When the group quieted, he spoke. "For those of you who don't know me, my name is Paulos.

He told them about his injuries and recovery. "I wasn't gone as long as some of you were—for instance, Mariah, here, was gone for ten long years. Has anyone here been gone longer than that?"

One man stood up. Paul guessed he might be in his mid-twenties.

"My name is Joshua," he said. "They took me eleven years ago. I might have been Bildad's first human theft. I was just a boy of fourteen, out in the hills with my father's sheep. Some men approached me and asked for a drink. I turned my back to get the water skin, and one of them hit me over the head with something hard. After that, they beat me with great regularity. My father tells me I was a rebellious young man. Perhaps I still haven't outgrown it."

A few of the men laughed, including a guffaw from his father. "I was among the first to return." He sat down again, receiving an embrace from his mother.

Mariah stood up, took a deep breath, and plunged forward, but her soft voice didn't carry well. "I have a story, too."

"Louder, Mariah, we can't hear you," shouted one old man.

She took another breath and spoke louder. "I had gone to the well to bathe early in the morning. Nobody was around at that time, or so I thought. As I started to remove my cloak, someone grabbed me from behind. I tried to scream, but the man held one hand over my mouth. He and another large man, whom I later knew as Bildad, dragged me into the trees, where they bound and gagged me. They took me to Jerusalem."

A woman with a baby on her hip stood up. "Mariah, you have two children born in captivity. What will you do with the children?"

Mariah smiled gratefully at Jonas. "My husband wants to be their father. He will adopt them."

The woman burst into tears. "My husband is unwilling to accept my little one."

The man sitting next to her shifted and scowled.

Jonas stood up. "My friend, I know this is hard for you, but think how hard life will be for this child if you don't keep her. What will you do, Bartholomew, sell the baby into the same bondage that your wife suffered under for so many years?"

Jonas walked to Bartholomew and placed an arm around the man's shoulders as he gazed at the young woman. "You must have known these captors wouldn't treat her gently. She didn't choose to become pregnant by another man, but she also doesn't want to kill this innocent child or sell the babe to a stranger. The fault wasn't your wife's or the infant's. Will you punish them for what they couldn't help?"

Bartholomew's stubborn scowl melted a little.

Jonas patted his back. "Accept this child. After the brutality your wife endured, she may not be able to have any more children. Would you not rather have one who has your beloved's blood than no child at all? Or even if you have more children, would you throw this part of your wife away?"

"I hadn't thought of the babe being a part of my Rebecca." Bartholomew turned to her. "Maybe we should talk again." He peered at the sleeping baby. "She does look like Rebecca."

Another young man, about twenty years old, stood up. "My name is John. I've been gone five years. While I was gone, my parents moved, and I don't know where. Maybe they wouldn't want me back even if I found them. I'm not a child any more. I have no home, no work … and I'm hungry." The young man's chin jutted forward.

Hamath turned to Martha, who'd been standing near the door. "Martha, would you show our guest where the food is set out? There may be others here who are hungry too."

Jonas cleared his throat. "I may possibly know your parents."

"I'm the son of Caleb and Dinah. My father was a gatekeeper."

"Ah, yes. I do know them. They haven't moved far, John. They are in Leontopolis, only a mile away. They were here just last week. I sent word to them of the meeting, but they didn't want to come. Your father was afraid that seeing so many people who had returned, except their own son, would be too much for your mother. Your father has missed you, but your mother has made herself sick worrying about you. They live on the street called Beth."

The young man's eyes were damp. He nodded and looked at Martha, who approached with a tray. "Thank you. I won't take much of the food, but a piece of bread will last me until I reach Leontopolis.

No one else stood up. By this time, Tamara had snuggled up in Paul's arms and drifted off to sleep. The other children had settled down too, sitting close to their parents. Perhaps people needed to get to know each other better before they could relax and open up. Finally, Paul, still seated, spoke up. "Would you all like another chance to get together?"

The people looked at each other, smiled, and murmured their assent.

"Then let's meet again," Jonas said. "Next Sunday afternoon, this time at my home. It's just east of the Jewish synagogue."

"Maybe we could each bring some food to share." Sarah suggested.

People nodded.

Paul grinned, wondering if this would be the world's first potluck.

"Each household could bring something. And could we meet at mealtime, since we would be sharing a meal?"

Jonas nodded. "At the sixth hour, then."

With more nods of agreement, the people gathered their children to leave, stopping to thank Hamath and Dorcas.

Paul noticed Tamara didn't have her doll. Startled out of his reverie over the meeting, he stopped and touched Sarah's arm. "Tammy's doll is missing."

The child yawned and smiled. "It's okay, Papa. I gave Abby to Zillah and Ezra. They don't have a doll, and they need her more than I do."

Paul squeezed her. "I'll make you another one, Tammy."

"Okay, Papa," she said, and laid her head back on Paul's shoulder.

Sarah's mouth turned down.

Their eyes met. Paul remembered how, while in the hospital, Tamara had given her favorite doll to a little girl suffering from cancer and a stuffed toy to a boy who had been burned. One after another, she'd given away her toys to other children in the hospital, as though she knew she wouldn't need them.

Paul felt a knot tightening in his stomach. He understood why Sarah's spirits had abruptly turned sour.

Chapter 46

September AD 30

Tamara'd had another bad night. Paul helplessly watched her downhill slide. She didn't play, she wasn't hungry, and she slept most of the time. Paul had made Tammy another doll to celebrate her name day. She acted excited for about five minutes.

Dorcas had begun having Shalisha prepare the meals so Sarah could stay with Tamara. After giving lessons to the other children, Paul always hurried back to be with his family.

Sunday was scheduled for the third meeting of the returned slaves. Paul didn't think Tamara should go, even if she did nothing but sit. Neither he nor Sarah wanted to be more than a few steps away from her. What if she needed them, or if she should go away with her friend, Jesus, again? Each moment with her was too precious to miss.

Tamara woke up from another nap just before noon. "Jesus says he'll be here today."

Sarah shot an anxious look at Paul. "Is ... is he going to take you away from us again?" Sarah asked.

"I don't know. He said, 'Don't worry. I'll be there today.' I don't know why he said, 'don't worry,' though, 'cause I'm not worrying."

"You don't have to, Tammy. I'm doing enough for both of us" Sarah said, brushing a strand of hair back from her little one's face.

"Mama, Jesus is coming. Everything will be okay."

"How about Papa? Is it all right if I worry?" Paul asked.

"Oh, Papa, you're so funny." Tamara giggled, almost sounding like her old self. "Papas don't worry!"

Oh, sure. Papas are always calm, cool, and collected. Not! Paul ran shaky fingers through his hair.

Tamara grew serious. "You have to go see him tomorrow, Mama. Jesus wants to talk to you."

Sarah's eyebrows shot straight up. "Jesus wants to talk to me?" Her voice was little more than a squeak.

"Why does Jesus want to talk to Mama?" Paul asked. "And where?"

"He didn't say where. He just said he wanted to talk to Mama tomorrow."

"Then we'll find out and take you to wherever he'll be," Paul said. "Even I remember the stories where he healed people. Before, I didn't believe the stories. I thought they were folklore, but after my experience with him, and after everything else I'm hearing, I've changed my whole outlook. Yes, I think we'll all go see him. Or better yet, invite him here."

Tamara shook her head. "No, Papa. You're supposed to stay here with me while Mama goes to talk to him."

"I don't understand why you don't want to go or why he wouldn't want you to go see him," Sarah pleaded. "He might be able to help you get well."

"I don't know, Mama," Tamara said. "I'm thirsty. May I have some juice?"

"I'll get some for you. Do you want to come with me?"

"No, it's too far to walk. I'm tired. Can I stay with Papa?"

"All right, Tammy. I'll get you some juice. I'll hurry."

Good as her word, Sarah was back in record time with not only fresh-squeezed pomegranate juice, but also some chicken, cheese, bread, and milk, enough for the three of them. Tamara ate only a small sliver of chicken but drank the juice.

After their midday meal, Paul left to lead the others through their Greek lessons. His morning lessons had been brief lately. Whenever he left before they were done, Dathan had stayed with the children until they were all finished.

This time, as soon as he'd passed out assignments, Paul returned to the house. After sneaking a quick look at their sleeping child, he joined Sarah in their room. "I'm going to go see Jonas. He might know something about Jesus's plans to visit Tyre. If Jonas doesn't know, I can tell him that Jesus will be in our city today." He shook his head and chuckled. "Odd, isn't it? We accept without question a little girl's pronouncement that Jesus is coming to visit."

Sarah nodded. "True. And that's a good idea. I wonder if he will stay for the Sunday meeting? Jesus's presence would make the meeting pretty exciting, wouldn't it?"

"That's putting things mildly."

When he reached the marketplace, he went directly to Jonas's shop. "Hello, Jonas. How's business?"

"Shalom, Paul. Business is good, my friend, very good. God has blessed me, and there is not one thing in business or life I can complain about. How is Tamara?"

"Not good, I'm afraid. She weakens. The fevers and convulsions don't just come at night anymore. The fever doesn't go away, and she has seizures a few times every day as well as several at night. Sarah doesn't get enough rest. Some of the servants are sure Tamara is demon-possessed. She had one fit in the middle of the courtyard yesterday. Before she was through convulsing, everyone in the household had gathered around her."

Jonas shook his head. "I'm sorry, my friend. Your eyes tell the tale of your own sleeplessness. If it's any consolation, we're praying for Tamara many times a day."

"We pray, too, but she just keeps getting worse. However, she tells us not to worry, because Jesus is coming soon. In fact, she says he'll be here today."

"That's interesting. Not only because Tamara says he'll be here—and she's so accurate in her predictions—but I also heard yesterday he's been seen nearby. I wonder if he'll come to the synagogue tomorrow morning. If he'll be here tomorrow, he'll need to be in Tyre before sundown this evening, due to our Jewish Sabbath laws. Jews aren't supposed to travel more than two thousand cubits outside their city walls on the Sabbath—in case you didn't know. I'll ask around, although that's seldom necessary in this city. Word travels."

"All right. I don't want to be gone for long. I'm uneasy whenever I'm away from Tamara for any length of time. She said Jesus said for Sarah not to worry, and she thought it was funny when I asked her if it would be all right if I worried. She said, 'Papas don't worry.' But I agonize over her illness as much as her mother does."

"If you will help me put away these materials, I'll close the business for the day, and we can go in search of this Jesus. Hamath told me of his experience with the man. Benoni is said to have had a personal experience with him. Then there's your story of seeing the man in shining white, and Tamara talks about Jesus too. I have to admit my curiosity grows."

Before long they had packed away the goods and were ready to go. Jonas stretched his back. "The best thing might be to check with the gatekeepers. At least there's only one gate into the city. He could arrive by boat, and we'll check that if we find out nothing at the gate."

Their first guess was correct. They found a crowd of people following a man walking straight toward Paul and Jonas. He greeted them with a smile, his hands outstretched. "Behold! My friends who helped bring so many home!"

Paul's felt his Adam's apple working up and down as he recognized the man who had pulled him through the windy web, but only a strangled sound came forth from his throat. He dropped to his knees. "That's him," he whispered to Jonas.

Jonas stared open-mouthed at Jesus. "You mean this the man in white?"

Jesus smiled at Jonas. "I am that man. I'm in need of a place for my disciples and me to stay this night, rabbi."

"My house is yours, Lord," Jonas said. "It would be an honor to have you come to our home."

Jesus nodded, then turned to Paul. "Tell Sarah to come see me tomorrow."

"Yes, Lord. Tamara told us you'd be here and that you wanted to see Sarah tomorrow."

"Good. Tammy has been faithful to deliver messages. For such a small one, she's made a good prophet."

"Lord, I have a request. She's so sick. I believe you could heal her, if you will. She is our only child."

"You shouldn't worry, either. Have faith, Paulos. You should return to your home now. You're needed there."

Paul rose to his feet and bowed to the Lord. Then he ran the whole way home.

Jonas stood in silence, unable to think of anything intelligent to say.

The Lord's eyes twinkled at him. "Jonas, I would like to speak at your synagogue tomorrow morning."

"Yes, teacher, I hoped you would. Even here in Tyre, we've heard of you." Jonas cleared his throat. "Oh—and on Sunday afternoon at my home, we will have a gathering of people who were captured by a slave trader and later released. Would you stay for our meeting, Lord? I think you could be a great encouragement to them. Some are deeply troubled because the man treated them so cruelly."

"Yes, I know, and I know of Paulos's role—as well as your own—in the release of the slaves. I'll be happy to stay and talk with them. Come," he said. "We need to go to your house. Your wife will want to know early there are so many extra people to feed."

Jonas nodded. "Yes, Lord. She used to chastise me when I brought my friends home to break bread without giving her warning." He had to smile at the memory, and then he winced. Now she acted as though she were afraid he might banish her—or beat her—if she said any small thing that might offend him.

As they walked toward his home, Jesus and his disciples joked as they walked along just as other men did. Jonas wasn't sure why he thought a group of people that included the Messiah would be always serious.

A loud voice sounded from behind one of the shops, and Hamath trotted out from a vendor's stall. "Jesus!" Hamath cried again. He ran up and fell to his knees in front of the master. Benoni, close behind, dropped to his knees beside Hamath. Tears streamed down the faces of both men.

"Lord, you're here!" Hamath pressed his forehead to the ground.

"Shalom, Hamath," Jesus said.

"You remember me?" Hamath lifted his head. His voice shook, cracking on the last word.

"Yes."

"You've made me want to change my bad ways, Lord," Hamath said. "I'm so ashamed of the things I used to do."

"Keep working, Hamath, and I will help you. Never stop. The road through life is full of pitfalls for those who quit trying."

"Lord, I have a request. There's a little girl in my household, a daughter of two of my servants ..."

"I know. Her name is Tamara."

"Yes, Lord. Please, she's so sick I'm afraid she'll die. Could you heal her? She is a precious child, almost as dear to me as my own daughter."

"Have faith, Hamath," Jesus said, and then turned to Benoni. "You're forgiven, my son. You were foolish, but be patient with yourself. One day you'll be able to live on your own."

"How did you know about my ... um ... foolishness?" Benoni asked.

"I know many things. Maybe even things you don't know about yourself. You have a strength from me that you haven't used yet." Jesus reached out and touched Benoni's shoulder.

"I believe you, Lord."

Jesus passed by the two men, the others following. They were stopped one more time before they arrived at Jonas's home.

"Hail, Jonas," Nicolas called from the doorway of his small brick house.

Jonas lifted his hand in greeting. "Shalom, my friend. Come and meet the Master Physician."

Curiosity shone in Nicolas's eyes as he approached. He bowed his head. "Shalom, sir."

Jonas had to smile. There seemed to be something about Jesus's eyes that drew attention from those who were observant.

Jonas smiled at Jesus. "Lord, this is Nicolas, the best physician in Tyre. Nicolas, this is Jesus, the Messiah. The Christ," he added.

Nicolas's eyes opened wider. He wasn't a Jew, but maybe he'd heard of the promised Jewish deliverer.

"Shalom, Nicolas," Jesus said. "Come with us."

"Sir, wait! If you are indeed the master physician, there is a case here which baffles and concerns me—a small child who is dying of fevers and convulsions, I believe because of a bad growth in her head. She needs someone wiser than I to bring healing to her. Her name is—"

"Tamara," finished Jesus. "Yes, I know her."

"Then, sir, is it possible you know of a way to heal her?"

Jesus smiled. "It's possible."

Nicolas's eyes glistened. He nodded and followed them.

When they arrived at Jonas's home, Mariah met them at the door. Jesus caught her eyes, and she started. Why did this stranger seem to peer deep inside her?

Jonas placed a kiss on her sparrow-shaped birthmark. "This is Jesus, Mariah, and these are his disciples. I'm afraid I didn't ask their names. They've been traveling all day, and I invited them here to spend the night and eat with us. They will stay until after the meeting on Sunday."

"Welcome, sirs," Mariah said. "Please come in and rest. You must be weary."

"Arbah," she said, addressing a servant walking past, "please fetch water and towels and bathe their feet."

Jonas led the others into a large room, but Jesus stayed where he was.

Turning to face her, Jesus spoke softly. "Mariah." As he approached her, he grasped her hands.

Mariah caught her breath, her heart jumping. "Yes, sir?" She backed away as far as his hands allowed.

"You are forgiven," Jesus said. "Your husband has forgiven you, and your Father in heaven has also, but you hold back from your husband and your heavenly Father. You're forgiven. Let it go."

"How did you know?" Mariah asked, her eyes filling. "Are you a prophet?"

"Some call me a prophet." He released her hands. A smile warmed his eyes, and then he walked into the room where the other men gathered.

Jonas strode back to her side. "Mariah," he whispered, "can you believe this? The master is in our own home!"

"The master?" Her eyes stretched wider.

"Yes, the Messiah. Mariah, this man is the Promised One of God."

"Is this One who is able to heal the sick?" she asked, a spark of excitement beginning in her heart.

"Yes, so I've heard."

Without another word, Mariah turned and ran into the room where Jesus sat with his disciples and Nicolas. She knelt at his feet. "Master, I've a favor to ask."

"Ask, daughter."

"There's a small child in Tyre who has a heart of pure gold. She cares for other children as if she were their mother, even though she is barely four years old. She gave my two children her only toy and comforted their fears, but she herself is so ill and probably afraid for her own life. Her name is Tamara. O Lord, would you please heal her?"

Ezra and Zillah also trotted up to Jesus and both patted his leg for attention.

"Please make Tammy better?" asked Zillah.

"Tamma thick," Ezra said, nodding solemnly, his soft brown eyes leaking tears.

Jesus laughed as he knelt and hugged the children. "Truly, truly, I tell you, there has never been a child so loved by those around her."

Chapter 47

Paul entered his house to find Sarah crying as she sat with their convulsing daughter. They had long since moved her pallet away from the wall, so the child wouldn't slam her limbs or body into anything that would hurt her. Wet cloths lay scattered on the floor. Finally, Tamara's seizure ended, leaving her limp and unconscious.

Paul knelt and pulled Sarah to him, stroking her hair while she sobbed, her shoulders shaking. When she calmed, Paul said, "I saw Jesus today."

"You what?" she asked, pushing away from him.

"I saw Jesus. He said to have faith."

"Didn't you ask him to come here? Paul, I don't think she'll live until tomorrow. She hasn't gone more than fifteen minutes without convulsing. She hasn't stopped since you left. How can she take anymore? Please, go get him and bring him here to her. Please!" Sarah's hands gripped his arms.

"I asked him, Sarah, but he said you had to go to him tomorrow. Maybe because both Tammy and I have seen him, and you haven't.

Maybe because there is something he wants to tell just you. Maybe because he wants you to invite him here yourself. Maybe ... well, who knows what reason? All I know is that he wants you to come to him."

"But I'm afraid to leave her," Sarah said. "What if she, if she ..." Sarah began to sob again, tears running down her face. Paul rubbed her back as he held her.

"You're tired. You should take a break for a while. I'll take care of her." Paul soaked a cloth in the cool water and put it on Tamara's hot face.

Tammy woke. "Papa, I'm so cold," she whimpered in protest, trying to push the cloth away.

"I know, my little love, but we have to get your fever down." Her face felt like it was on fire.

Sarah poured some cooled willow bark tea into a clay cup and held it to Tamara's lips.

"This'll quit pretty soon," Tamara said with a scratchy voice, licking the tea from her cracked lips. "Jesus told me so."

Paul smiled, his mind's ear repeating the memory of what Jesus had said. A small hope began to grow in his chest. "I saw him today, Tammy. He said we should have faith."

Sarah, tears still flowing, knelt by Tamara's side. "Oh, Tammy, I'm so afraid, and I don't feel one ounce of faith. I remember before."

"Before wasn't bad, Mama. Jesus was there, and he held me and warmed me up. I was so freezy, just like now."

"But you see, Tamara, we didn't know Jesus, and we couldn't see him. All we could see was our precious little girl who had ... who had ..."

"Mama, it's okay. Being hugged by Jesus is like being hugged by everybody who loves me all at the same time."

Paul cleared his throat and looked at Sarah. "I've felt his caring too. I have to tell you, in those few seconds while I was with the man in white, I remembered hundreds of bad choices I made in my life. Sort of a startling revelation, since I thought I was pretty near faultless."

Sarah stared at him, her eyes flashing sparks. "This is not a time for joking. Are you saying Tamara's death would be just fine with you?"

"Dying isn't bad," Tamara said softly, patting her mama's arm.

"I'm sorry. I'm not saying this very well." Paul spoke to both Tammy and Sarah as tenderly as he knew how. "Dying might not be so bad for the one who dies. As your mama and I know, though, death is pretty hard for the people left behind."

"But Mama, wouldn't you like for me to be with Jesus all the time?"

"No! I mean, yes, in a way. But what I want most is for you to stay with us. You have an eternity to spend with Jesus. I want you to stay with us now. Do you understand what I'm trying to say, Tammy?" Sarah gazed at Tamara as she stroked the child's hair back from her forehead, her eyes pleading.

"Remember when we were missing Papa so much when he was gone?" Sarah asked. "That is a little bit like how we felt when you ... when you ... went with Jesus before."

"I—" Tamara began, but a seizure gripped her again, and she couldn't finish.

Darkness fell, finally ending the seemingly endless day. Paul and Sarah pulled their pallet into the room with Tamara and took turns sleeping and caring for their daughter, who amazingly lived through the night. Nothing they did helped. When she was awake but not seizing, she was too weak to move or talk. Only the rise and fall of her chest and an occasional glance from listless eyes indicated the child still lived.

Unbelievably, Tammy lived through the night. At dawn, Sarah ran to the cooking area to prepare food for Paul and broth for Tamara. Nothing for herself. No appetite. Paul seemed rested and relaxed. Sarah resented his attitude. *Why wasn't he as concerned as she was?*

Is he giving up on Tamara and accepting that she could die again? I cannot, will not, accept it! Can you hear me, Jesus? Do you care so little for this child who has such unshakable faith in you?

Sarah brought the tray of food to Paul and Tamara. She lifted a goblet of broth to Tamara's dry, cracked lips. The child swallowed once but refused even a small piece of honey cake. Paul, however, ate the entire tray full of food she brought him. *How can he eat? The very thought of food turns my stomach.*

"Paul," she said, "I'm not waiting. I'm going to see him this morning. Now." She wrapped a scarf over her head and hurried out the door. Would he try to stop her?

He called something after her, but his voice was far away and vague. She marched toward the street, not even stopping in the villa to say where she was bound.

Sarah trotted toward Jonas's house. If only Tamara could last until she talked to Jesus. Surely Jesus would come if she told him how sick Tammy was, even if it was the Sabbath. She remembered from somewhere that healing the sick was considered work and couldn't be done on Saturday. *So unchristian! Oh, Christianity doesn't exactly exist yet. Still ...* Tears streamed down her face again. What if he wouldn't come? Tammy was too weak to last another day.

Why didn't Paul feel what she felt? How did he come by this calm? How dare he have such peace in the face of the horror of Tamara's illness? Sarah wanted to scream that he should be just as indignant as she. He should rant at the injustice of it, shake his fist at God, feel the same anger.

Arriving at Jonas's house, she pounded on the door until the servant Arbah answered.

"Where is everyone?" Sarah demanded. "I need to talk to Jesus right now."

"It's the Sabbath, and they are all gone to the synagogue, madam," Arbah explained.

"Oh, that's right. I forgot." Sarah turned and raced toward the synagogue, not even flinging a thank you to Arbah.

When she arrived, no one was there but one scowling old man, sitting on a bench just outside the large double doors to the building with his arms folded across his chest. *Now what?*

"Where is everyone?" she asked the man.

"Humph. They followed that supposed prophet out across to the mainland. Too many to fit in the synagogue, he said. Glad they left. Noisy, curious mob, all trying to talk at once. God will be angry, mark my words. They're dishonoring the Sabbath. Even the rabbi. Especially the rabbi! You would think at least a rabbi would honor the first commandment, 'Remember the Sabbath day and keep it holy.' Sacrilege! Wouldn't surprise me if we all got killed in an earthquake or a mighty storm."

"Where on the mainland?"

"How would I know? I didn't follow them. If you are wise, you'll turn around and go home, young woman. That Jesus is an evil man, pulling people away from the laws of Moses!"

Anxiety made her empty stomach churn. She detoured to their house before crossing the land bridge and tiptoed inside. Paul sat on the floor holding the shivering child, stroking her hair.

"Any change?" Sarah whispered.

"No. Did you find Jesus?"

"Not yet. The crowd was too big for the synagogue, so they went across to the mainland. I'll go there now."

"All right. I'll be thinking about you. Praying, too."

Sarah nodded absently and left for the gate. There were several places where a large group could listen to Jesus. Coming to the end of the long path to the mainland, she had to decide whether to turn north or south. It probably didn't matter. As weak as Tammy had been, it would probably be too late before she could talk Jesus into coming with her.

Sarah's legs were as heavy as her heart. The path yielded no clues as to which way to go, but her feet turned north, almost of their own volition. She hadn't walked far before she heard voices and spotted a large gathering. Then she saw Jesus sitting on a flat rock. The size of the crowd amazed her. It looked like every soul from Sidon to Jerusalem was present in the clearing. *There must be a thousand people!* Jesus's disciples gathered close around him, trying to hold the throng back. Sarah's stomach tightened even further. How could she possibly get to him?

Jesus began to speak about faith, and she felt like he singled her out.

"It only takes faith as small as a mustard seed ..."

Not that much in my entire body.

She worked her way forward as best she could, slipping in front of one after another. Even so, to break through the entire crowd gathered between her and Jesus appeared impossible. The crowd in front sat on the ground, shoulder to shoulder, backs to knees. They began to shout questions.

"Jesus, Son of David! Would you please heal me? I'm blind," a man pleaded, his plaintive voice wavering above the rest of the noise.

A man dressed in Pharisaical robes with bells on the hems, stood up, shouting louder than everyone else. "It's not lawful to heal on the Sabbath." The noise of the crowd silenced as they turned to him.

Jesus smiled. "If your donkey fell into a hole on the Sabbath, would you not pull him out? Is this man not more valuable than a donkey?"

"That would be questionable," the ruler sneered. "This man is a beggar and contributes nothing to the community, unlike a donkey ..." The sound of his arrogance faded as Jesus silenced him with a look of pure pity.

Jesus turned to the blind man. "Do you believe I can heal you?"

"Yes, Lord," the blind man said, and then he gasped. "I can see!" he shouted.

That began a massive movement toward Jesus. People surged toward him—some with twisted backs, some with withered limbs, some whose ailments were hidden from the eyes of the world, some who had to be carried.

Sarah pushed and grasped for a way to reach him, but she couldn't get through the crowd. For the first time in her life, she wished she were as tall and strong as Paul.

The big reddish-haired disciple's booming voice sounded above the noise of the throng. "The master grows weary. Those who have serious illnesses only! The rest of you, stand away. Especially you gentiles. If you don't believe only in the One True God, stand away and watch."

Suddenly, someone shouldered Sarah, knocking her to the ground. Several people stepped on her, crushing her hands, kicking, unmindful of the human form under their feet. She cried out with pain and terror like she'd never felt before. She had to get up! She had to make it to Jesus! *Tammy* ... Then someone kicked her behind the ear. Everything went black and she felt no more.

Chapter 48

Later as the crowd began to clear away, the disciples noticed Sarah's body lying motionless on the ground.

"Master," John said, "there is a woman lying over here. I'm afraid she's dead."

Jesus walked over and knelt by her limp body. Picking up one mashed and bloody hand, he murmured, "Sarah, wake up."

Someone called Sarah from far away. She groaned. *Where am I? How long have I lain here?* She rubbed her aching head. Who called her? She opened one eye in a pained squint—the other eye wouldn't open. Slowly, she raised her head and gazed into the eyes of Jesus. As she did, the sting of the breaks, bruises, and scrapes began to melt from her like butter from the sides of a warming pot. She blinked and opened both eyes. "You called me?"

"Yes, Sarah. Rise. You wanted to ask me something."

She sat up, remembering. "Tamara, my daughter. She's too ill to live." Tears washed down her face again. "It might already be too late."

"This woman is a Canaanite. I can tell by her speech," a disciple said. "Go away, woman. The master is tired and needs to rest."

She threw him a look that should have frozen him. She wouldn't be shushed, not now. "Jesus, have mercy on my daughter."

"Master," the disciple repeated. "Send her away. She's only a Canaanite."

Jesus held up his hand and shook his head. He said nothing, just gazed into her eyes.

"Jesus, please." She paused, remembering that people in this era believed convulsions were demonically caused. The remaining crowd had begun to gather around. Some wouldn't understand that seizures could result from disease.

But the physicians in the modern world hadn't been able to find a cure. Maybe these "ignorant" ancients could be right. Maybe cancer was demonic. She thought of the servants who had watched Tamara convulsing earlier in the week. She remembered his words about faith.

Jesus remained silent, his eyes full of love and understanding.

She knelt on the hard, rocky ground and swallowed her pride. "Lord, my daughter suffers from, from a d-demon. Please free her."

"It wouldn't be right to take the bread from the children of Israel and give it to the dogs."

His words were so in opposition to the look in his eyes. Did he want her to beg?

The light dawned! *Ah, I remember the rest of the story!* "Lord," she said, "Even the little dogs are allowed to clean up the crumbs under the table."

Jesus smiled.

She understood. Have faith. Even a crumb is enough. And humility. Oh, yes—and He alone is Lord.

"Woman, your faith is great. It shall be as you asked."

The disciples' mouths dropped open. Didn't they know one small crumb would be enough?

For a moment, Sarah froze. A smile spread across her face, even while tears, this time of joy, again spilled down her face.

"Thank you, master," she said softly enough that only he could hear. "Thank you." She rose to her feet and bowed her head toward him. Then she turned and ran toward home with wings on her feet.

Sarah walked into her house, knowing what she'd find. Paul sat by Tamara's bed, smiling. He held a finger to his lips. Tamara lay quiet, the flush and sweat of fever gone, a smile on her face even as she slept.

Paul whispered, "What happened? You were gone all morning, and your clothes look like you robbed a beggar."

"It's a long story, Paul."

"I have time."

Paul rose and placed an arm around Sarah as they walked into the common room.

"Soon. Right now, husband, I'm hungry. I haven't eaten anything since ... well, I don't remember when. Do you mind if I get something to eat?"

"I have a better idea," Paul responded. "Why don't I go talk Shalisha into letting me have enough for all of us? When Tamara stopped convulsing and lost the fever, she ate all the chicken that was left and drank her juice. Then she went to sleep."

"Shalisha might not be there. I seem to remember seeing her in the crowd around Jesus."

"Martha then. Even if they're not around, I'll bet I can find some food."

Sarah laughed. "I'll just bet you can, you honey-tongued man!"

Paul opened the door and nearly ran into Martha, who stood with one hand raised to knock and her other hand holding a big tray of cloth-wrapped food. The tray very nearly tipped over, but she righted it.

"Hello, Martha. What have we here?" Paul asked.

"I brought you some fish and bread and pomegranates and, and, well, some other things. How is the little one? Shalisha just got home and she said a man named Jesus said you were there ... oh, no, I mean Shalisha said Sarah was there talking to Jesus ... No, that Sarah was in the crowd listening to Jesus, and that she—Sarah—had been hurt or killed and Jesus lifted her up, and then Sarah bowed to him and she said—Shalisha, that is—that Jesus said the child would be delivered or healed or something like that. Is Sarah all right? Is Tamara better?"

"Thank you, Martha," Paul said, taking the tray. "Both Sarah and Tamara are fine. Come in and see for yourself." He opened the door wide, and Martha followed him in.

"Shalom, Sarah. You don't look so bad, that is if you don't take into consideration that your clothes are dusty and torn. What happened to you? Where is Tamara? Would you like something to eat?"

"Come see for yourself, but please be quiet. Tammy's asleep." Martha followed Sarah into the child's bedroom.

"Are you sure she is all right?" Martha whispered. "She is lying there so quiet she looks ... she looks ..."

Tamara opened her eyes. Martha clapped her hands. "She's alive!"

"Hi, Martha. I'm hungry." Tamara hopped up from the pallet. "Why are you crying? Did you bring me something to eat?"

Sarah picked Tamara up and hugged her tight.

"Mama, you're squishing me!"

Paul took her from Sarah's arms and held her above his head, making her laugh. He set her down on the floor. "Okay, giggle box, let's eat."

He turned to Martha. "You should stay and eat with us."

"Oh, no, it's not for me. I didn't bring enough, and anyway, I already ate." She patted her stomach. "I'm so delighted to see Tamara well again. I'll tell the mistress. How surprised she'll be! And the rest of the household too. They'll all be so pleased." She left, still chattering as she trotted out the door.

Paul, Sarah, and Tamara sat around the table. "If there's ever been a time when it would be appropriate to offer thanks, now is the time," Paul said. He took Sarah's and Tamara's hands and bowed his head. "Most High God, we thank you from the bottom of our hearts for restoring Tamara to us and for your provision for all our needs. Amen."

"Amen," Sarah and Tamara repeated.

Chapter 49

Sarah and Paul had to hurry to keep up with Tammy as they walked to their next meeting. Sarah chuckled as they followed behind. Word must have spread quickly of Tammy's recovery, because cheers broke out when they walked into Jonas's courtyard. Ezra and Zillah were the first to reach Tamara, and they both patted her and hugged her while she giggled. Orphah, then Darius and Gideon, weren't far behind.

As soon as Tamara spied Jesus standing in the center of the courtyard, she shrieked with glee and ran to him. Laughing, he picked her up and swung her around before setting her back on her feet. The rest of the children crowded close, all of them talking at once. The Lord's disciples and the children's parents were less than pleased, and they tried to shoo the children away.

Jesus chided them. "No, no. Don't do that, my friends. Let the children come to me. Having them near is like being in heaven."

His gaze took in the whole group, one at a time. "I want you to remember something. These children are precious in the sight of God. It would be better for you to have a millstone tied around your neck and be thrown into the Great Sea than for you to prevent them from coming to me, or to do any harm to one of these, my little ones."

Sarah's heart warmed. *So, he really did say that.*

Bartholomew's face reddened. He lifted the babe from his wife's arms and brought her to Jesus.

Jesus took the baby from him. "Will you accept this little one, Bartholomew?" he asked.

"Yes, Lord. I'll care for her as my own." Bartholomew swallowed. As if on cue, the infant smiled a large toothless smile at Jesus, wriggling and squirming like a happy puppy.

Jesus looked at the smiling child in his arms, then at Bartholomew. "That would be wise. Remember, this child is also mine, and you shall treat her as such." He handed the baby back to the young man.

Sarah wondered if they should move back into the crowd, but as though he knew what she was thinking, he raised his eyes to hers. All right, they would stay right where they were.

Jonas brought Ezra and Zillah to him. "These children, too, were born during my wife's slavery, and they are very dear to her. I want you to know they're also dear to me. Indeed, they've found their way into my heart."

Jesus nodded. "Yes, I can see that. Mariah is doubly blessed." He then focused on Jonas's older son. "Dathan," he said.

When Dathan didn't move, Sarah nudged him closer. He stared at his feet, his brow furrowed.

Standing, Jesus drew Dathan to him. At first, Dathan resisted, but then he collapsed on Jesus's shoulder.

Jesus patted the boy's back and then lifted his chin, looking into his eyes. "Dathan, you're no less loved because you have a new brother and sister. Your father and your mother love you just as much as before your mother was stolen away. Their love for you is not decreased by their love for these two little ones. And these children will need a big brother who can help them grow up to be as fine a person as you're becoming. Will you accept that charge?"

"Yes, Lord," Dathan said. He held out his hands to Zillah and Ezra, who trustingly put their hands in his to be led back to their seats.

Sarah watched as one family at a time brought their children to Jesus. With each, he admonished the families to be patient and loving with each other, especially those with children of slavery. He called them by name, parents and children alike.

When their turn came, Paul, who had been holding Tamara, placed her in Jesus's arms. He smiled and poked her tummy. "Well, my small friend, you caused quite a stir here today. How do you feel about being the one everyone is talking about?"

Tamara shrugged. "They probably won't even 'member in a few days." She took hold of his hand. "Jesus, can I ask you for something?"

Sarah started to pull Tammy away. Jesus had given them so much. Would He be angry with still another request?

Jesus smiled at Sarah and shook His head. He sat and pulled the child close. "What's that, little one?"

"My grandma. When we were in the before, first I went away, then Mama, then Papa. She must be awfully sad."

"What do you wish for me to do?"

"Could you tell her we're all right?"

"I can. But what makes you think that would console her? People grieve even when they know their loved ones go to heaven."

"But she doesn't even know that. She doesn't know about you."

"That's true. My Father has been calling her, but she hasn't listened yet. Perhaps I'll give her a message she can't ignore. Have your papa write a little letter to her. I'll make sure she sees it."

"Can you mail a letter from heaven, Jesus?"

"No, but I think I have just the messengers we need. One of them is your papa's friend, Evelyn. She's one of my own."

"Oh, I know her. Evelyn works at Papa's office, and she's nice. She always gives me a Tootsie Pop and lets me talk to her. Everybody else shoos me away."

Sarah chuckled. Bless Evelyn, the most patient of people.

"It's because she loves you, Tammy. She'll deliver the letter to your grandma. Oh, and I have a secret to tell you, Tammy." Jesus leaned close to her ear and whispered.

Tamara clapped her hands and looked first at Paul and then at Sarah. "Can I tell them?"

"Just your mama and papa, but wait until you're alone with them, all right?"

Sarah raised an eyebrow at Tammy but said nothing. The little girl made a zipping motion across her lips, looking smug and happy.

Jesus looked first at Sarah and then Paul. "You have begun a good work here. Continue to help others grow in their faith." His eyes sparkled. "And you don't need to wait for a need to talk to me. If I'm your friend, you can talk to me any time, any day, about anything. And Paulos, Tammy says we need to give a message to your mother."

"Yes, Lord, I heard," Paul said, "and I'll write her a letter today. I'm curious. How will you get this note to her?"

"Write the message to your mother on parchment, seal it in a small jar, and leave the jar in your house. Write Evelyn's address on the jar, and don't worry about anything else."

"Lord, you're amazing. Thank you. I've been happy here, but I'm like Tammy. I've also been worried about my mother after all the tragedies in her life."

"Never worry. Just give all your cares and concerns, as well as your joys, to me."

"Yes, Lord, we'll do that from now on."

Dorcas and Hamath were the last to come forward. After Jesus blessed their children, he sent them off to play with the others. "Dorcas," he said. "you might have noticed that Hamath has changed."

Dorcas smiled into her husband's eyes. "Yes, I noticed, Lord."

"Have you forgiven him?"

Dorcas's mouth dropped. "Forgiven him? Why should I forgive him? If I do that, he might go back to his old ways."

"Yes, he might, although I have faith in him. He'll try not to. I've forgiven him. Won't you also forgive him?"

"You've forgiven him? Whatever did you have against him?"

"Any time someone hurts one I love, he also hurts me," Jesus said.

Dorcas's mouth dropped open. "You love ... you care about me? You don't even know me. Uh, do you?"

"I knew you before you were born, Dorcas. Now, do you forgive him?"

She looked at Hamath, who stood red-faced, his chin drooping to his chest.

"Yes, Lord, I do," she said, her voice soft and tender. Hamath raised his head, joy lighting his eyes as he gazed into hers.

Sarah blinked tears away.

"Then this is a day you should celebrate. This is the first day of your new lives."

Jesus stood. "Now, my friends, my disciples and I must rest. We've enjoyed this time of breaking bread with you, but we have a long way to go. We continue our journey to Jerusalem in the morning."

Paul and Sarah looked at each other. Among all the people there, they might be the only ones other than Jesus who knew what this last journey would bring to him. Sarah's eyes burned. She exchanged glances with Paul, and they watched wordlessly as the master walked into the villa.

Jonas clapped his hands, and everyone turned toward him. "This day, you have all met the Christ. Do you not think so?"

Nods and murmured agreements came from nearly everyone.

"Then I think now might be time to burn your household idols that really are not gods. What do you say?"

Dorcas and Hamath smiled at each other. Some of the others looked startled, some scowled.

Jonas clapped again. "So ... we'll talk more next week. Shalom, my friends, and may the One True God walk with you until then."

EPILOGUE

June AD 2008

English archeologist William Fitzhugh-Brown, known to his friends and most of his associates as Liam, scratched his head. *What is this, some kind of hoax?* Liam had found, under a layer of hard-packed dirt, a small, sealed, clay jar with an English inscription. The inscription, scarcely readable but definitely there, was an address in Phoenix, Arizona, USA. He stood, intending to tell the rest of the crew what he had found, but he was unable to speak. Instead, he heard that silent inner voice which had become so familiar over the years: *Take this jar to Evelyn. Tell no one.*

"But, Lord, that would be illegal!" Liam shook his head as the same line rang again in his heart. "Very well, Lord, but I do hope you'll keep me out of prison." He glanced around and furtively slipped the jar into his bag.

Liam had made his discovery late in the day at the archeological site in the ancient city of Tyre. He informed his crew that he'd be gone for about a week and gave them that much time for a vacation.

The crew members' faces brightened at the announcement, their thanks profuse. Many were volunteers who came to this tell from other countries, and a few days off would allow them time to explore the surrounding countryside. The rest were locals.

Liam went back to his hotel and booked a ticket to the United States for the following day.

On the flight from Beirut to New York, Liam was still shaking his head. He had decided not to try to hide the small clay jar, instead carrying the object in plain view, although wrapped in bubble wrap. The scanners and custom officials took no note of the jar, as though of no importance.

In New York, the same thing happened.

"Do you have anything to report for customs, sir?" the customs agent asked.

"Just this," he said, stomach tightening into a knot. He held up the bag. "I found it in … ah … in the dirt."

"An old coffee mug?" The customs official looked a little puzzled. He took the bag from Liam, glanced at it, and handed it back. "I don't think declaring it will be necessary. Next?"

"Thank you, sir," Liam said and hurried off to his connecting flight to Phoenix before the customs official could change his mind.

Phoenix is hotter than the proverbial US Independence Day firecracker. Liam dabbed at his damp forehead with an already drenched handkerchief. He wanted nothing more than to find a shower and a clean bed. Nevertheless, he looked up the telephone number for Evelyn McPhersen, which, oddly enough, was listed under E. McPhersen with the same address as on the jar, confirming he had located the right person.

At eight p.m. Arizona time, he dialed Ms. McPhersen's number. He hoped perhaps she might be home and had not retired for the evening. He was in luck—the lady answered on the second ring.

"Hullo, madam. My name is William Fitzhugh-Brown. I'm an archeologist, and I've been on a dig in Tyre, Lebanon. I've found something that is addressed to you."

"What kind of scam is this, mister?"

"Wait!" Liam almost shouted. "Don't hang up, madam, please. This is not a scam. Is the name Paul Johnson familiar to you?"

"If this is some kind of joke, Mr. Brown, this is the wrong day to pull it."

"The name is Fitzhugh-Brown, and why in the world would you think I'd be jesting?"

"Paul Johnson was killed in a car wreck this afternoon," Evelyn said. "I was just leaving to go to his mother's house."

Liam stared in amazement at the telephone in his hand, his exhaustion evaporating like water off a hot pavement.

"Madam—Ms. McPhersen—may I come to your house and show you what I have? I'm at the airport, calling from a pay phone, and I would rather not share this with the people walking past me. If it makes any difference to you, I believe the Lord told me to tell no one but you about this find."

"The Lord?"

"I know it may sound a bit odd, but that's my belief."

"You're a Christian?"

"Yes, I am. For as long as I can remember."

"How about if I meet you there? There is a restaurant near the airport, and I'll take you to it. I live a very short distance away. I could be there within a half hour."

"That sounds good to me. I'll be in Terminal Four at the US Airways baggage claim. You won't have to look hard. I'll be the one melting into a greasy blob on the floor." He chuckled. "A blob with a tan shirt, a brown tie, and very wrinkled brown slacks."

He didn't have long to wait. Evelyn arrived, shook hands with Liam, and led him to her car in the parking garage.

Once inside the car, Liam handed her the jar.

"How do we get into this?" she asked. "It's sealed. And how on earth did you get this out of Lebanon? I heard it's against the law to remove antiquities. Especially one like this, all in one piece. It must be unbelievably valuable."

"I may be mistaken, but I think you and I are the only ones who recognize this for what it is. The customs officials at both customs checks thought it was a coffee mug. As to how to open it, I have a Swiss Army knife in my luggage. Which reminds me, once we've finished, could you drop me at a hotel, preferably one with functioning air conditioning?"

Evelyn laughed. "I believe I can find one, but I don't think we should be opening this in a restaurant. Maybe we should find the hotel first. The Crown Plaza is close by, and it has a restaurant too."

"If it has cool air and a bed, it sounds like heaven to me. Except for cat naps, I've not slept for over twenty-four hours, nor have I had a decent meal in that length of time."

Evelyn started the car and soon cold air blew on the blissful Englishman. In a few minutes, they arrived at the Crown Plaza. Liam had almost fallen asleep.

Once he was checked in and they were on the way to his room, Liam let out a huge yawn. "My apologies, dear lady," he said, yawning again. "I'm not bored, just a bit exhausted."

"I promise not to stay long, just enough to find out what's in this jar."

"I confess to an avid curiosity myself," Liam said.

He'd bought a newspaper in the airport, and they spread the want ad section from the Phoenix Sun on the bed. Liam pulled the knife from his luggage and removed the clay seal in the mouth of the jar, working carefully but efficiently. Inside was a small roll of parchment—no, two rolls, one inside the other.

He took two mugs provided by the hotel for coffee, filled them with water, and heated it to boiling in the microwave. He then placed the parchment scrolls inside the microwave with the steaming cups of water. He smiled at Evelyn. "These need to soften for a time. Shall we go have a bite to eat?"

An hour and a half later, they returned to his room and retrieved the parchment from the moisture-laden air in the microwave. He carefully spread the sheets of parchment, which were unbelievably well preserved, scarcely even brittle.

The first was a letter to Evelyn.

Dear Evie,

I must admit you're right. There is a God, and he does have a son named Jesus. We have met him—Sarah, Tamara, and I. The three of us are together again and happy. Don't ask me how, but Jesus took each of us back through time to approximately 30 AD. It seems we have an opportunity to get things right this time. And Jesus healed Tamara. Please take the other letter in this jar to my mother, but don't show this to anyone but her, okay.

Paul

The second was, of course, to his mother.

Dear Mom,

I know right now you must be reeling at what appears to be my death, especially on top of Sarah's disappearance and Tammy's death, but I want you to know I didn't die in that wreck. This will be hard for you to believe, but I'm alive and well in the time of Christ, living in Tyre, Phoenicia (Lebanon to you). Not only am I alive and well, but so are Sarah and Tammy. Tamara came here first, then Sarah, then me.

Something else I want you to know. Jesus is real, and he is the Son of God. We've all three met him face-to-face, and he's as wonderful as the Bible says. Tamara has been healed, and people's lives have changed, including Sarah's and mine.

We're happy here. You knew Sarah and I had been having problems, but we were given one more chance to get our relationship straightened out, and we have.

I know this is hard for you, Mom, but hang onto Evelyn and listen to her. She tried to tell me before about the Lord, but I wouldn't listen. I hope you will. Jesus said she will be the delivery person giving this letter to you. He wouldn't tell me how he'd preserve this letter or how he'd ensure you got it, but I know now he can do all things.

We send our love to you.

Paul, Sarah, and Tammy

Oh—PS: Tammy says Jesus told her we're going to be having a baby boy in the spring.

Evelyn was weeping, and Liam was close to tears himself. He handed her a box of tissue.

She rummaged through her purse and found her cell phone. She dialed Halena's number.

"Hello, Halena? This is Evelyn McPhersen, Paul's secretary. I know this's been a difficult day and it's late, but could I come see you this evening? A friend is here with an amazing letter from Paul that you must read."

About the Author

Anne Baxter Campbell is an author with a single-minded purpose: to invite you to come one step closer to the heart of the One God who loves you, bids you to accept His grace and forgiveness, and encourages you constantly. She's mom to three perfect children, grandma to lots of unparalleled grands and great-grands, and tight friends with the best step-kids and -grandkids. Plus perfect in-laws too, of course.

Anne lives in Northern California with the friendliest dog in the neighborhood and one occasionally affectionate cat with lots of black fur to share.

Made in the USA
Lexington, KY
12 March 2018